THE
MISSING
AND THE
DEAD

Writing as Elizabeth Cooke

The Damnation of John Donellan
Rutherford Park
The Wild Dark Flowers
The Gates of Rutherford

Writing as Elizabeth McGregor

Intimate Obsession
You Belong To Me
Out of Reach
Little White Lies
Second Sight
The Wrong House
The Ice Child
A Road Through The Mountains
The Girl in the Green Glass Mirror
Learning By Heart

Writing as Holly Fox

This Way Up
Up and Running

E.M. SCOTT

THE
MISSING
AND THE
DEAD

NO EXIT PRESS

First published in the UK in 2024 by No Exit Press,
an imprint of Bedford Square Publishers Ltd,
London, UK

noexit.co.uk
@noexitpress

© E.M. Scott, 2024

ISBN
978-1-83501-030-3 (Paperback)
978-1-83501-028-0 (Hardback)
978-1-83501-029-7 (eBook)

2 4 6 8 10 9 7 5 3 1

Typeset in 11pt Minion Pro
by Avocet Typeset, Bideford, Devon, EX39 2BP
Printed and bound in Great Britain by
CPI Group (UK) Ltd, Croydon CR0 4YY

1

IN THOSE TIME-FROZEN SECONDS, THOMAS Maitland saw three things.

The trees beside the road. The slope of the valley ahead. And the red Fiat turning in mid-air, silent, red against white and pale green and grey: as graceful as a dancer, and shocking in its irrationality.

Then he heard the noise. The astounding impact of the Fiat and his own vehicle colliding: deafening, slamming the breath from his body.

He must have stamped on the brakes of the van, because it swerved. He felt it roll about. The road rocked, shattered into fragments, reassembled through a crack in the windscreen. Through it, Thomas could see the sharp bend clearly again at the bottom of the hill. The green fields beyond. The melting snow under the beech trees.

He sat gasping for a moment, then reached in a panic to switch off his engine. He found it hard to turn the key in the ignition. He did not dare to look to his right into the wood. There were other sounds, he realised: car's brakes squealing as it crested the hill behind him, 40 yards away. Another impact behind him. He saw a lorry, stalled, that had been behind the Fiat; and he closed his eyes.

The Fiat had rounded the bend below almost in the centre of the road. He saw it again, coming towards him, steadily veering. He had put his hand on the horn: he had sounded it, he was sure. He recalled the noise of that and then nothing, a blank, only the elegantly turning Fiat in the air. It reminded him of the kind of car that he had owned at college. A beaten-up thing with a taped-together wing.

A man had been driving. As the car came closer Thomas had seen him looking directly at him for a moment before glancing down to his side.

Thomas had seen the white of the driver's hands, one skimming the dashboard, one on the steering wheel.

*

Thomas had left his house that morning at 6 o'clock. He had finished the commission for the large painting, and loaded it, with much cursing and difficulty, into the van the night before. He had to go to Gloucestershire via a customer in Claverton Down: it was likely to be a long day.

In the half-light of the morning, he had stopped in the garden to look at the field beyond, waiting to see if the deer would come back to the maize stubble.

A dawn light. Astronomical dawn, the sun 18 degrees below the horizon. Followed by nautical twilight, 12 degrees. Civil twilight, 6 degrees. He rubbed his forehead, frowning quizzically. Emptied of what mattered, his brain had become saturated with pointless information. He was a repository for it; he'd become a place where names and facts and numbers washed up.

Sometimes his old life intruded: 32 years in the police force.

Cases he'd rather forget than remember.

Leaving the force nine years ago, he had visualised what he did now: thinking of landscapes, his drawings alive with contours. Colours to block the grey.

Fran was there only occasionally. She crept back only when his guard was down.

His dog was at his side, and looked up at him expectantly. Thomas glanced down at the terrier, the appallingly named Fish, who had become his shadow, mirroring his footsteps and stance, a canine slow waltz. Fran had named him.

That had been four years ago. 'You can't call a dog Fish,' he'd objected, laughing, when she had stood at their back fence with it, wet from the stream and wriggling as she held him on her hip. They'd only collected him from Rescue the day before. 'It's what he was chasing,' she'd explained. The sunlight was fragmenting and re-forming on the grass under the apple tree.

Fish always sat next to him on the bench seat in the cab of the van, ears pricked. He was a very small dog, intelligent, with a calculating, knowing expression.

He liked to lie on a dusty bed in the studio workshop, watching the easel with half an eye. Only yesterday, he had stood for over an hour by the stepladder in the garden as Thomas tended Fran's roses while an icy north-east wind blew around them both.

Thomas had kept Fran's dog at his side at first from duty, and then from gratitude, thankful that his wife had possessed a soft heart. He'd never liked dogs, that was the truth of it; but now Fish lay on his bed, smelling faintly of the mud from the fields, and of wax and sawdust. Fish even lay next to him on the overstuffed couch as he read the evening paper. Thomas smiled whenever he touched him. You had to be grateful for that.

When the roses were done yesterday, neatly tied into their arches and loops, Thomas had stood back and looked at the pattern they made against the 18th-century red brick wall of the house. Then, he had taken the stepladder inside, and swept up the cuttings, sucking the scratches on the back of his hand. He wasn't by nature a tidy person, but in the last two years he had kept solidly and bloody-mindedly to a routine, the kind of routine in the garden and studio and house that Fran used to have. He was only partially convinced of its usefulness, even when the roses bloomed, and the grass grew, and the blackthorn hedges that he had trimmed became a wash of white in early May.

People had told him that was the secret, the way out of misery. As if they knew; as if anyone had the answer. Only he knew the cause of his sleeplessness, a cause much deeper than his loss. But all he could do was keep to time and routine.

So he kept the house tidy, and he kept the dog's ridiculous name, and he saw to the roses.

*

It was twelve minutes past eight that Monday morning when the traffic sergeant crested the rise outside Radstock. It was one of the busiest roads in the area: a main arterial route from Bath, north-south through open country.

They had received 14 emergency calls. The fourth had been from the driver of a lorry, saying something about a small red car crossing the road. The sergeant narrowed his eyes, registering a van at a 45-degree angle almost in the centre of the road facing north, leaning to the left, its offside wing and door caved in. The nearside tyre had blown.

There was a lorry with an unstable load facing up the hill, and a second crash facing north. He wove his bike through the cars, stopped and radioed in; got off the bike and walked towards the van.

A man was on his knees in the road at its side, holding something in his lap. He looked up, into the sergeant's eyes, seemingly perfectly calm, without any definite expression, and away again, shielding whatever it was that he was holding.

The sergeant turned his head. The driver of the lorry was running, waving his arms, shouting about the chemical load. Liquid waste, inflammable. The sergeant had already seen the problem. He looked to his right.

Three or four people were standing on the verge by the trees. A woman held up her arms, a kind of Biblical gesture of prayer, of pleading. He walked over to her, talking to Control on his radio, keeping up a running commentary.

The woman ran forward and grabbed his arm. She looked to be in her early 70s, her face the ghastly colour of shock, her hands fluttering. She was holding a twisted headscarf, and her body shook. He made a mental note to watch her, another potential fatality.

'A boy,' she kept saying. 'He's only a boy.'

*

It was not quite true. Although he did have a boyish look, with a full head of dark hair, the sergeant thought that the Fiat's driver was probably in his late 30s, maybe more.

The Fiat had righted itself so that it sat foursquare on its wheels, looking rather odd among the broken branches and the rotted leaves of the previous summer and the remnants of snow in the wood at the side of the road. The windscreen was shattered, and the roof dipped in an almost perfect arc. The driver's door was open. Someone – surely not this elderly woman – had tried to pull the driver out.

The traffic sergeant made his way across the small drainage ditch at the side of the road, and picked his way through the muddy ground beyond. He saw then exactly what the others involved had seen: that it was hopeless to try and help the driver. His neck was plainly broken. Incongruously, his hands still gripped the steering wheel.

The sergeant leaned carefully inside the car. He saw a CD lying in the footwell.

One visible word on the disc.

Concerto.

*

The angle of the sun had somehow shifted. Thomas couldn't remember how.

He closed his eyes against the colour.

He was sitting on the road, hoping to be left alone, to be ignored. He had a blinding pain behind his eyes, a migrainous shuttle of light and dark, and felt pressure on the left-hand side of his head. He wanted to lie down, and an incongruous yearning for sleep overcame him.

He didn't want to look at the ambulances or the fire crews: reds and yellows, green banding. The fluttering of blue and white tape. The jumble of the other vehicles. He rested his face against the cold metal of the open door of his van. A long time passed. Hours, or seconds.

Someone took his arm. 'All right, mate?'

He opened his eyes. A paramedic was crouching beside him.

'Yes,' he said.

'Mind if I take a look?'

Thomas thought that they must be talking about the dog. He looked down at Fish, lifeless in his lap. 'I think he broke his back,' he said.

'You,' the man replied, not unkindly. 'I mean you.'

'I'm all right,' Thomas repeated. A light was shone into his eyes. He winced.

'Okay,' the paramedic murmured. 'Can you stand? Can we stand you up?'

'I want to lie down,' Thomas told him.

'How about in the ambulance?' A gently cajoling voice.

Thomas looked at him. 'I can't go anywhere,' he said. 'There's my work in the van.'

'They'll take care of that.'

Who were *they*? Thomas wondered. Somebody among all these people in their reflective jackets? The large canvas in the van was important. He had spent five weeks on it. It was worth £3,000, the best commission he'd ever had. In fact, one of the few. It must be damaged now despite the restraints that he had tied to it.

He glanced at the van, and then looked around. A fire engine was alongside the lorry on the opposite side of the road. The lorry was leaning to one side; there was foam on the tarmac. More vehicles were arriving: a police car with a blue light flashing. More sirens down the hill.

On the other side of the valley, on what he knew was the same road snaking up towards Bath, he could see a line of stationary cars. *Shit,* he thought. *How will they get them all out of here?* There was nowhere to turn. No side roads. Only little one-track lanes in the deep green valleys of Somerset. They would have to back them all up, turn them all around somehow, send them back the way they had come. It would take all day, surely.

The paramedic's hand was gently under his elbow. 'Anything that hurts?'

It made him want to laugh. It was like something that you got asked at school after a fall in the playground. He looked down at Fish. The dog's eyes were still open. He put his hand on the narrow little chest and tested his ribs. 'My dog,' he whispered.

There was someone else now. Not wearing a uniform. A woman. He saw the edge of her jeans and her flat shoes, and heard a broad West Country voice. He looked up into her face. She was young, maybe in her 30s he guessed, young to him at least. She was dressed in a muddy Barbour jacket. She crouched down and held out her hands: hands reddened, raw from work. She didn't speak, simply held out her hands, nodding to him. When Thomas didn't move, she slipped her hands under Fish and scooped him up, and stood, holding the dog's body close to her chest.

Thomas got up.

He looked down at himself: not a scratch. Not a mark. Nothing on Fish either. He reached out and patted the dog's head. 'Checked out on me,' he observed. 'How do you like that?'

'You need someone to look at you,' the woman murmured softly. 'You're white as a sheet. Go along. I'll take care of him. I know it's important. I've got dogs myself.'

'He's called Fish,' Thomas told her.

'Fish?' she repeated, and gave a small smile. 'Cool name.'

The paramedic guided him towards the ambulance.

It was strange, walking across a road as wide as this. There was an instinct to watch for traffic. Thomas shook his head, bemused. There were clouds on the edge of his vision: encroaching dark spheres. He tried to blink them away.

He stopped and looked towards the woods. 'Did he get out?' he asked. 'The driver?'

The inside of the ambulance seemed stage-lit. Lights on the roof, light from the side windows. An opaque, undersea light. He shielded his eyes and asked to sit on the step.

'Sit for a minute,' the paramedic conceded, removing Thomas' coat, putting a blood pressure cuff on him.

A police officer came to the door, looked at him on the step, checked his name.

'I think I looked away for a second,' Thomas told him.

'Away for a second?'

'Just to look at my dog. He was next to me on the seat. I mean, it was just a second. Less than a second. A glance. I looked, and looked back straightaway. I saw the car.'

'Which car was that?'

'The red Fiat. I saw the driver.'

'You saw the driver.' His answers were being written in a pocket notebook. Thomas tried to make sense of the pen moving across the page. Quite suddenly, it seemed odd to him that the words in his mouth were appearing on the notepad.

'The driver of the car was looking at something on the floor,' Thomas continued. 'He had started veering in my direction. And then suddenly he came across. He just came across, right across, straight into me.' Thomas stood up abruptly. 'It rolled and landed in the trees,' he said, the importance of this only just occurring to him. For minutes now he had been looking at the tarred surface of the road and at Fish, his gaze flickering between the two. Colours, the road, colours, the suddenly lifeless eyes. Now, however, he saw the roll of the Fiat again.

'Is he out of the car?' he asked. 'Did you get him out?'

'No,' the policeman replied.

*

He kept thinking of other days.

There had been nowhere to park on the day that Fran got her news. She'd gone inside the hospital before him. He'd told her to wait for him before seeing the consultant. But she hadn't waited. Brusque, authoritative, turning her face from him. The way she'd been for some time, because shadows had come between them. And not just the cancer. As he ran across the car park – it had taken ten minutes to find a space, another five to find change for the meter – he saw her come to the main door. She looked composed.

As he walked up to her, she hoisted her bag across her shoulder. She looked relieved, and his heart had dropped, then leapt in his chest. She had been reprieved. That was what it meant, that small smile on her face.

'Come on,' she had said, 'buy me a drink.'

Another morning. A soft, weightless summer morning, a year or so later. The second course of chemo was finished.

He felt he knew everything then, everything you'd ever want to know about waiting and looking down at hospital floors, at stark fluorescent lights on ceilings, about sitting at bedsides, about buying flavoured ices for his wife to suck on as she sat on the edge of the chair. She never lost that small rueful smile that had so fooled him at first. It was as if she had a private joke about it. *So, it caught me. Damn.*

Or perhaps that smile was about him.

The way that he'd once betrayed her.

Another morning. He had come out of his cottage at three in the morning, and walked across the grass. There were a stream and a bridge at the bottom of the garden, and he had found his way there almost by touch. As he put his hand on the bridge parapet, on the grainy wood, he had felt a series of electric shocks run through him. He had sat down on the ground. Tremors coursed across his shoulders and down his arms. He sat and wept for a long time.

Dawn came slowly, and at one point he heard a faint noise, a breath of movement, and he looked up and found himself face to face with a dog otter, standing six feet from him across the bridge. The otter had looked at him impassively, and then turned and retreated into the stream. Thomas had sat for another hour, cold through to his soul – he would have given his soul, that worthless thing, to anyone who had offered a way out. He would have paid any price to rewrite both the present and the past. But nothing happened. No one came along and said, 'I'll buy your soul. She can live another twenty years'. The sky turned an empty blue, and he saw the first tracks of aircraft. Transatlantic flights approaching Heathrow for their 7 o'clock landing. He wished himself up there. Anywhere.

He had got up, uncranked his cold body and walked back to the house where Fran was still sleeping.

*

He lay on a bed in Accident and Emergency, staring at another hospital ceiling. He was overwhelmed with a sudden, desperate feeling that he must get out. He couldn't look at these walls again. He needed to be left alone. He had to get off the bed, and leave.

The clock on the wall showed 10.30. Beyond the flimsy curtain, he could hear voices. He was being discussed. He heard his own name. A moment later, a nurse pushed the curtain back.

'Still the same?' she asked.

He submitted to the observation readings again. 'I'm all right,' he repeated. He had been saying it all the way to the hospital, but it seemed that no one was taking any notice. He had protested that the pain on the left-hand side of his head was gone; that he could walk. He could string a sentence together.

Nobody listened.

They had told him that he was to have a scan. It was, they said, a formality. He wished that he had never mentioned the roving blocks of shadow in his sight, the pain on one side of his head. He badly wanted to go home. 'We'll take you to Diagnostic Imaging in just a moment,' the nurse had said. How long ago was that? He had no idea. His gaze strayed back to the clock.

He kept thinking about the woman who had taken Fish. He didn't know her name. He didn't know who she was. Had she been involved in the accident? She had seemed so calm. She'd come from nowhere, vanished into nowhere. Perhaps he'd imagined her. She'd walked away, carrying his dog. He ought to know where she had been going, what had been done with the body.

He looked at the nurse as she took his pulse, and he fought down sudden panic. It wasn't a thing to be asking; it was inappropriate and selfish. But what the hell would Fran say if she knew? He had given her dog to a stranger.

Fish had kept close to him for most of the last two years, and now he had lost him. Abandoned him. Fish shrank from his touch when Fran had first gone, and the poor animal had looked for her everywhere. He used to go to the door, waiting for the sound of her car. He would lie in his bed in the kitchen next to the range, not eating.

Thomas had sat down at the dog's side in the early hours of one morning. 'Come on,' he had told him, annoyed. 'You're not the only one. You're not.' In the dark he had tried to get Fish to uncurl and sit in his lap, but the dog had rigidly resisted. He had longed for company and even Fish, miserable, had rejected him. Weeks, it had taken. Two or three months for the dog to come when he called.

Suddenly, the loss made him feel nauseous, and he put a hand to his mouth. Jesus Christ, he couldn't be sick now. Not out of grief for a dog. He could hear a man crying. He thought it was a man; the tone was low. Yet he seemed to be weeping like a child. Thomas could hear the muffled gasps, the pleas. *Don't do that,* the voice kept saying, *oh, don't do that.*

Thomas lifted his hand and touched the nurse's arm.

'I had a dog with me,' he said.

'A dog?'

'He was killed…'

'Was he?' she said. 'Oh dear.'

He leaned back on the pillow. 'I'm all right,' he repeated. The motherly woman glanced at him, smiling sympathetically. 'I have a cat. I love her to bits, I really do,' she said. He couldn't help thinking, *love her to bits?* He hated that phrase. *Love to dismemberment. Who, you or the cat?* Abruptly, he swung his legs off the bed. 'Where are you going?' she asked.

'Home.'

'Oh no,' she told him, pushing him gently back. 'You're scheduled for a scan, so hold on tight there.'

'But I'm fine.'

'Probably. But just wait a little while yet.'

He despaired, biting his lip. He had to ring the client in Bath and explain about the painting. Five weeks of work, and money tied up in it; but it wasn't the money. It was the making of it, and now it would be unmade.

When the nurse left, he got up and pushed the curtain aside.

He saw a police officer on the far side of the corridor, a woman. She looked about 12 to him, her body hidden by a giant fluorescent coat, but her face was smooth, closed down, impassive, as if she'd seen it all before. Or had seen as much as she ever wanted to see. She nodded at him.

'Where's my van?' he asked.

'You're Mr Maitland?'

'That's right.'

'It'll be still there for a while yet,' she told him. 'Collision investigator, scenes of crime, principal investigating officer, all that.'

'Can I go and get it?'

'No,' she said. 'Not for a while.'

'Tomorrow?'

'No, sir. It'll go to a pound, or a secure garage.'

'There's something in it,' he told her. 'A canvas. A painting.'

Her gaze was noncommittal. He realised that she must think he was insane, worrying about a painting, of all goddamn things, in the midst of all this. It sounded utterly banal. He wanted to tell her that it was his hobby – no, more than that, his love – that he did these things, created these things for the love of it, for the slow desire in him to make something out of the chaos of himself. That was why it was important.

But he couldn't have put it into words, and he saw the young policewoman's face take on a slight expression of distaste, dismissal.

He turned away. *Not for a while.* How was he going to get home? It was 30 or 40 miles. Would anyone take him? Would he have to drive, hire a car, what? He lowered his head and took a long, deep breath. He was suffocatingly hot.

The curtains across the cubicle a little way down the corridor were pulled back and the bed behind them was wheeled out. He saw an old man, yellow in the face, clutching the hand of the woman who walked alongside. She must have been 75 at least, dragging herself along, shoulders squared, feet scuffling, face fiercely set as if she was thoroughly pissed off with the world. Thomas didn't blame her. He recognised them as the couple in the car that had been behind him.

She had flung open her car door as soon as they had come to a stop, and run about the place screaming, yelling about her husband, yelling about the Fiat driver. Thomas had been convinced that she would suddenly fall down stone-dead with shock, and, half-falling from his own vehicle, he had tried to stop her. It was the first thing he did: catch hold of her arms, which were freewheeling about as though independent of her body.

She'd stared at him, held still for a moment until he released her, and then she slapped him hard across the face. 'You were going too fast!' she'd cried. He'd stepped away from her. She'd run to the side of the woods, demented. He had climbed back into the cab and lifted the deadweight of the dog from the floor.

Where is the driver of the Fiat? he thought now. Pictures of a profiled face, a mass of dark hair, and the hands gripping a steering wheel floated into his head through a fog of disorientation.

What happened to him?

He began to walk to the exit.

*

He got home at 4 o'clock.

The house, at the edge of the village, was picking up the light from its neighbour's yard. He could see Christine, seeing to the chickens, as the taxi pulled in. She glanced up, and stood stock still, the feed bucket in her hand.

The taxi dipped behind the hedge and trees and pulled up at his door. He got out, paid the driver, stood with his hand on the door keys in his pocket.

Christine came running along the drive. It was a roundabout loop from her garden to his land; she had to go out into the road and come all the way round, and she was out of breath.

'Thomas,' she called.

He watched her approach, rooted to the spot, feeling dull-witted.

She was a nice woman in her 70s, although you would not

know from the active life she led. As she jogged along, she was wiping her hands on the seams of her old khaki jeans.

She reached him. 'What's the matter?' she asked. 'Where's the van?'

'I had an accident,' he told her.

'Oh, Thomas!'

'It's all right.'

She grabbed his elbow. 'I can tell by your face it isn't all right,' she said. She looked at him, scanning his body with concern. 'Are you hurt?'

'Apparently not.'

'Where was it?'

'Near Radstock,' he said. 'I can't get the van back. I don't know when I will.' He was aware of the slight mist settling around them: on the path, the trees dripping with moisture. Of a faint frill of green on the hawthorn, a colour he hadn't seen yesterday. *Spring is coming,* he thought, a propos of nothing.

'I think someone was killed,' he murmured. 'I went into him.' He shook his head. 'He went into me.'

'Oh, Thomas,' she whispered. She looked behind him, and back at the drive. 'Where's Fish?'

'I don't know.'

'What do you mean?'

He could see the same moisture on her long grey hair twisted into a plait that almost reached her waist, and he thought of Fran holding Fish on her hip and laughing. He closed his eyes momentarily. The light of the afternoon was rapidly fading. In an hour, it would be dark.

Like the seven-year-old he used to be, he felt a thrill of fear about the night, the darkness of rooms. He imagined himself putting his hand on the switch and turning out the bedside light, and he knew that he wouldn't be able to do it. He couldn't be alone in the dark.

It was only then that he began to cry.

2

CHRISTINE ALWAYS WOKE EARLY. IT was ingrained. She sat up and looked out over the fields that she could see from her window.

Yesterday morning at the same time, 6 o'clock, she had heard Thomas slamming the doors of his van. She'd sat on the edge of her bed and wondered how long it would take him to get across Bath, and if he would stop on the way. If he would make sure that he ate something other than the bars of chocolate whose wrappers littered the cab of the van. She had doubted it.

She got up now and automatically shrugged herself into sweater, jeans and padded jacket from the heap of clothes lying by her bed. One day she would tidy herself up, she thought. It was the same plan that had crossed her mind every morning for 70-odd years. And it was the same plan that she knew she would never be bothered to carry out.

On the landing, she looked out at the quiet slope of the grass beyond her fences, and the distant trees. The birds were singing. 'Bloody birds,' she whispered. She opened the landing window and breathed in the morning. 'No respecter of grief,' she warned the invisible wrens and blackbirds. 'Shut the hell up for once, why don't you?'

She went downstairs to the kitchen and put on the kettle. She ought to go and see Thomas today. She doubted that he would have had any sleep. Since he and Fran had moved into the cottage, she'd always regarded them as her family; she had no one else, and neither did they. And since Fran had died Thomas had become even more important to her. She felt an attachment to him.

She scuffed her feet on the floor of the kitchen, thinking. What should she do? Go and knock on Thomas's door? He might not be awake. He might have been up for most of the night and only just fallen asleep. She didn't want to disturb him.

'Sod it,' she muttered.

She made two mugs of tea and carried them outside.

*

She had her answer when she was only halfway down the drive to the cottage. At the far end of the garden, in Thomas's workshop, she could hear the whine of machinery.

Opening the gate, she glanced at the roses, severely pruned and tied back. At the semi-circle of gravel below the kitchen window, and the fringe of green that hinted at the spring renaissance. It was a formal garden. Much too formal for her. And Thomas cut it back too much, as if he were taking his annoyance out on anything that grew. She noticed the stakes and wires, the white nub of branches pruned with a hacksaw. The apple tree looked like a sapling, and in the border to one side was a pile of kindling taken from it.

He was a methodical man. Dutiful. Slow to anger, slow to humour. He would always frown when he was listening to her, and it didn't matter if she were telling him a piece of village news, or a joke. He would study her face as if he were trying to decipher the meaning of everything she said.

The door to the studio, hidden beyond a privet hedge, was half open. Next to it was a covered walkway with open sides that held stacks of wood, suspended in their long years of seasoning.

'Thomas?' she called, above the sound of the saw. 'Thomas?'

He hadn't heard her. She went in.

He was feeding a piece of timber through the blade and she waited so as not to distract him. He was making picture frames. As the noise died, he noticed her.

'I brought you tea,' she said.

He took off his gloves. She could see her breath in the air.

'Aren't you cold?'

'A bit.' He took the tea. 'Thanks.'

She propped herself against the counter. She liked the smell in here. The sap of the wood. The smell of paint. He was talented, but had no ego. Modesty, the old-fashioned virtue that she liked so much.

'What are you working on?'

He waved his hand. 'Just frames,' he told her. 'For Bingham Fair.'

It was their local spring show. Every year Thomas hired a stand and took his marquee out to the castle grounds. One year she had helped him and Fran set up in a day of pouring rain. The three of them had got soaked setting up that damned roof; an expanding mechanism that needed at least four people to erect. Last year, she and Thomas had managed alone, cursing the thing until it miraculously became a structure. 'What a bastard,' she'd complained. 'It's clever,' he'd responded. 'Yes,' she'd agreed. 'A very clever bastard, that's what it is,' sucking her hand where the steel frame had pinched it.

'You're still doing Bingham?' she asked. 'It's not long now.'

'I have to do it,' he said. 'People don't find me here. I've got to go to them.'

'I know,' she murmured. 'But after yesterday.'

He turned away from her, holding the mug of tea in one hand and randomly turning over pieces of sanding paper with the other. 'Life goes on,' he muttered. Suddenly, he turned back again. 'I didn't mean it like that.'

'I know.'

He put the mug down on the nearest surface and put both hands over his eyes, rubbing his face. 'I've been thinking about him. The driver.' He shook his head slowly. 'He'd been looking for a CD. I heard someone in the hospital say that. The police?' He frowned.

'That could explain it, couldn't it? His veering over?'

'There was something on the back seat, too. A musical instrument, apparently. I woke up an hour ago and I suddenly remembered. They said a big case on the back seat.'

'A violin isn't very big.'

'Well, what's bigger?'

'I don't know, Thomas. I'm not musical.'

'Neither am I.' They stared at each other while the ghost of the man walked past them; this unknown person who had been carrying music in his car, in his head.

'There's a concert in Pallingham this weekend,' she said, suddenly remembering. 'At the school. Margaret in the shop was telling me. She wanted to go.'

Thomas seemed disturbed, suddenly agitated. 'You think he was a professional musician?'

'No, I...'

'Somebody talented?'

'Thomas, I can't tell you. He might have been carrying the thing for somebody else. Delivering it.'

'Somebody talented,' he repeated dully.

She immediately went to his side and touched his arm. 'This wasn't your fault,' she told him. And a silence descended between them while he stared into the middle distance.

'Did you sleep?' she asked.

He seemed to shake himself, to come back into the room. 'A couple of hours.'

'Will you later?'

'I doubt it.'

She gazed sympathetically at him. He was so thin. The skin on his cheeks was red with a fine tracery of broken veins. He was drinking too much red wine, she thought. She saw the bottles when he put out the recycling bins at the end of the drive. Wine bottles and not much else. 'Come over for something to eat tonight,' she said.

'I'll be all right.'

She took the empty mug from him. 'Do you have to go and see the police?' she asked.

'See them?' he repeated. 'No, I don't think so. I have to wait until they get in touch.' He nodded in the direction of his mobile phone on the counter top. 'I think that's what they said.'

She nodded. 'Okay then,' she murmured. 'See you at seven this evening.'

'I'm all right, Christine. I'll fix myself something.'

'No, you won't,' she replied firmly. 'And it wasn't a suggestion. It was an instruction.'

3

John Lord walked into the hospital and saw the Family Liaison Officer whom he had arranged to meet.

She came forward immediately. 'Mr Lord?' Just for a second, she looked shocked. He knew that it was because he was an almost identical copy of his twin.

He held out the piece of paper on which he'd written all the details. The place of the accident. The time. The address of the hospital. 'It can't be my brother. He wasn't due on the road. Not then.'

'Okay,' she murmured. 'Is somebody with you?'

'No.'

'You've driven down this morning, by yourself? That's quite some distance.'

'Yes.'

John stared back at her, remembering the empty roads until the outskirts of Birmingham. It was 310 miles from just outside Ambleside. According to his car. He'd kept checking the dashboard information all the way down the M6. Temperature. Average mileage. Mileage itself. Time. He'd kept looking at it because it made sense, had logic to it. It offered him a piece of reality.

Blue signs lit garishly against a black sky. Mountains behind him, dark fields either side as clouds threatening rain swept over Cheshire.

'Oh John,' Liz had said, 'let me come with you. You can't go there by yourself.' He told her to go back into work at the school – she had come home when he had rung her with the news. They had stood in their kitchen, immobile, not knowing what to say to each other after she had hugged him.

'Go back to work,' he'd told her. 'There's nothing you can do.'

'I can be with you, John,' she'd repeated, crossing her arms.

'I'll ring you later.'

He kept seeing her puzzled, affronted face all the way south. A surreal journey. Tewkesbury Abbey floating in green meadows as he passed it, lit by sunshine. A service station crowded with coach parties at Bristol. The bright holiday colours of the coach logo as he walked by. His mouth too dry to taste his coffee. A sandwich bought and uneaten.

And Mike ahead of him.

It had always been just him and Mike. Always them, then the rest of the world. In that order. They might as well have been joined at the hip. They spoke on the phone three or four times a week. Twice a year, Mike would come and stay, and walk the fells with him.

Only last Saturday they had climbed Scafell and looked across the shattered rocks of the summit towards the Irish Sea. Mike always said that being back in the Lakes was his piece of sanity. And so he felt that he owed it to his brother to do this alone, to go and meet him. This was a private thing.

*

'Look,' he said now. 'Maybe he loaned the car to somebody.'

The LNO gave a small smile, a sympathetic look. 'Would you like to come this way?'

In the lift, he saw his shaded reflection on the brushed steel wall. Like seeing Mike. Older by two minutes, the only difference was that he was taller by half an inch or so. And he was always the more outgoing one, as if first entry in the world had awarded him more confidence.

They had fought over who went first all their lives. As kids trying to get through doorways. Trying to get to a girl first. Running for a football. Over who could lift the heaviest object, throw something the farthest, run the fastest.

He ran a hand through his hair. They had the same thick dark hair that grew low on the forehead, and each of them had a double crown on their scalp, and a birthmark to one side of that crown. People said that they looked young for their age. They possessed the same colour eyes, the same double frown lines, and the same fleshy mouth. They were identical in more than looks, too; they both possessed the same slightly weakened knee, a genetic fault. Aged nine, he'd fallen from a rocky outcrop and buggered up the cruciate ligament, and an MRI scan had showed the shallow define that would always cause them both trouble. His knee ached after long car journeys. It was aching now.

The lift doors opened. 'Just down here,' the woman murmured.

A heavy door opened into a hushed, softly lit atmosphere. They'd put him in a chapel. Mike would have thought that was hilarious: right up by the altar as if it was already his funeral. On a trolley covered by a white sheet. Mike, who played so much church music and didn't believe in God. Mike, who sang in a choir in the cathedral but didn't believe in any greater power or an afterlife. Mike, who had sung at Cambridge in the aching loveliness of King's; he'd gone to hear him one summer evening and been moved by it all, and kneeled and prayed, and afterwards Mike had mocked him for it.

John's skin prickled with outrage. Why the fucking hell was he here, in such a public place? Wouldn't somebody come in? Didn't they have a private room like he always saw on TV dramas, one with a window so you couldn't get close to the body? He'd counted on that, he realised, not being too close, because being close would force him to look at his brother like a real human being, instead of being protected against it. Something behind glass had no texture, no sense of flesh and bone. It would have been like looking at a painting in an art gallery or clothes through a shop window.

He started to cry. Mike would have done the same. They were both soft at heart: marshmallows, easy prey, teased all their lives for their inability to be stoic. Neither of them had believed that a man couldn't weep, and their father – long dead – had been the same, the easy emotion running through their characters like a seam of coal runs through stone. Yet here was Michael, stiller than he had ever seen him, relaxed so far into himself that he wasn't there at all, with no expression on his face except a slight smile.

John stood gasping, his fists clenched at his side, tears running down his face, like a bloody tap had been turned on. He resisted looking at the ceiling, because he wanted to look away and felt that he shouldn't; he surely owed Mike that much. He couldn't bring his hands up to his face; he was solid, paralysed. Felt only the weird, unaccustomed movement of his mouth. His nose began to run. Finally, that made him wipe his face. Clumsily, like a child, with the back of his hand. 'Jesus, God,' he muttered. 'Jesus, God.' Anger was rapidly replacing grief.

Eventually, he turned away. He gave the officer a slight nod and then he saw that someone else, some other official, was at the back of the chapel. He sat down in a pew and stared at the profile of his brother while a murmured conversation continued behind him.

When the woman returned, he looked up. 'Where's the viola?' he asked.

'We have his possessions. We can let you have them.'

'Thanks.' He stood up. 'He plays professionally,' he said. 'It's expensive. An expensive instrument.'

'I'll see to it.'

'Not that it matters, the cost,' he added quickly. 'I mean, it was his pride and joy. He'd ask the same thing – where is it, you see?' he paused momentarily. 'He plays in an orchestra. There's a concert tomorrow. Did anybody ring them?'

'I don't think so. Would you like me to?'

'No,' he said. 'I'll do it.'

He took one lingering look behind him, and then walked briskly out.

Ten minutes later he found himself on an outside terrace by a café. It was a cold, sunny day and there were daffodils blooming in containers around the fringes of the tables. He had realised that he'd had nothing to eat, and had bought another sandwich, but found that once more he couldn't touch it. Instead, he was nursing a black coffee.

Above him to one side, the hospital buildings rose up five floors. He walked as far away from the café entrance as he could, and leaned on the rail and phoned Liz. It went straight to voicemail; it was 1.30. He knew that she'd ring him back as soon as she saw the missed call. After a moment he shut down his phone and remained where he was, staring out at the car park and leaning on the rail of the parapet.

'You're just like him,' a voice said. 'You must be his brother.'

He turned around.

An old woman was standing beside him. She was short and broad, and had a heavily lined face. He recognised it at once as the face of fury, perhaps a fury she had carried all her life. It was the sort of face that you would see and immediately think, *Better not mess with this one.* Or just, *Trouble.*

She held out her hand. 'Joan Somerton.'

'John Lord.'

She finally let go of her fierce grip. 'I was there yesterday. We were in the car behind. My husband's in there.' And she inclined her head briefly towards the hospital building.

'I'm sorry,' he replied mechanically.

'He's broken his pelvis,' she told him. 'God knows how.

Except that he was waiting for a hip operation. For months now. Whole thing weak, maybe. They don't give an opinion. They just humour you, especially at my age.'

He doubted that anyone could humour her. 'I'm sorry,' he repeated. He started thinking again of Liz, and turned his phone over in his pocket, wanting to make another call.

'It was the van driver,' she said. 'It was his fault.'

'The van driver?'

'A scrappy old white van in the middle of the road. He'd gone into your brother. It was your brother?'

'Yes.'

'We came over the rise and we saw your brother's car flying through the air. The van had hit him. We saw the car go into the trees.'

The words 'flying through the air' and 'into the trees' struck him in the solar plexus. He had no memory of having been told those details. He looked around for a chair.

'Oh, you didn't know?'

'I know there was a collision. Of course I know that.' He found somewhere to sit and she promptly sat down next to him, leaning forward.

'I thought my husband was all right. He stamped on the brakes. We stopped. I got out, I was so annoyed, and I just flew out. Broken glass, that's how bad it was. Windscreens don't shatter do they, as a rule? Not now. A stone or something must have hit us, or something off the car. So you can imagine. We have a son and he used to drive up and down that road to university, and he'd had a red car too, and he'd had an accident just three miles further on when he was only nineteen. Broke his arm and he's still got a scar on his forehead. Some man coming the other way had been drinking, at midday! You see? I had to go over.'

He didn't see. He wished that she would go away with her self-important outrage.

'So I immediately... I don't know what I thought... I saw that van driver and I slapped him. Hard! And I ran to that car and

I got down that slope.' She stopped. Her mouth gave a little twist. 'And the van driver was just standing there like an idiot. Staring. Didn't care. Then he sat down and he had a dog in his lap...'

John put his hand to his head. Too much information. He closed his eyes and a mental image of the road came into his mind. There were a lot of hills between Mike's flat in Bath and Dorchester. Rolling hills. Green hills. And then he imagined Mike's car turning mid-air. There must have been a lot of noise.

'A lorry got smashed up,' the woman was saying. 'And others. Someone went into the back of us while I was down with your brother.'

At last, he looked at her. 'Accidents happen,' he murmured. It wasn't really what was in his mind, but to be like her suddenly seemed so pointless.

'Accidents happen?' she repeated incredulously. She gazed at him and then placed her hands firmly on her knees in exasperation. 'It had to be his fault, an old van like that,' she told him. 'He just stood there. Not a care in the world. No reaction, nothing. Cared more about his dog. These people are despicable. It's just typical of these vans. Vans and lorries think they own the road. They bully you. Don't you find that? We have it all the time. For two pins they'd push you out of the way. Some woman came and took the dog and then he got in an ambulance and I swear I would have gone over again and knocked him out. I would. Because your brother...' Her voice trailed away momentarily. 'Some people just don't care. They're not human.'

He said nothing. She looked at him for a good few moments, and then reached down and took a scrap of paper from her handbag. 'I wrote down the licence number. And the words on the side of the van. There was a bit of a messy sign on it. He's a painter. Artist.' She snorted in disgust. 'You'd probably find him on the internet?'

He took the piece of paper, looked at it, and put it in his

pocket. He had no idea what she wanted him to do with the information.

'He should be in court. He should be done for dangerous driving. You need to get on to the police and tell them. You want to ask them if he'd been drinking. If he was breathalysed. People have got to pay for acting like that. They just don't care. I'd put them in prison, all of them.'

'Thank you,' he said, because she seemed to be expecting it. He wanted to say, *Why don't you do me a favour and just fuck off.*

After she'd gone, he sat staring into space, seeing Mike's car turning in mid-air. Minutes passed and he found himself looking at the tubs of daffodils, his gaze riveted to the colour.

He wanted to sleep.

It must have been going at one hell of a speed, he thought.

4

THE WEATHER ON THE COAST that morning was beautiful. There was a mist inland, and trails of grey out to sea, but the small bay, ringed by chalk cliffs, sat in pale sunshine. Alice Hauser had looked down from her house and seen that the beach was empty at 7 o'clock, and she had taken her coat from the peg and left.

She preferred to walk alone. She did everything alone.

She used to live here ten years ago, but it looked different to her now. She had started to walk every morning because she wanted to get it straight in her mind. For it to look to her as it always had done.

She wondered if something in her had been knocked askew after Helen disappeared. If she would never see this place, this coast, this beach in the same way again.

When she had first come back here last December, it had been coming up to Christmas. Three months ago. Dark streets washed with rain. Tinsel in the shops, and twinkling trees in people's windows. The time of year that she hated, dreaded. There had not been too much on the market.

'What is it that you're looking for?' the estate agent had asked.

'Something quiet.'

'In a quiet street?'

'No. Not a street. Somewhere off on its own.'

'In the country, you mean?'

'Yes.' She had looked at all the photographs in the estate agent's window, and at those pinned up on the wall inside.

'Have you anything at all like that by the sea?' she had asked.

'Not really. Properties don't come up all that often. When they do, they go quickly.'

'Well, would you put me down as wanting…'

The man was keying the computer. 'By the sea?'

'Yes, by the sea. I like Asham Ferry.'

'Good choice. Budget?'

When she told him, he typed the figure, but with a slight frown. She wasn't in a bracket that would earn him much commission. Then he gazed at her. 'You seem familiar. Do you live nearby?'

'No,' she told him.

'I seem to know your face.'

'I lived here ten years ago.'

There. Well, so they might eventually connect her. Let them.

On the way out, she had glanced again at the photographs. She couldn't live in a street. They looked so like the places where she had once lived, an onlooker, a locked door against the tide. The last thing that she had done when she left Haltby Road - her childhood home in another time, another life - was to throw the key away. She had left the windows open, the door on the latch, to show its empty face to anyone coming inside. She had been only 18, her mother dead.

Afterwards she had sometimes dreamed that she was standing in the room at the back that overlooked the long, steady slope to the field, and there had been random letters, magnetic letters, spilled all over the floor.

'We've been trying to make sense of it,' her brother had said in the dream.

And she would start to laugh until William laughed too. 'Make sense of it? Really?' The room beginning to whirl. 'But there is no sense in it.'

She had spent most of her life alone since then. Alone from 18 until 22, when she had met Helen. Only a year with Helen. Then alone again for ten years.

Just one year of being loved.

And after Helen, after the investigation, she had gone to live for eight months in a small town on the east coast, far away. Blind running. Hundreds of miles away. A place that she had never been before, where she knew nobody. Looking for anonymity. As far east as she could get, in flat country, flat as far as the eye could see, insignificant under a painter's wide and empty skies.

But the town that she chose had proved to be a mistake. Too lively, with its Saturday market, and a high street of independent shops, and an arts centre. 'We are different,' her landlady had told her. And eyed her speculatively up and down. 'Are you an artist? We have a lot of artists.'

'No. A refugee.'

The woman's thickly pencilled eyebrows had shot up. 'From where?'

'Not from where.'

'Oh, from a *him?*' A broad smile. 'We've got something in common then! I'm one of those.'

Her landlady was a nuisance from that moment. She would wait for Alice to go out, or come in, and ambush her. 'I'm just making tea…'

'I'm fine, thanks.'

She had only wanted to be by herself. Stay in bed all day thinking of Helen. Of their last argument. Of all the questions that she had been asked, to which she had no answer at all.

That summer, the summer nine years ago, there had been a party that had been impossible to avoid. Almost at once, she had been cornered by a man breathing fumes of real ale. 'What do you do?'

'Not much.'

I hide. That's my occupation now.

'You must do something.'

'I don't.'

'You must lead a fucking boring life, then.' His teeth were unusually white, gleaming in the shadows of the lamps. 'Get out and be someone!'

In the morning, the reek of curry permeated from below and she left. Packed her bags, threw them into the back seat of the car.

'Holiday?' her landlady had called from the door.

She'd left an envelope with a month's rent on the ratty kitchen table that rocked as she leaned on it, split Formica under her palm. Electric heater on the wall. Bed with hardboard over the springs.

Writing *in lieu of notice.*

She left that place in the same way that she had left Haltby: door open, windows open.

Months passed. She kept moving.

She worked as a temp. Barmaid, cleaner. Weeks, months, years.

What was the saying? *'The days are slow. The years are fast.'*

There was so much truth in that. A morning could last for ever. An afternoon washed slowly through a century, like the tide of an estuary irrevocably turning. And then suddenly it would be night.

There would always be an hour, the hour that she needed to sleep, when she dared not close her eyes. If the mornings or afternoons were endlessly long, that hour was cruelly sharp.

Helen invaded those minutes. 'Come on to bed, it's late.' Following Helen to their room. Lying down with Helen in a warm bed, curled into each other. Quiet, sleepy conversations. The feel of a hand in hers, fingers curled against her own, wrist to wrist, her head in the curve of Helen's shoulder. The security of the night, the pleasant waking in the morning, knowing that you were going into the day together.

Always the small things. Helen had not been easy, so she had tried to please her. The kind of tea that Helen had liked would be as clean as a blade in memory, staring at her from shop shelves. Or the bread that went into the supermarket basket was Helen's rye bread that she herself had never liked, but that she automatically chose. Cooking for one. She had never really got over that. In ten years, never got over it.

Her brother would come back to her then, too. She'd be back in Haltby Road in the cold house. Staring at the things she cooked on their rickety stove. The same stove that their mother had used. Her 16-year-old hands moving around the plates and pans. The same long view out of the kitchen window: rolling hills, empty sky, mountains in the distance. A glimpse of the single-track lane and the windswept trees. The occasional hiker going by. Cooking for William and herself. They were both just lost children at such times, feral almost. Children who had never been taught or cared for.

She'd found cruelty leaking out of her mouth, just like their mother.

'You won't like it, Will.'

'What is it?'

'Boiled cats and snails.'

And William would cry, and she'd take him into the next room and sit him down.

'What have I told you, Will?'

'Not to ask.'

'That's right. Don't ask. And what else?'

Looking at her from under his frown and confusion. 'And don't tell.'

'Yes, that's right,' she'd answered. 'Don't ask and don't tell. You don't tell anyone at all.'

*

Ten years of anniversaries, birthdays. Christmases, Easters, summers, winters, lived without Helen.

The days are slow. The years are fast.

The middle of the night, wakeful, pressing her face into the pillow whispering *I miss you, I miss you.* So sick of her own grief.

She travelled. Around and around, stuck in her loop. Stopped in out-of-the-way places. But never too long in any of them. Never so long that she became familiar either with the place or the people.

She was engrossed in some sort of journey similar to a long-distance slow train that stopped at, or slipped by, nameless places. A never-ending formless journey, as placid as a daydream, while she sat disengaged, letting the earth slide past her. Whenever she stopped somewhere she would go walking, and to libraries, and to matinee showings of films. Walking for hours sometimes. But nothing came into focus.

If she got a job – petrol station, corner shop, care attendant – after a while people always started asking questions.

'Have you family?'

'Do you have children?'

'What brought you here?'

People and their curiosity. They would not leave her alone.

'Are you here long?'

'Where are you staying?'

And the dreams.

One particular and horrifying dream out of many.

*

She returned to the south coast in the winter, driving down through the Midlands, out to Bristol. Down through Dartmoor and eventually down to Devon, as if being pulled back towards her old home on the coast. All the while, Helen was calling her. A relentless voice saying

I was here all the time, didn't you find me? You can find me if you come back.

Alice chose a cheap hotel this time, a white block on a river estuary.

She told them not to come into her room. She kept the windows open, and sea mist came in, and sun, and February fog, and the scent of the gardens outside, and rain sometimes in while she sat and she let it soak her face. She was very good at keeping still.

In fact, she felt so still that the world froze when she walked in it. By the fifth or sixth year after Helen's disappearance, she had found that it could possess a pleasant blankness. She refined loneliness to a delicate, opaque art. The world was empty and she found herself bleakly calm.

She would have loved to have a great white wall, or a great grey wall, a bulwark beyond which there was only muffled sound, like the sea heard from a distance. She never turned on a radio, and it was peaceful, and the most peaceful part of all was driving along small roads through small towns and inconsequential landscapes.

Perhaps I'm crazy, she thought one day.

She knew the oblique looks that she got in the hotel - the perplexed curiosity of the staff and other visitors. Maybe she *looked* crazy. She would stand staring into the mirror. But she couldn't see any obvious signs. All her life, she'd hurried to catch the ordinary, knowing that she was different. There was no choice – there had never been a choice – about that.

And then a text came from the estate agent. There was a property for sale above the bay 20 miles away. Asham Ferry. It had been owned by a 90-year-old woman who had died. Alice had turned the idea over and over in her mind. It was almost – but not quite – the same place. It was on the hill above the seafront and the café. They'd often been along this bay and this piece of coast and she could feel Helen nudging her hand, her shoulder. Felt her breath on her face.

Come back.

She arrived to view the house in the first week of January,

and the light was extraordinarily bright that morning, as if the place were stage lit; and the wind howled, tossing the tails of the cattle in the fields, whipping branches on to the roads. From the coast road she could see the white breakers rolling in.

She drove over the ridge of hills. Cars had to be parked in the dead-end lane. A hundred yards down, there was a National Trust gate – the coast was in the remit of the Trust for two miles either side of a winding mud path that led between scrub-like, dense trees. You could hear the sea making a roaring sound far below.

'It isn't often like this,' the agent reassured her. 'This bit of coast is sheltered. You never really get gales.' His handshake was warm, but too long. 'Miss Hauser, is it?'

'Yes.'

'Alice Hauser?'

'Yes.'

'I hear that you know this area.'

'I lived here a while ago. Ten years.'

They had walked down through the dripping tunnel of trees. 'Here it is,' he told her.

She felt a rush of recognition. On their walks, she and Helen had passed it a few times, and it had always looked like this: deserted. A green-roofed hut with a verandah and an outbuilding behind. A garden border grown high and as thick as the trees and shrubs in the lane. A couple of apple trees and a path that ran dead centre to the door.

'It was only ever meant as a temporary building,' the estate agent said.

'How old is it?'

'Mrs Franklin and her husband built it in the 1930s. As a holiday home, I believe.'

'But she lived here?'

'After her husband died. It's been empty since she went into care.'

'And how long ago was that?'

'Her daughter did say...' He glanced at his notes. 'Eight years?'

They went inside. The verandah was deep and ran right around the building. Inside, the smell of cedar. And damp. There was a wood stove against the wall, a galley kitchen. Nothing else.

'No bathroom?'

'No. And the toilet is outside.'

She walked to the sink. More wood, warped and white. Two ancient taps.

'He was a carpenter, I think. They made everything in here.'

'Water?' she asked.

'Water and electricity, yes.' He shivered slightly from the cold.

They went back out to the garden. She inclined her head, listening. 'How far is the cliff edge?' It was impossible to tell because of the garden, but she could feel it drop away, sense that there was nothing beyond the scrub and trees.

'About a hundred and fifty feet. There's no erosion. The cliff is solid.'

'And the nearest neighbour?'

He waved a hand casually over his shoulder. 'Bantam Wick, by the road. The big house you'll have passed.'

Half a mile. That was good.

She closed her eyes.

*

When the estate agent got back to his office, he threw his coat across his chair and said, 'Some woman's taken Cliff Cottage.'

'No,' said the girl nearest him, laughing in disbelief.

'She's buying it cash.' He stood, chewing on his thumb, frowning. 'I know her. I know her face. But I just can't place her.'

5

JOHN LORD PARKED HIS CAR at the roadside.

He checked again from the piece of paper in his hand that he had the right place. Then he looked in his driving mirror at the long stretch of country lane behind him, as straight as a die between high hedges.

It was the day after the crash.

He got out and walked to the top of a tarmac driveway. There was a sign here tucked into the grass. He checked the name of the house against the piece of paper, which he then folded carefully and put into his pocket. Looking down the drive – more like another narrow lane than the entrance to a property – weeds were pushing up through the surface. Trees hung overhead. He could see a house a hundred yards away, a very old house hiding in the dip of the land. Part thatch, part tile on the roof. Your typical country cottage. Chocolate box stuff. Gritting his teeth in the silence and the faint sunshine, he began to walk.

On the phone last night, Liz had warned him not to come.

'John, leave it to the police.'

'I'm not going to do that.'

'You *have* to do that. They know what they're doing.'

'This isn't their business. It's Mike's. And mine.'

He had heard a long exasperated sigh on the other end of the phone. He could imagine her sitting in the garden, cigarette in hand, a cup of coffee by her side. At the end of the day she was always exhausted. But in a good way, tired out by the teaching job she loved. Different to him. He was always wrung out through frustration. From the sense that the business was sliding gradually downhill.

'I owe it to him,' he told her.

'You owe it to Mike to arrange for him to come home,' Liz said. 'Not take it out on someone else.'

'Take it out on him?' he'd repeated incredulously. 'I'm not going to take anything out on him.'

'You're sure?' She sounded anything but.

'I'll be home in the afternoon.'

'John…'

He breathed in deeply when he put the phone down. He was inhaling the air of their home, imagining it.

The driveway here reminded him of their own lane. Flat instead of uphill, but with that same country feel. Land spreading out on either side. This place smelled of the overnight rain. As he got closer to the house, he could see an old rose clipped and trained to the wall, just starting to come into leaf.

His eyes ranged over the place. Very nice. The tiled roof dipped in the middle from the weight of years. The thatch looked relatively new. Money, then. It took a lot of money to replace a thatch. The windows were set back in stone frames. Maybe 300 years old, and what looked like two front doors, one facing the lane and one to the side. He tried the first and saw immediately that it hadn't been opened in a long time, was painted shut despite being half glass. Frowning, he went along the side to the next. There was an open porch with a stone shelf. On the shelf was a dog's lead.

He knocked. He heard the sound echoing through the rooms. There was no reply.

He questioned himself then. He had no idea what he was going to say. In the back of his car was Mike's viola and his clothes – the well-worn stuff that he had been wearing, not his concert clothes. They had been in a case. He had opened the case and inspected the viola, and found it horrible to see things neatly folded, and the beautiful instrument unmarked. Horrible because Mike had packed those clothes – the black jacket, the pressed white shirt. It was Mike who had put the viola in the case. His were the last hands that had touched those strings; it was he who had packed the music.

It had even felt odd taking them away, because John felt that his brother would need them. Placing the viola on the back seat of his car had felt as if he were packing a precious child into a harness as he had fastened the seat belt around it.

Mind that thing, he heard Mike say.

It broke his heart.

Horrible, terrible. World out of joint.

And the man who lived in this house was responsible.

John walked away from the door, looked up in frustration at the upper windows, and retraced his steps. He could see a gate leading to the back, alongside the garage.

Big garage, he thought. Triple garage. *Very* fucking nice. Probably got a Range Rover in there, bastard. His thoughts seemed to bang inside his brain, as if his skull were empty and his ideas were knocking against bone.

He pushed open the gate.

The garden was large. It was level for a while and then sloped dramatically. There was a little stream and a footbridge at the bottom. He could see the roof of a shed behind a privet hedge, and as he walked towards it he realised that it was some kind of workshop or studio. On the outside, in open shelves with a corrugated iron roof, were stacks of wood.

He'd heard about that somewhere. Seasoned wood, allowed to expand and contract with the seasons. Here was a man who stored sections of trees and then cut them further and shaped them. Suddenly the cutting of wood seemed to him unutterably senseless and cruel. Taking down trees and splitting them, bending them to a frame.

He knew that Maitland had some sort of talent, supposedly. But all of an instant it seemed to him the worst occupation on earth, using what used to be living trees. Living to dead, living to dead. And then making a painting, putting the living world on to paper. It didn't seem clever to him at all in that moment. It was false and pointless.

It was a grassy path, and slippery. He made his way slowly. There were still no words in his head, but there was a hard fist of resentment in his chest. Lovely house, nice workshop, country home. He couldn't say exactly what his feeling was, because he had never experienced it before. It was as if something that he had eaten had gone bad and wouldn't move from under his ribcage.

The door was half open.

There was a mixed smell in the crowded space. Varnish, wood, oil paint. The sight of the man sitting by the easel surprised him, stopped him in his tracks. He'd imagined that it would be someone young or middle-aged. Stocky maybe, from sitting at his work. Stocky and square. But this was an old man.

Maybe he'd got the wrong place.

'Are you Thomas Maitland?'

The man looked up. It was obvious that he hadn't heard John coming. He wasn't painting. He had simply been sitting, slumped forward slightly, his hands folded, his head bowed.

'Yes.' Maitland stood up very slowly, his whole body telegraphing fatigue.

'I'm John Lord.'

No reaction. Maitland shrugged in a puzzled way and spread his hands as if to say, *So what?*

'I'm Mike Lord's brother. The man who was killed yesterday.'

There was some reaction then. Maitland stepped forward, and took a pair of glasses out of the pocket of his fleece. Once he had them on, his face changed. It couldn't have got paler, but it went through a series of oddly emphatic expressions. Realisation. Puzzlement. Fear. Almost like a theatrical mime of those feelings.

Maitland looked past him to the door.

'There isn't anyone with me,' John told him.

'Did the police send you?'

'No.'

'No,' Maitland repeated. He seemed to shuffle out of his apathy, realising his mistake. 'No, of course not.'

In the silence, a paraffin stove in the corner creaked. That was the oily smell, John thought. Paraffin. You hardly came across it these days. One of the first offices he had worked in when he was a teenager had used these stoves if there was a power cut.

'How did you know where I am?' Maitland asked.

'One of the other people told me.' John took the piece of paper out of his pocket and showed it. 'She took down your name from the side of the van.'

Maitland nodded. 'I see. Was it an elderly lady?'

'Yes.' John thought he might choke if he couldn't get away from the smell of the paraffin.

'The police called you?' Maitland asked.

'I came down from Cumbria.'

'Cumbria? That's a long way.'

'I was sure it wasn't him.'

'But…'

'But it was.'

Maitland nodded again.

You fucking nodding dog, is that all you can do?

'I wasn't absolutely certain that he was killed. I thought so. But no one told me exactly that morning,' Maitland murmured.

'But they told you afterwards?'

'Yes, they told me afterwards. I'm very sorry for your loss.'

John stepped forward. He wanted to hit him. He wanted to plant his fist in that face. More than that. He wanted to kill him. Visceral. It surprised him how plain and strong that feeling was, how justified.

'I just spoke to the police,' he told Maitland. 'He cartwheeled into the trees.'

'Yes.'

'The car turned over. It landed on its wheels by some fucking miracle, in the trees.'

Maitland looked at his feet.

'Are you paying attention to me? It went into the trees and quite a distance from the road. Have you any idea of how fast you were going?'

'Not fast.'

'No? Not fast? Faster than he was, I bet. Wouldn't you say? You coming downhill in a van, and him driving a fucking little Fiat coming uphill…'

'I wasn't speeding.'

'No? How fast were you going, then?'

'I don't know exactly.'

'You don't? Coming downhill and what, you had stock in the van maybe?'

'Yes.'

'A fully loaded van?'

'No. It was just one large canvas.'

Maitland was frowning now. Christ, he looked sick. What was wrong with him?

'I wasn't speeding,' he repeated. 'As soon as I realised, I braked. I swerved.'

'You *swerved*? What, into him?'

'No.'

'You swerved into him. You hit him.'

'That wasn't how it happened.'

'Well, how did it happen exactly?'

Maitland sighed. 'I can't say.'

'My brother is driving his car, a little car.'

'Look,' Maitland said suddenly. 'I can't discuss this. I just can't tell you. You ought to speak to the police, if that's what you want to do.'

'Oh,' John said, nodding. His skin was hot. The skin on his face. Hot, like sitting in front of a fire. 'Oh yes, I'll do that. You can be sure of it. This woman.' He brought the piece of paper out of his pocket again and waved it in front of Maitland's face. 'This woman says you hit him, smashed into him...'

'She's not right. He hit me.'

'Oh, like you remember now? A second ago you couldn't say.'

'I'm sorry,' Maitland told him in a quiet voice. 'He came straight across the road into me.'

'That's your story?'

'It's not a story. I saw him coming up the hill. The car began to veer towards me. Slowly veering.' The older man put a hand to his face and rubbed his forehead. 'Not sudden. I thought he'd correct himself. I glanced down at my dog. And then he was...'

'You weren't looking.'

'I was looking.'

'Not paying attention! You looked at your dog.'

'It was a second. Half a second. Just a glance.'

'But you looked at your bloody dog!'

'Half on the dog, half on the road.'

'What was the dog doing?'

'I don't understand.'

'You heard me. Moving about? Big dog moving about? I bet it wasn't harnessed. Dog bumped you, did it? Made you look away, maybe pulled on the wheel?'

In his mind's eye, he could clearly see this happening. It revealed itself to him suddenly now as a fully blown picture in vivid detail. The dog being some sort of nuisance, probably a large breed, unsecured on the seat.

He was close to Maitland now, standing slackly, apologetically. If he realised that he was going to be hit, he didn't show it. He was just one great slack body, shoulders drooping. And silently shaking his head from side to side.

'What are you? Sixty? Seventy?'

'Pardon me?' Maitland asked.

John waved his hand. 'Age.'

'I'm fifty-six.'

John heard himself laugh briefly. 'You look like shit.'

Maitland blinked once or twice.

'Really, like shit. Maybe you shouldn't be driving at all.'

John turned away. He wanted to get out of the workshop. Out of the corner of his eye, he saw a half-finished picture, some sort of abstract image about five feet square, standing in front of a lot of other frames, next to a table of brushes and bottles of turpentine. He stared at the painting for some moments, thinking that it was beautiful, and that Liz would like it.

'Jesus,' he muttered. He turned around again, staring at the man. 'You're sick, are you?'

'No, I'm not sick.'

'You look it. You look like you've got something wrong with you. You're taking medication? Maybe you were half asleep yesterday morning.'

'No.'

Exasperation swarmed through John. He walked over to the painting and laid his hand on it. 'My brother is dead,' he said quietly. 'My twin brother. I don't suppose that you know what that means.'

'I'm sorry...'

'I don't suppose you've lost anyone. I don't think you know what that means.' He looked up, away from the painting. There was a tiny window in the wall, an old-fashioned kind with wire threaded into the glass. Through it, he could see the edge of the thatched part of the house. 'Living here,' he murmured. 'In the country. In your expensive house.'

Maitland didn't reply.

'Got a nice family, I suppose. Nice little business.' He looked down again at the painting. 'Sell much?' he asked, and looked back at Thomas.

'It's more of a hobby.'

49

John looked around at the equipment. 'This stuff must cost a bit.'

'Some of it.'

'Expensive hobby, then. Expensive house, expensive hobby.'

'Well, at times.'

'Oh yes,' he decided suddenly to himself. 'Altogether a nice set-up.' A thought occurred to him. 'Retirement hobby, is it?'

'It's something that I always wanted to do.'

John raised his voice. 'Maybe you didn't hear me. Maybe you're not paying attention. I asked you, is this your retirement hobby?'

'Yes.' Maitland glanced at his phone lying on the workbench.

'Retired from what? What did you do?'

'Look, Mr Lord…'

'From what!' He was at Maitland's side in half a dozen strides. He didn't give a damn what career Maitland might have had. It was just something to say while he considered how much he was going to hurt him. He stood so close to him now that he could feel the other man's breath on his face.

'Listen,' he said. And he tried to keep his voice under control, tried to lower it. And as he did so, he thought of the last argument with Liz. He thought of her saying, *You want to take a breath John, because you're frightening me. Please, John.*

'Listen,' he repeated. A kind of tremor ran up his spine. He thought he was beginning to shake. He bit the inside of his cheek. 'Do you know what's going to happen? I'm going to get you charged with death by dangerous driving. I'm going to get you convicted of that, do you understand? I'm going to make sure that I see you standing in the dock and convicted for murdering my brother.'

'That's a case very hard to prove,' Maitland said.

Easy and calm, and quiet as you like.

John snatched up the nearest thing to him, a heavy spirit level. It looked old, antique. Maitland stepped back. But there was nowhere for him to go. He had his back to the easel.

John, you're frightening me.

John turned away and strode back to the painting with all its vibrant colours – *Hours of work is that,* he thought, *hours of work, how long does it take to make that, a long time* – and he brought the spirit level down on the surface and tried to split it. There was not much of a mark. Not as much as he'd like. He threw the thing down and stood there sweating, retching almost, sick to the stomach.

'Mr Lord,' Maitland murmured.

He looked behind him. Maitland had his phone in his hand.

'Don't bother,' John told him.

He went to the door and breathed in the clean air of the morning.

'This is just the beginning,' he said. 'Do you understand me? You're not going to forget this day. Because this is just the start.'

*

John didn't go home that night.

Instead, he went to the Pallingham concert.

It was in a beautiful place, a private school set in glorious grounds. He parked some distance from the concert hall and walked through the parkland as the light was draining from the sky. He had never been here before and the school and the enormous chapel seemed exhaustingly vast to him, floating in the green countryside like a sepulchre or memorial, a chalky colour against the woods.

When he got inside, he was met by a woman who grasped his hands. 'Oh, Mr Lord. We're so very sorry about Michael.'

'Thank you.'

'But really… Such a terrible loss for you and your family, and of course to music. Such a wonderful talent.'

'Thank you,' he repeated.

They sat him in the front row. After a while he got up and went to the back, where he sat down again and listened to Bach, looking intently at the female musician who had been brought in to take Mike's place.

Then, at the end of the second piece, he got up and left.

He walked back through the inky darkness, the formless-seeming shadowy mass of the park, carrying his misery all the way.

6

Helen Elizabeth McAllister had disappeared in July.

The beginning of July ten years ago.

It had been a warm, beautiful day. She'd been due at a meeting with colleagues. They had waited in the school staffroom on a sweltering morning, all the windows open on to the playing fields and the tennis courts. St. George's was a private school, one of several in this wealthy county, and the grounds were well-kept; the line of 100-year-old chestnut trees along the drive had cast less and less shadow as the sun rose higher in the sky. There was no breath of breeze.

'We'll get on without her,' the Head had decided.

In truth, nobody minded. Helen wasn't well liked. She could spin a conversation out until she had beaten down the other person, like a terrier worrying a bone. That's what she was to most: sarcastic, undermining. She never told anyone about her personal life.

On that July morning, they had had the meeting without her, but afterwards the Head had made a phone call. He didn't like loose ends.

Her mobile rang out unanswered.

He had tried again in the afternoon. It went to voicemail.

In fact, he was relieved not to talk to her. He left a message instead. 'Miss McAllister, I wonder if you forgot our meeting today? Would you send me an email? Thank you.'

He didn't like her, but that was irrelevant. She was an asset to the school. You could depend on her. Most pleasing of all was that she had never come to him with any personal problem, the sort that resulted in time off. No children, no partner, no parents in tow. He knew that from her application five years before.

He sat back in his chair and considered the pleasant view from his study window.

Helen McAllister had never been late or absent for anything.

*

At 3 o'clock the next day, Alice Hauser had walked into Brimham police station. The weather was truly sweltering, a fierce heat that was to last all month. She had stood at the desk, both hands flat on the counter as if to steady herself.

'I want to report a missing person,' she said.

The officer who came to talk to her, Richard Ellis, thought that she might be sick because she was so pale, sitting in the interview room turning her car keys over and over in her hands.

'Can I get you anything?' he asked. A glass of water.

'The weather's so warm,' she whispered, drinking half of it and setting the glass unsteadily on the table. She sat tugging at her T-shirt to ease it from her shoulders.

She gave her name, and spelled it.

She lived in a single-storey house, she said, right on the beach at Asham Ferry. 'In one of those odd-looking ones with the plate glass fronts.' The car keys had clanked in her hands until she laid them on the table.

'And how long has she been missing?'

'Since yesterday. Her name is Helen McAllister.'

'And this lady…'

'She's my partner,' Alice Hauser said. 'We are partners.'

Traffic noisily passing on the road outside. Heat pressing

down hard on the room. She gave her address. 'Do you know it? You must know it. Near the beach café. The one with the boards outside.'

He knew it. The café perched on the edge of the shingle.

'I work there.'

'Does she?'

'Oh, no. She teaches at St George's. She's been there...' Her voice had trailed away. 'A long time. I mean, she's taught for a long time. English literature. And she helps at sports. She likes sport.'

'Age?'

'She's thirty.'

'And you, your age?'

'What does it matter?'

'Just for the record.'

'I'm twenty-two.' She took her hands from the table. 'She had a meeting at the school yesterday, but she never turned up. Nobody rang to tell me. I rang them today. I rang the Head. He said that there was nothing on file that gave my number as a contact...' She gave a strained little laugh. 'I can't believe that.'

Ellis considered her. Her accent was not local; he couldn't say what it was. North country somewhere. He'd once had a girlfriend who came from Sheffield, and remembered the definition, the burr of it.

'Are you from this part of the world?' he asked.

She didn't miss a beat. 'Yes, I work in the café. I told you.'

'No. You said you lived near it.'

'I live just behind it and I work there,' she explained, irritated.

'I see.' He paused. She hadn't answered his question. He let it go. 'We will speak to Miss McAllister's school.'

She looked down at his notebook, and added, 'She left at eight thirty.'

'How?'

'What do you mean, how?'

'Did she drive? Has she got a car?'

She gave him the make, model, year and registration. 'Red,' she murmured, and put her head briefly in her hands, pressing them to her face so hard that when she put them down again there were small white arcs of fingertip pressure on her forehead. 'She bought it last year. Not long after we met.'

'Has she any family that she might be visiting?'

'No.'

'Friends?'

'We just have each other.'

'Can you give a description?'

'I can do better,' she said. She reached into her handbag and took out a photograph. It had been taken on the same beach that she had just described, the unmistakable arc of glowing sandstone at Asham Ferry. There was the café in the background. Helen McAllister was standing in the surf, hands on hips, laughing.

'It was taken last summer.'

Helen was slim, tall, blonde, and pretty. In the photograph she looked very happy. Outgoing, independent.

'She was daring me to get in the sea,' Alice explained.

'And how long have you two known each other?'

She paused again, scrutinising the officer. Her face took on a guarded expression. 'We are together,' she repeated. 'It's not a passing thing. We've been together for a year.'

'Past relationships?'

'I'm sorry?'

'Is there anyone in her past who might be looking for her, might be trying to find her, want to get in touch?'

'No.'

'Parents, siblings?'

'I've told you… nobody. She's an only child. Her parents are dead.'

'Uncles, aunts, cousins? Children of her own?'

'There's nobody for either of us.' And she gave a shudder and looked down at her clasped hands, not meeting his eye.

'She never mentioned anyone special?' The officer glanced back at his notes. 'She's thirty years old and never married, never had another long-term relationship?'

Alice Hauser had paused. 'No.'

Ellis said afterwards that he couldn't make Alice Hauser out. There was something about her that didn't sit right. She was fidgety and distracted and anxious, but she didn't have that hollow-eyed look of horror that he had seen in others reporting missing persons.

'Are you very worried?' he had asked her.

'Yes, of course.'

'But you didn't think of telling us last night?'

'I just sat waiting for her.'

'Or first thing this morning?'

She frowned, and sighed. 'I kept thinking all the things that you've just asked me,' she murmured. 'Had I missed something? Did she say that she wouldn't be back? Had I got something wrong, missed something that she had told me? Usually I would be in work at the café, but this morning I felt ill, so I stayed at home, waiting.'

A silence settled. Alice crossed her arms as if to comfort herself, rocking slightly back and forth.

'How had she seemed lately? She didn't talk of having a break, a holiday?'

'No. We were looking forward to the summer together. Now that the school… The school is on holiday now, you see?'

'Had anyone new come into her conversation?'

She was silent for a long time, looking into her lap. 'No.'

'And had there been any problems that you can think of lately? Health? Money?'

'No. We don't argue.' She leaned forward then, arms on the table, an urgent tone in her voice. 'We are happy,' she said. 'There's no reason that she should go. Don't you realise? Something bad has happened.'

'Why jump to that conclusion?'

'Jump?' she repeated loudly. 'I've been waiting for her for more than twenty-four hours, since she ought to have come home. I haven't *jumped* to any conclusion.'

'Might she have planned to leave without telling you?'

She gave a momentary start and seemed insulted, pained. 'No.'

'What about her phone? You've rung her?'

Her mouth set in a hard line. 'Yes,' she said, almost hissing the word. 'Of course I've rung her. What do you think? *Of course.*'

Ellis reassured her that they would begin to look. The woman had been gone for nearly 36 hours. Not necessarily a cause for alarm. People did just up and leave their partners without explanation. Thousands disappeared in the UK every year. With a child, the danger signals would be ringing loudly, but not for an adult.

Ellis got up and indicated the open door. He murmured a few words. Platitudes belonging to the situation.

But Alice Hauser wouldn't leave the room. She stood with her bag clasped to her chest, breathing shallowly, audibly drawing in air.

'Who will investigate her disappearance?' she asked. 'I mean, who personally?'

It was an unusual question. On the whole, people didn't care who did the job, as long as someone did. 'We'll be in touch shortly.'

She hesitated as if she wanted to say something else, then sighed.

He watched her leave.

*

At 5 o'clock, barely two hours after Alice Hauser had been at the station, a red car was spotted by a police patrol on the coast road.

There was a point where the hills ran down almost to the beach, and here the road rose up on the side of the hill. It was a beautiful place and on either edge of the road was a lay-by, a place where tourists and locals would stop to take photographs, or simply admire the view of the curving shoreline far below.

The hill was an ancient ridgeway, here and there dotted with Bronze Age graves. The path was so worn at the top that the chalk showed through the turf. From the highest point, just beyond the road, miles of coastline could be seen, and the enormous geological divide became obvious – chalk to the east, sandstone to the west. Distantly, across the huge bay, the cliffs were a golden colour.

Helen McAllister's car was facing west, having come – it seemed – from the direction of the village at the bottom of the hill. It was the wrong direction to be facing if Helen had left it there on the way to work.

In the passenger footwell was a light jacket. But no bag and no phone.

There was no sign of trouble. The doors were locked. In the glove compartment were her insurance documents, papers for a breakdown service, an MOT certificate and a satnav zipped into a black plastic case. There was no luggage, no mess, no receipts and no marks. The boot was empty, as were the door pockets.

An ice cream van was parked in the lay-by most days, and the owner told the police that the red car had been there when he had left at five the previous evening, and had still been there in exactly the same place when he had come back that lunchtime. He told the officers that he had been thinking of reporting it.

'And why didn't you?'

'People park here and go for walks,' he said.

'Not overnight walks, though.'

'No,' he conceded carelessly. 'Not overnight walks.'

The police constable glanced up at the hill behind them. The man was right. People did park here, go through the gate, and follow the path up to the top to get the best view. From there you could see right along the coast and also into the countryside behind, spread out like a green patchwork. It was shimmering today in the unaccustomed heat.

He wondered if Helen McAllister had done just that – gone through the gate and walked to the top of the hill to take in the beautiful view – and if anyone had been with her.

'Was the car here when you got here yesterday morning?'

'I wasn't here until the afternoon,' he explained. 'So I couldn't tell you if it was here in the morning or not. But it was definitely there by the time I got here at midday.'

The car was about six miles from Helen and Alice's home at Asham Ferry, and eight miles from St George's. But it wasn't facing in the direction of the school. It was facing in the direction of Asham Ferry, as if Helen were coming back. But, if so, she had turned back sometime before noon, when the van had arrived.

It was impossible to say whether she had turned back on the way to school, having forgotten something, or whether she had turned back later in the morning. Turned back towards home without having arrived at the school. If so what had she been doing in the hours between 8.30 in the morning and midday?

'If she forgot something, why park here?' the officer asked his mate. 'Why not go home?'

'Something wrong with the car?'

It was checked. The breakdown service hadn't been contacted, and there was no mechanical fault.

It appeared that Helen McAllister had simply got out of the car sometime the previous morning, taking her keys and bag and phone with her, and walked away.

7

Ten years can be a long time.

Or it can be no time at all.

On Saturday, Alice Hauser drove from the clifftop house to Brimham, 20 miles inland. The journey took her through changing countryside: green rolling valleys interspersed with flat and fertile fields. Crops beginning to show, faint lines in the soil. Trees in first leaf. All the promise of the year.

Coming down the hill towards the town, her heart was in her mouth. She was nervous of remembering. She and Helen had always liked Brimham; they had come here often. It was why she had gone there ten years ago to report her disappearance, knowing that there was a police station there but hoping still that she might see her walking along the street. Hoping for that miracle.

She didn't know what she had been expecting – some momentous difference in the place, some discolouration or distortion, reflecting her own absence and the greyness of her life – but Brimham hadn't changed at all. Nestled in a wide valley, it looked both peaceful and beautiful, with the spire of the abbey marking its centre in the morning sunshine.

Parking her car in a side street, she looked up towards the abbey green. She and Helen had looked at a flat in the road next to the church. Her heart turned sluggishly in her chest, like a small animal turning in its sleep.

Oh, don't wake me.

Make it ten years ago.

Make it that day that we came to look at the flat.

God, memories were so hard. She was tired of being ambushed by them. She wanted to know if seeing Brimham would be as hurtful as she'd imagined. Wanted to know if she could lay the ghost to rest. The ghost of being part of a couple – that far-off dream of being two.

That Saturday morning in autumn, they had not been together long and everything was painted in an improbably rosy glow, even the inconsequential things in the street: kerbstones, shopfronts, the lettering on signs. Alice had never received affection like this, except perhaps for the doglike devotion of her brother. But she tried not to think of William as she had clasped Helen's hand. For once in her life – for the first time in her life, in fact – she had been happy to the roots of her soul.

Alice paused by her car now, breathing shallowly. In the next street along was somewhere that she knew almost as well – the shabby 1950s building where she had been questioned, twice, a fortnight after Helen had disappeared. The place where she had come to first report her missing. A week after their home had been searched. She had not been taken to the headquarters further west in the county – a new glass and steel centre in manicured grounds – and she had never known why. Perhaps they thought that the cosy, old-fashioned familiarity of Brimham would reassure her, even lull her into a sense of false security.

It was another place that had its ghosts, ghosts that she had given up trying to lay to rest. Even in a warm sunlight on this beautiful morning, she had a conviction, ten years in the making, that some ghosts would never stay in their graves. They would always rise up and suffocate her, and she would never be free.

Just a few questions.

We'll take them at Brimham.

No need to drive to HQ.

Despite every intention – despite the lure of the memory of the café where Helen had held her hand – Alice found herself now going to the next street, standing at the corner, and looking at the police station. It looked the same. A single-storey block with aluminium window frames, and a patch of lawn outside. The door had not been repainted. 'Would you like a cup of tea?' That had been Richard Ellis. He had always shaken her hand whenever he'd seen her. Ellis had always been the smiling one behind that blue painted door.

It was Thomas Maitland, Ellis's boss, who had been her tormentor.

As she watched now, the door of the police station opened and a man came out, shrugging himself into a coat. He looked angry and frustrated. He turned, stumbled and as he passed Alice, he looked at her blankly: seeing but not seeing, and his shoulder brushed against hers.

The sun felt hot on Alice's neck. She realised that she had begun to sweat. She turned away and absentmindedly followed the man, sunlight half blinding her as she reached the abbey. She shaded her eyes as she looked up at the huge church.

She felt nauseous at the memory of coming out of that blue door after speaking to Maitland. Ten years ago, she had been sure that they would somehow pin Helen's death on her, even though a body had never been found. Crossing the road, still breathing heavily, she crossed the green and went into the cool and quiet of the abbey.

She walked slowly along a side aisle through the colours cast by the stained glass windows, waiting for her breathing to slow.

Waiting for her heart to stop racing.

On the same morning that she and Helen had looked at the flat – in those first days before it all went wrong – they had come here afterwards and sat down in a pew near the altar. All that time ago that was really no time at all. It may as well have been yesterday, and all her travelling and evasion of the past nothing more than a dream.

That day, Helen had quietly put her hand into hers, pressing her thumb against Alice's palm. They had smiled at each other. Helen had a familiar expression on her face – smiling at some inner stratagem or joke, a catlike, sideways smile. It was part of her appeal: she was unknowable even in her closeness, and she was strong. Opinionated and cajoling. Everything was possible to Helen. She circumnavigated obstacles, and could call you out for being afraid of them.

On that Saturday, they had been talking about partnership. Civil partnerships had come in two years before, but Helen had wanted a big flashy wedding.

'I'll wait,' she had told Alice.

Alice had already been reeling at the mention of a wedding, at the thought that this woman wanted her for life. For ever. 'Wait for what?' she had asked.

'Until we can get married in the abbey.'

Alice had laughed. 'But that's never going to happen!'

'Yes,' Helen had told her. 'One day it will happen. And then we'll come into town and have a day of it.'

'A day of what?'

'Of getting married.'

'You think they'd actually marry us here, in the abbey? No way.'

But Helen had been right. She was generally right about things. Eleven years later it had become legal to marry here, under this great sandstone arch, next to where Anglo-Saxon kings were buried, under the glorious roof bosses, in the colours pooling from the windows. She and Helen. Helen and her.

But when that law was finally passed, Helen had been missing for nine years, and Alice had taken herself far away.

She looked up at the altar, at the enormous brass cross, at the silver, at the white cloths. It was all so imposingly clean and ordered. It seemed to bear down on her suddenly: an atmosphere taking on human form with an accusing voice. She got up and stared at a future that had receded – she and Helen standing by that altar, under those windows – snatched away from her.

She still remembered the question she'd dared to ask. 'Helen… has there been anyone else?'

Helen had grinned. 'What are we, jealous?'

'No, but I…'

'Darling, I'm thirty years old. What do you think?'

Alice had felt herself colouring up. She'd glanced away.

Helen had put her arms around her from behind in a bear hug and rested her chin on Alice's shoulder. She whispered, 'We can't all be angels.'

'A woman?'

She felt the breath of Helen's laugh on her neck. 'And a man.'

'What man?'

'Oh,' Helen had murmured. 'Maybe I'll tell you all about him. I'll tell you all about it if you're good. Would you like that?'

'No.'

Helen's lips on her skin. 'I think I will. Every detail.'

'Please, I don't want to know.'

'Don't you, my little green-eyed monster?'

As she walked slowly back down the central aisle, Alice saw the man who had been in the police station. He didn't look as if they had helped him in any way. Rather the opposite. He looked defeated.

She would have walked past him but that despairing posture.

'Excuse me,' she said.

He glanced up at her, then looked away.

'You were just in the police station.'

He didn't reply.

She sat down beside him. 'I don't mean to disturb you, but…'

'Then don't.' But he looked up almost immediately, and seemed to focus on her for the first time.

'What did you want?' she asked.

'What do you mean?'

'Of them. The police. I don't think they'll help you. Not in my experience.'

'I know that now,' he replied. John Lord gave a laboured sigh, staring up at the vaulted roof and then around him at the memorials on the walls and the carved oak pulpit. Then he looked back at her speculatively. 'Do you believe in all this?'

'What exactly?'

'Religion.'

'No,' she said.

'Not raised in it?'

'Oh,' she replied. 'I was raised to fear God and retribution, yes.'

'Do you any good?'

'Never.'

'Nor me.'

They gave each other a faint smile. But she was tempted to stand up and move away, because she had recognised his accent.

John sighed and looked down, shaking his head wearily from side to side. 'I must go home.' He governed himself, arranging his feet as if they didn't quite belong to him, seemingly willing himself to stand.

'You ought to,' she murmured. 'You look very tired.'

He stood up and plunged his hands into his pockets, shrugging his shoulders as if he were cold. 'I used to sing in a church choir,' he told her distractedly. 'Not in a big place like this. Just the local church. Even communion at eight o'clock on a Sunday morning. A country church. There were more sheep outside than congregation inside.' He nodded, remembering. 'We liked doing it. Me and Mike. Can you credit that?' Then he spread his hands. 'With my brother, when we were kids. He was musical. I wasn't. I was tone deaf.'

'But you sang?'

'I was asked to leave.' He gave a sad little smile.

They walked together towards the door. At the back of the church was a small table holding prayer and hymn books.

As they passed, he picked up a Book of Common Prayer. 'Remember this? From when you had religion?'

'I never had it. I hated it.'

'Remember the Confession?'

'No.'

'You had to say that there's no health in you. "And there is no health in us." At least, you used to. I wonder if they changed it. Not a great thing to teach your children, is it? That there's no health in them.'

'You have children?'

'Two girls. You?'

'No.'

He put the book down. 'I used to look at Mike and think – I mean, I'm a boy here, I'm eight or nine, you don't understand much at that age, do you? I used to wonder, how can Mike not be healthy? Look at him. Look at me. We're fine.' He ran a finger over the cover of the discarded book. 'He died two days ago.'

'Oh… No! I'm so sorry.' She automatically wanted to reach out and say, *I know that, I know that feeling, to lose someone –* but she stopped herself.

'He died two days ago and the man who ran him off the road and killed him is walking about fit and well. And these buggers here—' he cocked a thumb towards the town, 'say that it's police business and I'm not to get involved with him. His name is Maitland.'

Alice gave him a long hard stare.

'Sit down a minute,' she murmured.

*

Back at the station, Richard Ellis picked up the newspaper that his sergeant had been reading before John Lord had come in.

There was an article on an inside page about the accident on the Radstock road.

A man of 44 was declared dead at the scene.

Several casualties were admitted to hospital.

Collision with a white van.

The driver of the van, a 56-year-old man, was unhurt.

Ellis flicked the paper dismissively. 'John Lord reckons the old man was to blame. That there's witnesses to it.'

'Never,' the sergeant retorted.

'You'd think.'

'When did he retire?'

'His wife was ill. She died two years ago. But he retired seven years before that.' Ellis rocked backwards and forwards on his heels. 'Of course, he was finished long before he retired.'

The sergeant looked up, surprised. He had only recently come to the area. He knew of Inspector Maitland, but only by name. 'Finished? Why?'

Ellis looked out of the window. 'There was a disappearance case ten years ago. A woman from Asham Ferry. She just vanished one morning. We found the car – no sign of trouble. All neatly locked up. But the woman was gone.'

'What was the trouble with the boss?'

'The woman who disappeared had a partner, and that partner – strange, quiet woman – she kept on and on. It all became… well, trouble.'

'Why? What did she say?'

Ellis gave a sigh, frowning. 'You don't want to know. You really do not want to know.' He snatched up his car keys from the table. 'She broke him into little pieces.'

8

FOUR DAYS LATER IN DOB Gill woods, the stream had broken its banks and water tumbled down the stones between the trees. In light but relentless rain, John Lord trudged uphill despite the slipperiness of the path.

Occasionally, he looked back down through the dense canopy, broken in places where old conifers had been cleared. Thirlmere lay below like a flat grey sheet, no ripple on its surface and no reflection from the leaden sky. Every now and again when he stopped, John looked at his feet, his hands plunged in his pockets.

The woods around Thirlmere weren't the most popular walking place in the Lake District even in summer. Under Thirlmere lay the long abandoned villages of Amboth and Wythburn, flooded when the reservoir was created in the 19th century. There were houses under there somewhere, and a church, all drowned to give Manchester water. John stood and thought of the pipes running south under the valleys, and his mind raced with them, back down through the country until his concentration hit a road near the coast.

He had been in to see a funeral director that morning, confused at the instructions that had been left in Mike's will for a woodland burial. But despite the long conversation, he still couldn't get his head around the fact that the arrangements were all for his brother. It was too surreal.

Eight years ago he had done the same thing for his father, and that had seemed right – sad, but right. His father had been 81 and in poor health for years. But Mike – Mike had been fit and well. John couldn't stand the thought that his brother was lying in some hospital drawer, cold to the touch. It had woken him in the night. Two images: Mike's icy flesh, and the expressionless face of that bastard, Maitland.

Liz had come downstairs and tried to get him to come back to bed. But he had shrugged her away. How could she understand what he was thinking, how could she know what it was like?

Part of him was dead with Mike.

A good part. The best part.

*

He reached Harrop Tarn at midday.

It had stopped raining. At the mouth of the lake, a tree had become lodged at the makeshift crossing. He skirted it, walking in the direction of Tarn Crag. Here, where the trees became less sparse, he sat down on a boulder and stared at the tarn.

Liz had asked him this morning if he was going to the office this afternoon and he had told her yes. But he had no intention of going into Keswick.

'Will you be all right at work?' she had asked. 'And will you be okay this morning?'

Her concern irritated him. Worse than that. It made him angry. She was like something scratching at his skin. It was an intrusion. When he had at last gone to bed, he had turned away from her and after a while she had curled into him and put her arms around his waist. Something that she hadn't done in a very long time. And he knew that it was just out of pity.

'Leave go of me,' he'd told her.

He had heard her sigh, and she had rolled away from him.

Eventually, at 6 o'clock, he had got up again, gone back down to the kitchen and stared at the greyness of the garden in the dawn.

He couldn't get what Alice Hauser had told him out of his head.

*

They had sat for a long time in the abbey. She had told him the story of her partner's disappearance, and how Maitland had pursued her.

'And all the time, it was his fault,' she'd said.

'What was?'

'My partner disappearing. Helen.'

'Why?'

She had bitten her lip and looked away.

'You're not saying he did something to her?'

She had shaken her head slowly from side to side.

'She knew him,' she said.

'Who, Helen? Your partner? She knew Maitland?'

She was still sitting half turned away. He tried to gauge more of the expression on her face by sitting forward in his chair. 'How did she know him?'

'He had come to the school,' she murmured. 'Some sort of police visit to the school. You know... engaging with the community and all that.'

'But...' He had been trying to get his head around it. 'You're saying that she met him at the school, and then... well, what?'

'She talked about having liked him.'

'How is that anything to do with her disappearing, though?'

'Then she *stopped* talking about him.'

'I don't understand.'

At that, Alice Hauser had turned to face him. 'Haven't you ever heard that?' she asked. 'When people have affairs they keep mentioning their name. Because they like them, and they're

71

impressed by them, or amused, or attracted or whatever. They keep telling their partners or friends about them.'

'And that's what she did, she talked about him, did she?'

'Yes. But then she stopped. She wouldn't tell me anything else. She said it didn't matter. She got angry if I asked.'

'So she wanted to forget it?'

Alice leaned forward and wagged a finger slowly at him. 'Don't you see?' she asked. 'He meant too much to discuss with me.'

'She said that?'

Alice had looked away, biting her lip.

'Jesus Christ, you're not saying that Maitland had an affair with her?' Alice didn't reply. She looked back up the aisle at the elaborate altar.

'*Are* you saying that, that they had an affair? She actually said that they did?'

'I know that she had met him several times. For work, she said. Putting on some sort of exhibition, and then a talk for the sixth formers. Careers.'

Her evasion drove him crazy. 'But did she *say* so, this affair?'

He almost missed the next few words. He had to lean forward again to hear them.

'Yes,' she murmured. 'She told me that.'

*

John sat on the shoreline going over and over the conversation in his head.

He didn't know if he believed Alice Hauser or not. Helen had been gay, after all. Why would she go with a man, and a married man at that? A man who had been so much older than her, too? Perhaps Helen had just been taunting Alice Hauser, teasing her. He didn't really understand and couldn't even guess. Maybe she was bi, then. Did Helen McAllister sleep around with anyone who took her fancy, was that it? She sounded a nice piece of work.

Alice had taken a photograph of Helen out of the canvas tote bag that she was clutching on her lap. He took the image from her, seeing Helen standing in the waves, laughing. She had been a pretty woman, he decided.

He had glanced up at Alice Hauser. A small, inconsequential-seeming person. When she sat down she had tucked her skirt modestly under her knees. She was very pale. Unusually pale. He had a sudden thought that she had no idea about being attractive. Probably didn't think that she was. Abruptly, he was overwhelmingly sorry for her.

He gave the photo back to her. A real, old-fashioned photograph. Not something on her phone. He watched her hold it for a moment, gazing down at it, rubbing the edge with her thumb, and he realised that she wanted a physical image to hold, to caress. He turned away, looking up the aisle and away from this glaringly intimate moment.

'It wasn't her fault,' she said.

He looked back at her. 'What wasn't her fault?'

'Maitland,' she replied. A tinge of colour appeared on each cheek. 'He made all the running. She didn't want to.'

'She told you that?'

Alice tilted her chin in a gesture of defiance. 'He bullied her.'

He bit his lip momentarily. 'She doesn't look like someone that you could bully.'

She put the photograph away. 'It was all show, the confidence,' she told him. 'She was different with me.' She said it with a sudden show of defiance, as if expecting to be corrected.

He ran a hand through his hair. He was so tired.

'So Helen went missing, just missing out of the blue one morning? She'd said nothing out of the ordinary to you?'

'Nothing. It was a normal morning.'

'She wasn't worried? Sad? Angry?'

'No.'

'She got in her car and left for work…'

'For school, yes.'

'And she never came back.'

'No.' A slight tremor in her voice.

'They found her car...'

'Facing the wrong way. As if she *had* been travelling to the school, and then changed her mind, and started back.'

'But she didn't come back to you, back home?'

'No. She parked on the coast road.'

'But why do that?'

'I don't know.'

But she looked as if she did know, or suspected the reason. 'You've got a theory,' he murmured.

She looked up at him sharply. 'She stopped for some*one*, not some*thing*.'

'Okay. Who?'

'Maitland. I think she was meeting Maitland. I think it was him who called her back.'

'To do what, say what?'

'I don't know,' she muttered. She raised a hand to her face as if she might be brushing away a tear, but her eyes were dry. It was more a gesture of confusion.

'Had she mentioned Maitland that day, or the day before?'

'No. It was all over.'

'Since when?'

'A long time.'

'So...' He tried to untangle the story. 'So just a minute. She had an affair with Maitland, something she didn't instigate and didn't particularly want very much, and it had ended long before she disappeared?'

'Yes.'

'So why would it be Maitland that she was meeting that day, then?'

She turned slightly in her seat so that she was facing him directly again. 'Because I think he wouldn't let go,' she said. 'He wouldn't let it be over.'

'Jesus, seriously?'

'You don't believe me.'

He pondered it for a second through his haze of fatigue. 'He just didn't strike me as that sort of man, I suppose. He looked to me like a washout. Nobody who would...'

'Be vindictive?' she asked. She was blushing furiously now. 'But that's exactly what he is. He came after me, he questioned me, and he had me taken into...' She glanced behind her. 'To that place back there. Hours and hours. And he came round to the café, and the house. I used to swim in the sea in the morning in summer – it kept me sane, you know? It cleared my head, the shock of the cold – and he would come and stand on the beach and watch me. And I made a complaint against him, and told them. I couldn't stand him anymore, so in the end, after three or four weeks of this – this stalking me – I went and complained to his bosses. I told them about him and Helen.'

'You did?'

'Yes.' Her mouth had set in a stubborn line, full of bitterness. 'And what happened?'

'Nothing happened,' she said. 'Nothing at all.'

*

Before they had parted company in the abbey, Alice Hauser had given him her phone number.

And, in exchange, he had told her where Maitland lived.

He frowned now, crossing his arms and staring down at his feet. Perhaps he shouldn't have done that. She was a complete stranger, and he didn't know, couldn't guess, if she were even sane. She gave off this strange brittle aura, the expressions on her face and the tone of her voice shifting all the time, like clouds chasing across the sun.

He struggled with that and felt an instinctive sympathy for her. She looked like someone who was always ignored, passed over.

Maybe she had a grudge with Maitland because he'd brought her in for questioning after her girlfriend's disappearance. But it was a bloody huge leap to believe in the supposed affair. More still to think that Maitland might have actually killed this woman, which she had hinted at. Maybe nothing had happened at all. Certainly, as she'd said, it couldn't be proved that Maitland met Helen on the morning she had disappeared. That was one hell of a conclusion to arrive at, and it obviously had no evidence behind it or Maitland would have been implicated at the time.

Who was lying?

Alice, Helen or Maitland?

She'd looked away from him when she was telling him that Helen must have met Maitland that day, as if she were not quite telling the full story. He had a feeling that he couldn't quite pin down, that floated just out of his grasp, that it was a story she had told before and that she was telling it again to make it sound real. He wondered, confused, if she knew what it was that she was saying at all; people went crazy after losses. He should know that. But to *never* know what had happened to someone you loved – that was a loss that he couldn't even begin to imagine. If Alice Hauser had suffered that for ten years, who could blame her if she had lost track of the truth?

But whatever had actually happened, he had now got himself in between them.

He tilted his head back and looked at the grey sky overhead. Could he bring himself to care about any of it, really? It was nothing to do with him.

Except in one important respect. He didn't really care what had happened, or if Alice Hauser was some crazy, obsessed bitch who simply hated Maitland for hauling her in over her partner's disappearance and thought that he might have murdered Helen McAllister.

No. What he really cared about was that Maitland was guilty of killing Mike.

And maybe he had killed this woman.

Or maybe not, who knew?

But Mike. He had killed Mike for a fact.

John groaned out loud, straightened up, and looked out across the water. Grief mixed with fury made his stomach churn.

'Oh God,' he whispered.

The lake and the fells looked implacably back at him as if saying, *You work it out.*

*

In the summer this was a great place to swim. Through the reedy shallows, striking out to break up the blue reflections and the shape of the mountains in the water. Chasing clouds, scattering them with the splash of strokes. He had always been ahead of Mike. Because he was the tough one. The footballer and swimmer. Sometimes he'd grab Mike's arm and pull him down, and for a moment or two he'd see his brother's face an inch below the water, half laughing, half shouting. A greenish disc before he came up. The slither of his brother's skin in the peat-stained lake. He closed his eyes in the concentrated act of remembering.

He had been there about 20 minutes, sitting thinking about Mike and Alice Hauser and Maitland, thinking about all of them with the same sick constriction in his gut that he had had now for days, when a walker came down from the direction of Long Moss and Watendlath higher up in the mountains.

There was a dog with him, a brindle collie that immediately ran towards John. It stood a little way off, wagging its tail slightly, unsure. He wondered if the dog could sense his feelings. The dog's tail dropped, and it lay down, its eyes fixed on him.

'He's looking for food,' the walker said cheerily as he got close. He was a middle-aged man, well-dressed against the weather in an outfit that looked new. He was carrying two walking poles;

expensive ones by the look of them, John thought. Perfectly kitted out for the cold and wet.

'He's out of luck, then,' John told him.

'Aye, well. Not above trying.'

John gave him a smile. He was now being scrutinised by both man and dog.

'Have you got soaked?' the man asked.

He looked down at his clothes. He pinched the wet material of his jeans. 'They'll dry.'

The man glanced up at the sky. 'If you're lucky.'

'Well,' John said. 'That's what I am, lucky.'

His tone of voice wasn't good. He knew that. He made his smile wider. 'I'm heading back down when I've had a breather.'

The walker paused another few seconds, then called the dog to his side. 'Well, good luck,' he said. 'As long as you're okay.'

'I am.'

The man glanced over his shoulder. 'Pint in the Breakstaff, that's us. Hope they've got a fire going.'

John wanted to say, *Enjoy it.*

But the walker was already too far away, striding out fast to Dob Gill in the direction that John had come, the dog at his side.

He waited until they were out of sight, and then he stripped down to his underwear and waded out into the water. The cold took his breath away. He struck out, shocked at the temperature; it was much colder than he had anticipated. But that was what he wanted. Something cold enough to get the last three or four days scoured from his system. Of a sudden, he remembered that this was what Alice Hauser did after Helen's disappearance. Swam in the cold sea. He understood it. Blasting feeling away. Blasting memories that wouldn't let him out of their grip.

He had a strange feeling that if he kept on swimming the lake would never come to an end. It was an otherworldly moment. Dreamlike. Intense.

This is what people must feel out at sea if their boat sinks, he thought. Fishing boats that go missing in the North Sea. When they get so cold that they don't feel real anymore. Drifting, frozen. Such things had happened, and the wrecks never found. He wondered if he would eventually sink to the bottom when his strength gave out. He saw himself as he once used to see Mike. A disc disappearing below the surface. Face, hands, body. A disc sinking down into the mud. Fading away. The ice of winter coming back and covering him.

He thought of his wife, wondering if Liz would miss him. Their marriage was no marriage, after all. If he died, would she get used to his absence, meet someone else, realise how bad it had been? Would she mourn, cry, make a scene? He didn't think so. He could almost see her alone, dry-eyed, thoughtful. He'd seen that look on her face sometimes when she was sitting at the kitchen table marking books, one hand hesitating over the page, her gaze elsewhere. A look of complicated preoccupation.

He had got home at 8 o'clock a few days ago. Flinging his bag down in the hallway he saw her come out of the back of the house, from the old scullery that they laughingly called a utility room. She had wet laundry in her arms and she put it down on the table and came towards him. 'I've been worried, John. Where have you been?'

'Well,' he told her. 'I'm here.'

'Was it terrible?'

'How else would it be?'

She had made him a meal, poured him a drink, and encouraged him to take a shower. He had taken his drink upstairs with him, and looked around their room, and it had felt anonymous. For a moment, he couldn't actually remember living here.

They ate together, and he told her everything about the hospital.

'Then I went to see the bastard.'

'Who?' she asked.

'Who do you think? I went to see the man who drove the van.'

She looked horrified. 'John, you didn't? I said not to.'

'Well, I fucking well did, so what?'

'What did you say to him?' She had gone white in the face. 'How did you know who he was?'

'A woman in the hospital told me the name on the side of his van.'

She frowned at him. 'You should have left well alone,' she said. 'You don't know what actually happened.'

'But *she* did,' he told her pointedly. 'She was in the car right behind him.'

'Oh, Jesus, it can't do any good,' she breathed.

'It did *me* good,' he replied coldly. 'I told him…' He had paused, looking down into his glass. 'I told him I'd make sure he was prosecuted.'

She didn't reply. He could see her trying to work out what must have actually been said. Then, quietly, 'Nothing else?'

'What else would there be?'

'I don't know,' she murmured. She got up and took the plates to the sink. In the scullery, he heard her put up the drying rack for the wet clothes. He went to the door and watched her.

'They're doing an autopsy,' he said.

She frowned. 'Why, if this man went into him?'

'I don't know.'

'Do they think that Mike had a heart attack?'

'He was forty fucking four, Liz! My age.'

'A brain haemorrhage, something like that, something that made him…'

'Made him what?' He stepped towards her, angry.

'I don't know either. But if they're doing an autopsy?'

'It wasn't his fault,' he told her. 'He didn't have a heart attack and he didn't have something wrong with him.'

'You don't know that, John.'

He thought then that she was braver than she used to be.

Once she wouldn't have replied. She would have agreed with him, if only for the sake of peace. He felt the world tilt a little, trembling on its axis. Whole fucking world going backwards. Shifting, rolling.

He went back into the kitchen and downed his beer in two or three gulps. 'Someone told me who he is,' he muttered. 'He's in the police. Or was. He's a retired inspector.'

Liz had come back to the door and stood looking at him.

'How the hell do you know that?'

'Police,' he muttered under his breath. 'How fair is the investigation going to be?' he demanded. 'Look after their own selves. But I know what happened.'

'You do not know that at all,' she pointed out.

'Yes,' he replied. 'Yes, Liz, I do. This woman told me.'

'What, the woman from the accident?'

'No. Someone else. She told me that this Maitland, he was in charge of the team that searched for her missing partner ten years ago. Her name's Alice Hauser. Her partner was Helen McAllister. And she said that Maitland did a bloody horrible job.'

'What woman is this?'

'Just someone I met.'

'And she said…'

'They never found this woman who went missing, her partner. Can you believe that? This woman just disappeared off the face of the earth and Maitland's crew never found out what happened.'

'But how is that this man's fault? People go missing all the time.'

'Haven't you been listening? It was the same man. Maitland.'

'I heard what you said. Don't get fixated on him, John.' Liz sat down again, facing him. 'Or her, this Hauser woman.' She leaned her head on one hand. 'And what is this to do with Mike?'

'Can't you see? The same man! The incompetence…'

'Where did you meet this Alice Hauser?'

'She'd seen me come out of the police station, and saw me again when I was sitting down in the town.'

'And she told you all this, just like that?'

'Yes.'

'But why? To a complete stranger, a terrible case like that?'

He stopped himself, trying to sort it in his own mind. 'She just did, all right?'

'Had she followed you?'

'Not followed,' he said. But in fact he wasn't entirely sure whether Alice had followed him or not. It had never occurred to him until Liz said it.

Had Alice deliberately come after him? Did she already know who he was somehow? It was all getting so ragged in his mind.

'John,' Liz had murmured. 'Don't get involved. It won't help Mike.'

'Yes,' he said. 'It bloody well will.' He turned away. 'Anyway,' he muttered. 'I gave her Maitland's address so that she could find him too. Least I could do.'

He had gone to bed then, consumed by frustration.

He turned over now in the water and the cold was so savage that it sent a pain over the top of his head. His neck ached. His shoulders ached. He felt as if he'd been curled, foetus-like, in an agonising cramp, not only since last night but for ever.

Just a child curling up against the cold, afraid of monsters.

9

PETER THOMPSON CAME INTO THE estate agents' office almost at a run.

It was 8.30 in the morning, and the office was gearing itself up for the onslaught that always began after Easter; holidaymakers wanting to see properties that they had no intention of buying, but who were either insatiably nosy, or indulging their fantasies at the expense of the staff.

The street outside was almost empty, but it was looking to be another bright day. Peter's drive into work was pleasant at this time of year: 15 miles through farm lanes and along roads where the hedges were full of blackthorn flower.

He had been at the agency longer than most. He'd joined when he left school, and he liked it. He was – as he embarrassingly admitted – a *people* person.

This morning, driving along the coast road, he suddenly – like a flash of light in the centre of his otherwise vacant mind – remembered.

'I've remembered!' he announced to the office.

Only three staff were in. The youngest, Jan, was on her phone, but Alan Whitteson looked up, and Margie Bennett, coming out of the kitchen with tea for them all, smiled.

'What's that then, love?' she asked.

'That woman.'

'What, yesterday?'

'No, no,' Thompson told her, taking off his jacket and pulling out the chair behind his desk. He switched on his laptop. 'The one who bought that cottage above Asham Ferry a while back.'

'Did she?' Margie had been out that week, on holiday. 'What, the wreck?'

'Yes, the wreck,' he confirmed. He sat back, luxuriating in his feat of memory.

'And?' Alan prompted.

'Alice Hauser.'

'Who?'

'It's *the* Alice Hauser. Ten years ago.' He waited for a reaction that did not come. 'I thought I recognised her, but I couldn't think where from.' He sighed, and tapped his index finger on the desk. 'You must remember it now? She was a suspect in the case of that teacher who disappeared. Found her car on the coast road. I passed the lay-by yesterday. It was summer when it happened, I think. She just vanished.'

'They never found her,' Margie suddenly recalled. She put her hand to her face. 'It's the same person?'

'Her partner. Alice Hauser, the very same. Correct.'

'How do you know for sure?' Alan asked.

'I told her I knew her face. She just said she'd been here ten years ago. But it wasn't until today when I passed that lay-by...'

'What's this?' Jan asked. She had finished her phone call.

Margie turned to explain to her. 'Alice Hauser. She bought that horrible dilapidated shack above Asham Ferry. She used to live with a woman who disappeared ten years ago. They arrested her but they never charged her. It was big news at the time. Well, I'll be damned. She's come back?'

Peter nodded. 'But they didn't arrest her,' he corrected.

'Well – they took her in for questioning,' Margie admitted grudgingly. 'It was in the paper.'

'What for?' Jan asked.

'Murder,' Margie told her.

'No way! What, a body and everything?'

'No,' Peter said. 'No body. They never found the woman. She just vanished into thin air.'

'But they thought that this Hauser person had murdered her?'

'They must have done,' Alan murmured.

Peter started typing quickly. 'And then they released her. A couple of times, in fact,' he murmured, repeating *Alice Hauser, Alice Hauser* under his breath as he gazed at the screen, waiting for the search results.

'And then *she* disappeared,' Margie added.

'I always wondered if she'd committed suicide, you know,' Peter said.

'Because she was there one day and gone the next,' Margie agreed. 'My sister's boyfriend worked at the garage at the top of the hill and he used to sometimes go in that café where she worked. She had a single-storey place just along from the café, and the landlord said she'd cleared out. No notice or explanation. Just gone.'

'Here it is,' Peter announced. 'I found this last night.'

He turned the laptop screen round for them to see.

Alice Hauser had been caught by the camera as she exited Brimham police station. Head down, clutching a bag to her chest defensively. She wore a T-shirt and jeans. In a subsequent picture, she was opening a car door, eyes downcast and her expression guarded.

'She doesn't look like a murderer,' Jan observed.

'What does a murderer look like?'

She shrugged. 'Women don't murder, do they? Not often.'

'Of course they do.'

'The serial killers are always men.'

'Nobody's saying she's a serial killer,' Margie replied. 'But the police don't have people in for questioning unless they think something's wrong, do they?'

'Look at this,' Peter Thompson said.

There were two or three other photos of uniformed officers. A group was pictured walking up the path on the opposite side of the road, looking carefully – it seemed – at the ground. Above them rose the ridgeway, a short climb whose top was only a quarter of a mile from the car. Other figures could be glimpsed on the ridge, most probably walkers being directed back to the road by the way that they had come, from the direction of Asham Ferry. There appeared to be another small group a few yards to the left of them, and a knot of people coming down an adjacent hedge line suggested that they had been told to come back to the road rather than retracing their steps through the fields.

'So what exactly were they all looking for, all those police?'

'Clues to where she'd gone after that,' Peter guessed.

'Blood or something?'

'Probably. Clothing, anything like that.'

'But they never found anything?'

'Nothing.'

He was staring at the last photograph. Helen McAllister's car was being loaded on to a trailer in the lay-by, which, like the other side of the road, was cordoned off with blue and white tape, and a small team were standing by to examine the ground around and underneath it.

'It says the hillsides were searched,' he told them. 'Up to the ridgeway, and down to the beach. It's just a mass of brambles that way. Must have been fun.'

Margie seemed to have lost interest now. She had picked up her phone to call a client. Outside, two or three people were already peering in through the windows. 'Here come the darlings,' she muttered under her breath.

Jan, her arms crossed, was staring into space. 'If she wasn't guilty she must have been like frantic, yeah?' she said. 'Imagine someone you love just vanishing, and nobody believing her. Like, imagine that.'

Peter looked across at her, smiling. 'You think she wasn't guilty?' he asked.

10

THE BINGHAM FAIR WAS ALWAYS held in the grounds of a country house, and ever since taking up painting, Thomas had a little stand under an awning in the beech avenue at the border of the park.

Fran had encouraged him, despite everything he'd put her through. 'Let people see how talented you are,' she had said. 'Start afresh.'

In that first couple of years, working in the garden studio, he had warmed to it. He'd surprised himself. He'd always liked art but never tried either drawing or painting until now. He took three or four courses and began to turn out things that people sometimes wanted to buy.

'You're not to think of it as a failure,' Fran had told him sternly. 'It was a good decision to retire.' And, as he had looked at her sitting across the kitchen table, she had added, 'Put the past to sleep. Bury it.'

He thought that he had done. He had hoped they'd managed that together. But then the illness came along, and it was now two years since Fran had died. It had been a summer's day – scented and warm and clear – but all he had been able to think of was that it bore the stench and misery of the oncology ward.

He wished that Fran had wanted to be cremated, but she had been adamant that she would happily lie in the churchyard a mile from the house. It used to be a routine – flowers from the garden, sitting on the bench opposite her grave underneath the cherry tree – but he hadn't gone for months now. Ever since the ground over her had sunk slightly. He hadn't been able to rid himself of the thought that the coffin lid had cracked with the weight of earth and the winter rains, and that the small branch of apple blossom that he had put in Fran's folded hands was crushed and wet with the valley clay.

*

Bingham Park wasn't far from the cottage: he often passed it if he went to the supermarket in the nearest town.

One night last winter, he had come round the bend in the road, the trees at the park edge making a large dark shoulder on one side, indistinguishable in the darkness, when he had been forced to brake hard. Right there in the centre of the road had been three or four deer, a stag among does, and the stag's head turned towards him. The animals had stood their ground.

He drove at a crawl, expecting them to move, picked out in the headlights. He had been worried that another car would come around the corner in the dark and crash into both himself and the deer. He had flashed his lights. The stag stamped and made a movement of his head. Its eyes were brilliant reflective discs, yellow, glassy. The does began to walk slowly across the road into the wood. But the stag remained.

He could almost feel Fran's breath on his hand as he raised it and put it on the dashboard.

'How beautiful, Tom,' she would have said.

And then he had wished for another car to come round the corner, fast. He would have liked to have that sight of the stag as his last thought. But eventually it did move, and he drove on, rattled, disoriented by the apparition.

He'd had to pull over the next chance he got. He was choked by the strength of his wish for that other car to come. He'd wanted it so badly. He had put his head on the steering wheel, breathing heavily, thinking of the collapsed grave and the silent animals in the road, and the strange stamp of the stag's foot, staring him down with those yellow eyes.

The irony of it didn't miss him. There had been a real road accident, and he was the one left alive, and the other man was dead.

*

He had arrived at the fair yesterday, and put up the new white gazebo, much smaller than the usual one that was still in the van.

'Why can't you use the old one?' Christine had asked him.

'I don't want it,' he told her.

She'd raised her eyebrows in surprise. 'What do you mean?'

'I don't want it anymore,' he'd repeated. 'It's too big. I haven't got as much as I'd planned.'

He spent the Thursday afternoon making the display. He laid down a tarpaulin, and arranged a stand of drawings – country scenes – and positioned a central table with a portfolio of prints, and cards giving details of how to contact him. Around the edge he showed half a dozen paintings, large abstracts that he knew wouldn't be to everyone's taste, but which he preferred to the pretty drawings. He managed as best he could, until Christine had arrived, tut-tutting over the arrangement on the table and moving things in her brisk, no-nonsense manner. When she had finished, he had to admit that it looked nice. As a finishing touch, she had put a spray of apple blossom in an art deco jug.

It wasn't her fault. She wasn't to know.

'There now,' she'd said, happy.

'Thanks, Christine.'

'I hope you sell a lot.'

'Yes,' he had murmured. 'Thanks.'

She patted his arm. 'I'm always here for you, Thomas. You know that. I'll give you a lift to the pub.'

*

It was just after 11 o'clock the next day, the first day of the three-day fair, when he saw Richard Ellis walking down the row of tents towards him.

'Hello Richard,' he said, returning Ellis's handshake. 'What brings you here?'

Ellis looked around. 'Big set-up, isn't it?' he remarked. 'I had to wait twenty minutes at the gate. Line of trailers right out to the main road. You've got great weather for it. Proper spring day.'

'Yes,' he agreed. 'It's always busy. Friday's for the livestock, really.'

Ellis smiled. 'Fattest pig and all that?'

'Something like that.'

Ellis walked into the stand and gazed around him. 'This is what you do?'

'Yes.'

'It's all yours?'

'Yes,' he replied.

'They're really good. Professional.'

'Thanks.'

Ellis turned back towards him. 'That's where you were going when you had the accident, wasn't it? You were delivering something.'

There was a pause before the reply. 'A big canvas. That's right.'

'Ever get it back?'

'Yes, when I got the van.'

'Was it all right?'

'It was all right.'

A couple of customers wandered in and spent a few minutes looking at the work, exclaiming at its skill, asking Thomas if he were local. He gave them a card, and they went away, smiling at him, waving goodbye.

'Do you sell a lot?' Ellis asked.

'It varies. Art is hard to sell.'

'And you've carried on. Since the accident? Couldn't have been easy.'

Thomas pulled out a chair for him and they settled themselves at the table, gazing out at the crowds for a moment, and the patches of sunlight under the trees.

'Thought you might want to know something about John Lord,' Ellis said.

Thomas shuffled his feet and sighed, gazing at the floor. 'So that's why you're here.'

'Has he been back to you?'

'Maybe.'

Ellis frowned. 'What do you mean, "maybe"?'

'I think that he gets in touch, in his way.'

'I don't understand,' Ellis replied. 'What way?'

Thomas gave his slow, slightly twisted smile. 'I've had two packages this week. Postmarked Cumbria.'

'And?'

'Very well wrapped. Foil and bubble wrap. Not bulky; they fitted through the letterbox.'

'What was in them?'

'Human faeces.' He gave a shake of his head. 'I'm supposing it's human, at least.'

'Jesus!' Ellis considered just for a second. 'John Lord?'

'Who else? But there's no proving it.'

'Give us the envelopes.'

'I've thrown them out.'

'Tom… sir… let us have a look at them.'

Thomas stretched his legs in front of him and crossed his arms. 'No, Richard. He'll tire of it. It's grief.'

'Bloody hell. It's not grief. What if he ups his game and sends something worse?'

This time Thomas gave a short laugh. 'There's something worse than shit?'

'You know there is.'

'No, no. He's not a terrorist, Richard. He's not going to do that.'

'He's fucking deranged, though.' Ellis let out a long slow hiss through his teeth. 'I mean, Chrissake, sir. It's not on.'

Thomas smiled at him. 'Don't call me sir, Richard. That's all over. Been over for years.'

Ellis hesitated. 'We'll go and see him.'

'No, you won't. Let the man alone.'

'It wasn't your fault that his brother died.'

'Wasn't it?'

'I don't need to read any bloody accident investigation.'

'I'm telling you to let it be.'

Ellis leaned forward, lowering his voice and leaning on his elbows. 'John Lord's got form,' he said. 'Assault.'

Thomas said nothing. But it got his attention.

'On his wife. She called the locals out, they took him into custody. Blind drunk. She went to hospital with a broken cheekbone. He'd hit her. She wouldn't press charges.'

'Are they still together?'

'I can find out. You see what kind of man he is. Short fuse. You told me he'd been round to see you and was aggressive.'

'He didn't break *my* cheekbone. Only tried to damage a painting.'

'I'd have had him in for that.'

'No, no.'

'I can't understand why you're so blasé about it. Let me look into him. Let me ask. I know his kind.'

Thomas looked away. He watched the crowds strolling past with their kids and dogs and backpacks and ice creams. He looked for some time at a Jack Russell terrier idly scratching, then plonking itself down on the grass, the kids pulling on its lead. A dog that looked like Fish.

'I'm not blasé,' he said. 'What is "his kind" anyway?'

Ellis wordlessly spread his hands as if it was obvious what sort of man John Lord was.

Thomas broke his gaze and looked back into the crowds. Looked at the dog again. Sighed. 'What's the truth?' he asked. 'Only what we show to the world. That's all we know. People like us take it as gospel if we have evidence to back it up. But what's in the heart of anyone, at the root? You can't really know. Not for sure. Not for certain. Nobody can.'

*

The afternoon was busy.

He hardly had time to eat the couple of sandwiches that he'd brought with him, and a cup of tea from the Thermos grew cold. The crowds began to dwindle at 5 o'clock, and there was suddenly a chill in the air.

Thomas started to roll down the sides of the gazebo to secure them for the night. He was working on the last one when he saw her.

She was standing on the other side of the double row of tents between two displays of flowers. She was standing with her back to the sun and was quite motionless.

His first reaction was that it was only someone who looked like Alice Hauser; she had her hands clasped in front of her around a large shoulder bag.

She hadn't changed at all. It might as well have been that summer. It might as well have been August and she standing in the same way on Asham Ferry's beach.

He hadn't given a thought to her – not a single thought – since Fran had died. In the years after Helen McAllister vanished, he and Fran had talked about Helen and Alice, particularly after all the trouble that Alice had caused between them. To give Fran her due, she hadn't believed anything that Alice said, even when it got impossible. Even when he retired because it had soured police work for him. The lies and accusations, the investigation of him personally. But Fran had been steadfast, even accepting his resignation. 'It's what you need, Thomas. We have to move on.'

He blinked, staring into the sun. He couldn't see Alice now. He looked down for a moment to secure the last strap, fumbling with it.

His heart was in his mouth. Ten years! She'd disappeared, gone away. There'd been no sign of her since they scaled down the investigation. Why had she come back?

If she had been there at all.

What was she, a ghost? A fragment of memory? Stirred by what?

He ran over to where she had been.

He began to run up the aisle between the displays, and under the shadow of the trees. He was out of breath when he got to the top, and he turned in a full circle trying to see her.

But there was no sign of Alice Hauser.

11

TEN YEARS AGO, A SWELTERING afternoon.

Heat shimmered from the coast road; the whole countryside seemed asleep. As Thomas came closer to Asham Ferry the sea came suddenly into view as he drove over the hill: a hazy flat calm beyond the yellow shingle. He had picked up the case from Richard Ellis, and was here to gauge Alice Hauser for himself.

He had parked in the public car park near the beach: a gritty expanse on the edge of a field. He walked along the narrow front, just 100 yards of tarmac. Beyond the scatter of buildings, the cliffs showed a curious division – grey on one side, yellow sandstone on the other. The state schools hadn't broken up yet and there were only a few people on the shingle. Not many came here even in the height of the summer: there was no pub, only one café, and no sand, and the sea current was strong. It had an air of genteel shabbiness that Thomas liked.

He could see the café perched on the edge of the shingle. There was a red sign outside enclosing a blackboard. *Fish and chips. Cream teas. Ice cream. Hot and cold drinks.* It looked as if it hadn't been painted for a while, and the café was the same. A few determined walkers sat on the only bench. The place was on the South Coast Path, and the strange geology drew some from the easier roadside car park at the top of the hill. There were always customers, but never crowds.

He pushed open the door of the café, walked to the counter and showed his warrant.

'Alice Hauser?' He'd been told that this was where she worked.

The woman cutting a slice of cake glanced up at him and then at the warrant. 'Not me, love.'

'No, I meant is she here?'

'She's not in today.'

'Are you the owner?'

'I am.'

'Does she work regular hours?'

The woman sighed and raised her eyebrows. 'Yes. But of course, with all this yesterday... I wouldn't have expected her in.'

'All this?' Word was out, then. He had expected it.

'Her friend missing.' She paused. 'Are you ordering anything?'

'Just a glass of water, please.'

She passed the glass across the counter. She looked him up and down.

'How is she?' he asked.

'What, today? I haven't seen her today, like I say.'

'No, usually.'

'Oh,' she said. 'She's... well, just Alice.'

'Is she good at her job?'

'Never stops. And never talks.'

'Really, she never talks?'

'Not about herself. Never socialises. Doesn't talk to me except – you know – taking the orders, clearing up. Work.' She suddenly stopped and leaned on the counter. 'Funny little girl. Shy. But she perked up a bit when she met her friend.'

He drank the rest of the water, and thanked her. 'Do you know where she is now?'

'At home, I should think, don't you?' She looked over

his shoulder. 'That old blue Ford is hers, so she's not driven anywhere.'

*

He walked back from the beach and café towards the glass-fronted houses. There was a line of six, single-storey, and built in a staggered line. The sort of places that should have been torn down years ago. Like the car park and the café, they backed on to gravelly areas and the line of low cliffs. He knew that Alice lived in the first, and he knocked on the door.

He could hear movement inside, but it was some time before she answered the door. He stood there waiting patiently, the sun beating hot on his neck and his shirt sticking to his back.

She answered eventually, standing in the doorway but holding on to the door as if for protection. No one had told him how small and slight she was. He showed his warrant. 'Miss Hauser?'

She looked at the card closely and then whispered 'Thomas Maitland,' almost to herself. She opened the door to let him through.

He was straight into the living-room.

In his experience, you could learn a lot from someone's living space. He'd been in too many homes to count, but still remembered a few: an over-furnished flat with a line of dolls propped up on the windowsill, and an elderly husband suffocated in a chair; a young man struggling with a demented father in a manor house with a vast garden; two brothers sitting at either end of a kitchen table in a rundown terrace, both bleeding after a violent row, and both crying. Mothers and sons and fathers and lovers, sisters and brothers. You could make a song out of that. Mothers and sons and...

He smiled at her. She was standing in the centre of the room, blank-faced.

'You've come round very quickly,' she observed. 'I thought it would be you. But I supposed it would be later.'

At that moment, he thought no more of it, assuming that she meant the police. She showed him the couch. She took the chair. Such a sparsely furnished room, he was thinking. Very clean and neat. No sign of disturbance. Nothing out of place. There was a faint tang of bleach that raised the hairs on the back of his neck, out of habit.

'We've found your partner's car.'

'Oh?' She sat forward a little. 'Where?'

'On the coast road. On the ridgeway, before the village.'

'Yes,' she murmured. It was an odd reply.

'You don't sound at all surprised.'

'Oh,' she said quickly. 'Well, I…' She looked away from him. 'I was very confused yesterday when I came in to tell you all that she had gone.'

'You'll have to explain that to me,' he said. He sat back, considering her and waiting for her to elaborate.

She looked out of the window, then back at him. 'I didn't quite tell the truth.' She squared herself, took a breath. 'I was with Helen that morning on the coast road.'

'Two days ago?'

'Yes.' She had folded her hands in her lap. The knuckles weren't white. She seemed relaxed. She glanced up at him, and then down again. 'I met her there and we walked up to the ridge.' There was a distinct defensive tone to her voice.

'What time was this?'

'About half past nine.'

'In the morning.'

'Yes.'

He watched her for a moment. 'You told my officer yesterday that you hadn't seen her since she left for the school.'

'Yes, I know.'

'Why did you say that?'

A silence. Then, 'We were arguing. I thought if I said that,

you'd think she'd left me. And I know that she hasn't left me.'
Her mouth opened, then shut rapidly again. She gave him a
look that was almost a glare, a sudden flare of feeling. 'She
wouldn't leave me, not for anyone. And I thought that if I
said I'd been with her, you'd think I'd done something to her.'
This last sentence was delivered with a narrow-eyed sulkiness,
almost defiance.

Why would you think that? he thought.

He let a moment or two pass. 'Let's start at breakfast two
days ago.'

'We had a disagreement and she left for work. I followed her
in my car, but I stopped in the village to phone her, to reach
her before she got to school. I asked her to come back. I left a
voicemail telling her that I was on the ridge. I parked in the
village and thought she'd see me as she drove back through.
When she didn't come, I walked up to the ridge from the
village. From there, I saw her come back and park below the
ridge on the coast road. She must have driven right through the
village without seeing my car.'

'What then?'

She shrugged slightly. 'She climbed up to the ridge. It was
somewhere we often walked. We talked for a while…'

'What about?'

'Does it matter?'

'Yes. What were you disagreeing about?'

'She wasn't the same. Not the same as she had been.'

'In what way?'

'She didn't always want to stay with me lately,' she continued
slowly. 'She has a house, you see? In Bloxley. It was rented out
last summer. She's lived with me here for nearly a year. Then a
few weeks ago, the tenants had gone and she was talking about
going back.'

'To live?'

'Yes.'

'Did she give you a reason?'

99

'She said it was too cramped here.'

He could believe that. The place was tiny. He couldn't imagine two people living comfortably in the three or four rooms – living-room, kitchen, bathroom and bedroom, he guessed. He glanced out of the window. The edge of the beach could be seen. On the other hand, there were worse views.

As if reading his thoughts, she added, 'It's bleak in the winter if you don't like the sea.'

'Did Helen not like the sea? You showed my officer a picture of her standing in the waves.'

'We both like to swim. She's better at it, of course.'

'But not in winter.'

She followed his gaze, and looked oddly bitter suddenly, but didn't reply. She was biting her lip so much that her mouth was a straight line.

'So what happened when you were on the ridge?' he asked.

'She just told me again that she'd made up her mind to go back to her house. That she didn't want to talk about it anymore.'

'That must have been upsetting.'

'Yes.'

'Was that the last thing she said to you?'

'Yes.'

'Then what?'

She shrugged. A helpless spread of her hands. 'I went back down to my car and drove away.'

'And she walked back down to her own car, in the opposite direction?'

'I suppose so. I didn't see her. I walked away and left her and you can't see the coast road from the other side of the ridge.'

'Were you angry?'

A pause. 'Yes.' She paused. 'But I was more confused. She'd never shown me the house in Bloxley. I couldn't visualise it. I didn't know why I couldn't go with her if she was moving back there.'

'Did you ask her?'

'She didn't give me the chance.'

'It seems a perfectly reasonable question.'

Alice didn't reply for a moment. Then, quietly, 'When Helen made her mind up about something, there was no saying otherwise.'

'That must have been very difficult. Did she say she'd see you later?'

'We still had things to discuss.'

The obvious conclusion that Helen McAllister *did* have somewhere else to go hung between them.

'Did you expect us to find the car?' he asked.

She sighed. 'I'm glad that you found it.'

'But did you expect us to?'

'What do you mean?'

'You must have passed it on the way to see us yesterday.'

'No, no… I went up towards town. Not on the coast. If I had seen it, I would have stopped, wouldn't I? I would have told you where it was.'

'You haven't driven along the coast at all?'

'No… I've just been waiting here.' There was now a strong ripple of irritation across that blank face. 'I've been here,' she repeated.

He sat forward. 'You haven't asked me about the car.'

'What would I need to ask? Like I say, I'm glad you've found it.'

'Don't you want to know what was in it, or if it was unlocked, if it was as you last saw it?'

'I've been waiting here…' She stood up abruptly. 'Do you know what it's like to lose someone? Do you know what it's like to be awake all night and sit here? I can hardly think straight. And then you come here cross-examining me. But nobody rang and told me about the car. Why didn't someone ring me?'

'I've come to tell you now.'

She was swaying slightly. 'Helen said that you were a bully.'

'I beg your pardon?'

'She told me about you. Coming to the school and taking charge. I know who you are.'

Bright spots of colour had come to her pale cheeks. Her hands dropped to her sides. He thought, bizarrely, that she might hit him. Fury was rolling off her.

'Miss Hauser,' he said slowly. 'I might have visited the school. But I don't know Helen.'

'Oh,' she exclaimed, and laughed.

'I can assure you.'

'Oh God,' she murmured. She walked across the room and opened the door to the street. 'Please go.'

He walked over to her, frowning. 'You've made a mistake,' he said.

'Have I,' she intoned. It was not a question.

'I'm afraid so. Perhaps you've mixed me up with someone else.'

'I don't mix anyone up,' she told him. 'Thomas Maitland. She told me.' Her bottom lip trembled momentarily. 'She *liked* to tell me.'

'Then it was Helen who made a mistake.'

'Go away, for Christ's sake,' she said. It sounded like a threat.

He took a step across the threshold, and paused outside. 'I understand that you must be very worried. We'll be back to talk to you very soon. If there's any news, we'll let you know immediately, of course.' He was about to step away when he thought of one last thing. 'Do you have a key to Helen's house in Bloxley?'

'No,' she told him.

'You haven't been there at all?'

'No. I told you.'

'Really?'

'Look, just find her,' she said. 'If you're capable of it.'

*

He went and sat on the sea wall watching the walkers and the few people at the café. He felt rattled. Disturbed. There was something wrong with Alice Hauser, but he couldn't put his finger on it. She was both blank and bitter. She had switched between that odd stillness and flashes of fury, suppressed but still all too obvious. Like two different people talking to him. And she was angry with him personally.

All the time he was thinking, if she left Helen on the ridge, and she knows that the car never left the coast road, why didn't she ask me where Helen could have gone from there? Why didn't she ask me where we were looking?

Was there something wrong with her? He'd heard about cases where two personalities – or more – lived in the same body. And none of them knew what the others were doing. But he thought that sounded too far-fetched, and Alice Hauser wasn't *quite* vacant even in her stillness: she followed a train of thought.

No. She was sitting on some terrible rage, though.

Rage that was directed at him.

There were uniforms out in the village at this moment going door to door. This afternoon, there would be search teams along the ridge and in the overgrown paths down to the beach. The forensic teams were busy with the car. But Alice never asked, never showed any concern or interest. All she had shown him was anger.

After about half an hour – which he spent considering every aspect of her and their conversation – he saw Alice come out of her front door. She walked to the beach, head down. He stood up so that he could keep sight of her as she went down the slope of the shingle. At the water's edge she peeled off the skirt and T-shirt that she was wearing to reveal a swimming costume.

She went into the water without hesitation. He saw her strike out from the shore in a few fast strokes. She swam out a hundred yards, and he knew that she would have to be working hard to keep herself at the same place, such was the current. But she made no move to come back. She stopped, and stayed upright in the water and looked back to the beach.

And he and Alice Hauser stared at each other for some time, while the bright sunlight fractured the water and turned the waves white.

12

JOHN HADN'T KNOWN THAT MIKE wanted to be buried.
He was sure that they had talked about this more than once – agreed that they would both be cremated and their ashes scattered on one of the Cumbrian mountains. Somewhere they often walked and climbed together. He thought that they had even chosen a place above Borrowmere.

But he had been wrong. Mike had made a will, and in it he had stated that he wanted a burial, and he had even found the woodland burial site on a farm out towards the coast with a view of the estuary.

When he had first heard the news – reading the will with a mounting sense of surreality – John had found it impossible to understand. He had been utterly dumbfounded. He hadn't dreamed their conversations about this, surely? Somewhere high up in those mountain passes. Somewhere relatively remote. Somewhere with an unbroken view of the sky and the winding path below, up in the clear air, up in the silence. Faced with the evidence of a different ending, John had been choked with another wave of grief. But here was Mike's signature on the bottom of the will – that strong, looping hand. Evidence of Mike's wishes, but completely foreign and incomprehensible. It was like being cut adrift from his brother all over again.

The day of the funeral dawned calm but grey. It was a long drive out past Ravenglass. Past what John thought of as their home. They went through all the familiar little villages, all the farms, all the little clusters of stone houses huddled together here and there at crossroads, under the vast slopes and shadows of the peaks, out towards the sea. The estuary there was all mud flats and bird reserves; a lot of the sea and part of the coast was military, action forbidden because of the shooting ranges. They had eventually found the site and John had recoiled at the crowds gathered, waiting for them, waiting for Mike. He had wanted to push them all away and carry Mike's body himself. He resented even the other pallbearers who gave him such sympathetic looks, who even put their hands on his shoulder, or held out their hands to him. He wanted them all to vanish. This was his day, his last day alone with Mike. Why did no one understand that?

Mike was carried out into a tidied-up field, a place where other people were evidently lying for eternity, a place of no privacy. He had felt bile roiling up from his stomach, and had to swallow it. To his horror, the grave for Mike was close to a silver birch that had been decorated with ribbons by some other grieving family. It took all his strength not to tear them down.

'It's lovely,' Liz had said in the car on the way back from the burial. 'I can see why he chose it.'

Just another example of how far apart they were.

He knew that his wife was trying to be consoling. But he didn't need her to be. He was past that first sickening rage, past the feeling that he carried a stone in his gut. It had settled into something quieter and more fluid, as if the injustice of Mike's death had infected his bloodstream. It circulated inside him, an invisible virus. Now, added to that, was this loneliness, this dislocation.

He had been mystified after reading the will. Once he had fully grasped what Mike wanted, he couldn't bring himself to be involved, and Liz had more or less taken over the arrangement. 'You can choose all kinds of coffin,' she told him gently one night. 'Which one would you like?'

'I don't know,' he had muttered. 'Oak. Or mahogany.'

She had the printout from the website. 'Let's go and see them,' she'd suggested. 'They could explain better. You can't have that sort of thing, John. You see? It has to be biodegradable. Cardboard, wicker. Something like that.'

Her soft, concerned expression in the dull light of the kitchen.

'*Cardboard?*' he'd replied. 'You want me to bury my brother in a cardboard box?'

He hadn't raised his voice. It wasn't her fault. But everything was her fault. Nothing was her fault. Back and forth in his head. But oh God, the softness infuriated him. She was all woven into a pattern that had spoiled him, and if that wasn't her fault, then whose fault was it? Nobody understood, not even the psychologists he'd been forced to see when he was a teenager. The world was so mediocre. So dull. Just like her. Her fucking goodness. Her forbearance. His life was her fault.

He wished she would hit him, hard. He'd have welcomed it. He wanted to be on the receiving end, just to see if it shocked him out of his stupor.

She had pushed the pictures across the table towards him. 'It doesn't *look* like cardboard, John.'

He had sat back in his chair and spread his hands, helpless. 'Humanist,' he said. 'That's not church. No vicar.'

'They call them celebrants.'

'They're going to come and stand over my brother buried in some field and they're going to celebrate?'

'You know that isn't what it means.'

He had got up and poured himself a beer. With his back to the worktop, he looked out through the uncurtained window.

It was the tree that did it.

The funeral over, they had been driving to the wake. There would be more music, more soft applause. They said that they were going to play some of Mike's recordings and he was sure that he wouldn't be able to stand it. He'd taken all of Mike's CDs out of his own car.

They had got as far as Eskdale. Liz was driving. 'Pull over,' he said.

'Why?'

'Can't you just do one thing, one thing for me on this day, of all days?'

'They're expecting us back at the Legion Hall.'

'Will you just pull over!'

She didn't stop until they began to climb Hardknott Pass, and then when he slammed his fist on the dashboard, she finally turned into the parking spaces by the Roman fort.

He had got out, breathing deeply of the cold air. He walked out of the parking space and into the fort, trudging over the long grass, skirting the 2,000-year-old walls, until he got to a viewing point. You could see all the way back down the valley. See the River Esk winding down there in the green. It came down off the Scafell range, the mountain walls rearing up beyond the river, the great stone shoulders of Great How, High Scarth and Great Moss hiding its beginnings.

Looking east, in the opposite direction, you were facing his favourite place, Langdale Valley: Stickle Ghyll to Stickle Tarn and on to Pavey Ark. That was a hell of a climb past the tarn, nearly vertical in places. And the flattish common of the tops beyond. He loved these places more fiercely and for longer than he had loved Liz.

But here at the fort was the beginning of the end of the great mountains. Why had Mike chosen to be buried on those flat marshlands and wetlands and muddy expanses? Why would he want to look at them, and not at the places where they'd had a life together as boys, as men, all their lives, all the things they did together?

Their places were important. More than that. They were holy in their way. He remembered climbing up towards Haystacks, watching Mike's feet in their scuffed boots ahead of him, for once, and the pair of them standing on the top looking down on Buttermere. It wasn't a hard climb – there were plenty higher and more difficult – but it had been a good day every single time they climbed it, coming round to the peak via Green Crag, and back down to Peggy's Bridge, and it was like the whole world was laid out in front of you when you stood up there, and it was special to them both. It meant something. They talked about the tops as if they owned them, and they did – it was their country, and all the mountains were owned by them, and they were kings.

But Mike had forgotten all that, apparently. He wanted to be buried on the flat near the sea. It was as if he was telling him that none of it had mattered.

Liz had followed him and stood slightly to one side. Not touching him, not looking at him.

'That tree,' he said.

'What tree?'

'In that place. The one nearer him.'

She knew which tree.

'It's supposed to be natural, isn't that the point?' he said. 'All those bloody ribbons aren't natural, are they? I suppose at Christmas we'll have the whole fucking works, tinsel and fairy lights.'

'John, people have to grieve.'

'That's not grieving. It's show.'

'I don't expect they'll always be there. The tree will grow.'

'The next time I go there, I'll take them down,' he told her.

'You'll do no such thing.' She turned and looked at him. 'You're not the only person in the world to lose someone.'

'I'm the only person in the world to lose *him*!'

'No you're not,' she said. 'We all lost him. All those people who played with him in orchestras. All the ones playing by the grave today. The singers. And our neighbours. His school friends. All the people waiting back in the Hall for us now. All the people who heard him play, and who wanted to hear him play in the future. Your mum and dad. He was their son, even if they're not here now.'

'Then they can't bloody lose him, can they? They're dead.'

She leaned on the wall, shaking her head. Long moments passed. 'What does it give you, John?'

Far below, in one of the distant houses, a dog was barking. The sound floated up to them like a voice from another world. 'What does *what* give me?' he demanded.

'This anger all the time. This hatred.'

'I don't hate anyone.'

She laughed briefly. 'That's a lie, John. You hate the world. You always have.'

He started shaking his head. 'For someone who's supposed to know me, you know sod all,' he told her.

She was looking at him closely, with an expression of such sadness that he had to turn away. 'I take it back,' she said. 'You just hate yourself. That's what it is, isn't it? I don't know why. Your parents adored the pair of you. Not just Mike. You too. You couldn't put a foot wrong in your dad's eyes, for a start. He gave the business to you, not Mike. Your mother couldn't string a sentence together without prefacing it with how wonderful you were. It was always "the boys, the boys".'

He crossed his arms, staring down at the valley. The dog was still barking: insistent now, repetitive.

'You've had what you wanted, John.'

One moment he was caught in the stillness of a second; and the world had stopped. He was inside a room that had been drained of oxygen. He was drowning, weightless, in the dark. He floundered out of it as if breaking the door of a cell, or rising to the water's surface. He saw his arm floating in mid-air as if he were looking at an entirely unrelated object.

She staggered backwards and slipped against the wall, falling to a sitting position, her hand to her face.

He thought of a poem that she had once read to him,

something about hiding behind a wall and how it was bad for you, and you had to get up.

It was because of the tree.

That was the reason.

He couldn't stop thinking about the tree.

13

S HE IS DEEP IN SLEEP.
    Somewhere beyond the house on the cliff, the sea is breaking, a rhythmic rushing noise in the night. As the wind pushes up the slope it bends the trees, and they add their voices to the rumble and roar. The old cabin creaks in the assault, grumbling under the pressure. The wind finds its way under the corrugated iron roof, slapping the sides, pushing at the windows.

But Alice isn't here. She doesn't hear the sound.

She's 300 miles away, and she is 16 years old.

She has climbed the fell behind the house, following the line of the beck. There's no proper footpath here, and the ground next to the stream is waterlogged, spongy. She slips more than once, and the gradient gets steeper. There are stunted hawthorn trees after 20 minutes or so, and she stops next to them, holding a branch as she lowers herself to the ground and sits on her haunches, staring back down to the house.

Hearing the sound of the latch.

Haltby Road comes in from Penrith and sheers down into the valley. Tourists rarely come here, because the valley road stops after three miles – stops at the big triangular cleft of the mountain. There's a way through to the next valley on foot, a 1000-metre climb that gives a spectacular view at the top, a glimpse of the distant peak between the rise and fall of the land. She's only been there once, up the long climb to the shattered summit, picking her way over boulders where the path is only visible from the smooth-worn polish of other feet.

It's hard to think of what she has to do next. But she has to do something. She just can't leave the bedroom the way it is. The shape under the sheets. The water on the floor. The suitcase still on top of the wardrobe. The garden is big enough, ragged enough. It can all be hidden there. No one will look. And she and William have been alone so much before.

In her sleep Alice is rigidly still, but her heartbeat quickens.

A long way down the incline comes William, following her. He's struggling, his heavy body dragging him to a snail's pace. Even from here, she can see him huffing and blowing. Only panic has driven him up here. Usually he's in the kitchen or on the couch. When he's at the table, he's tied there. It's been that way since he was tiny, and he accepts it now, waiting to be fed or for the TV to be switched on.

There would have come a time when he would have broken free of that chair or that couch. He would have realised that he was possessed of a far greater strength than their minder. But for now he only sits, his mouth open, sweet of temper, shaking sometimes from the Parkinsonism of the CDD. He had been okay until he was about five, although his face had been unusually flat and broad. And then he had fallen away from them, retreating into himself. He seemed not to listen to them very much; he would repeat small movements of his hands – build up bricks, take them down, build them up, take them down. Noise and light frustrated him. Thunder made him scream. Even the sounds outside finally made him wretched – sheep on the fells, dogs barking as they ran down the lane. The radio was turned off permanently, and Alice had learned never to sing.

She wonders often what goes on in William's head. If he can tie the scraps together and make it whole. If he tries to ease the pieces out of the tangled puzzle. They both had blows from their mother, blows that sent a shower of speckled light across her sight. As a little girl, Alice often wondered if William saw the same, and if it frightened him. But she'd put that question away long ago. Stopped thinking about it. It was just how the world was. Bedwetting terror. The voice that made her eardrums ache.

She had been three years old when William was born. No man claimed either of them as their father. By then, she'd already learned how to be quiet. How to restrain herself and be restrained. How to be alone when her mother went out and the house was dark. Where to hide and what not to touch.

The understairs cupboard was safe and she was out of sight there, out of the line of fire. She had a friend in the patterns of the red-grey lino that lined the space like a plastic tomb and was filthy with the dust of years. Fear was footsteps and the creak of the stairs. Her mother going up, coming down. Domestic terror in those stair treads, each with its brass stair rod keeping the bare blue carpet in place.

But the one thing that she was really afraid of was touch. Hands. She knew every inch of her mother's hands: the long fingers that someone might have said were artistic, the square nails. The smell of them: the lily of the valley hand cream. It was impossible to predict what they would deliver: a slap or a smothering hug. Impossible to know which was coming. Or holding her tight in her mother's lap, her hair stroked and pulled by turns, hearing but not understanding the rambling monologues.

When she was anxious now, she held her own hands for comfort.

The same adult hands would propel her into the cupboard. 'For your own good.' Before William was born, her mother had got herself a job in the local shop, and Alice knew that around this time she inherited an auntie. People would say to her that it was nice that her auntie came to look after her while her mother was working. She didn't understand. She didn't trust their faces. She couldn't smile – her face felt peculiarly stretched if she tried. 'Where did I find such a bad girl? What did I do to deserve her?' her mother would say, savagely brushing the tangles out of her hair and swiping at the crown of Alice's head with the same brush.

She is breathing heavily now, deep in the dream. Smothered by a dead voice, her scalp tingling.

In the talk about her auntie – the one who was supposedly with her at home – the pressure of those same hands tightly holding hers would tell her that she was not to ask who her aunt was or to say that she hadn't seen her. Just as she was not to say that the latch of the cupboard made a scraping sound when it was closed.

That conversation had been in the village too. The elderly lady that her mother had been talking to had leaned down. 'It makes a noise, does it?' she had asked, frowning.

The sound of the latch, the sound of the latch. While she sleeps now, the noise of the wind carries the latch into her. The scraping latch, once painted white, the brass now showing through, glimmering in the half-light of the cupboard.

There was a line of light under the door. The angle would change. Sometimes she could hear rain. Sometimes voices out on the road. When she was let out, she would go up the garden, scuffing her feet among the overgrown vegetable patch that had gone to seed years before, where cabbage stalks grew high and seed heads flourished in season, and there was a smell of blue-green earth. Sitting in the wilderness she could see the mountain rising up beyond. It was the last thing to be in sunlight in the evening: bright when the valley was dark. She wanted to climb the wall into the field and walk towards it, had it not been for her mother's warning. 'Don't talk to people,' she'd told her. 'People will lock you up and throw away the key. That's what people are like. And they eat little girls for breakfast.'

When she had been very young, before school, she had thought that was true. She would watch the postman out of the corner of the kitchen window, hands gripping the edge of the sink, shrinking back if he knocked, because here was a man who would cook her and slice her into little pieces, or boil her. He would put her in a pan with eggs and watch her rattle around like they did when the water was hissing and spitting. At the edge of the sink, there was a line of mould under the Formica of the worktop. Dirty people in here. Dirty murdering people outside.

When William came along, suddenly there were other people in the house. Women who came in twos or threes and looked at him but didn't pick him up, and declared him very nice, and smiled at her. 'You have to look after your baby brother now, Alice.' There was some sort of consensus that her mother could not. The same women came in every morning for a while. 'Oh, but he can't help his little face, can he, poor love?'

There was a social worker – looking back as an adult she supposed that was what she was – a social worker in a bright dress with a red belt, who got down on the floor with her and asked what games she liked to play.

Dumbstruck, she had gazed up at her mother standing behind. Her mother raised a warning finger to her lips.

'She's such a quiet child, Mrs Craig.'

'She's peculiar.'

The woman had stood up. 'Peculiar?'

'She can speak if she wants to.'

The woman had looked back down at Alice. 'Are you shy?' she asked kindly.

But in the end, the visitors stopped coming. William was a placid, expressionless, heavyweight baby. He wouldn't cry, but he whined most of the time: a monotonous high-pitched drone. The Moses basket he was laid in stank. There was an argument one day between a woman and her mother. Alice had gone to the understairs cupboard and covered her ears. When the house fell silent, her mother had come and dragged her into the light and clutched her in one of those wordless, terrifying embraces. 'They don't know,' she was muttering. 'They don't know, do they Alice? They don't know.'

All that evening, Alice had sat on the floor between the Moses basket and the kitchen table, where her mother sat with her cigarettes, smoke drifting into the shadows when the light went from the sky, her foot tapping on the floor.

Terror was an immeasurable thing, a phantom in the air.

It hissed like perpetual tinnitus.

She could hear it all day.

She could hear it all night.

The only way to get through living was to exist deep in her head with a cast of people who were kind to her. And when at last she went up to bed, more nights than not she'd stand looking out of the landing window, waiting for her real parents to come and get her. Because it was only logical that there had been some terrible mistake. Mums were loving. She knew because she'd seen it. Seen other mothers scoop up their children and kiss them or hug them or hold them on their knees, sitting on the bench by the village shop talking to each other over their children's heads. Babies kicking their legs, and toddlers wriggling to be set down. She had never been able to fathom why they didn't sit still. It was so dangerous to move about.

Sit still, or else I'll teach you to sit still.

*

Alice woke with a gasp and a cry.

For a second or two, she thought that there was some animal running about in the roof over her head until she realised that it was just the wind battering the flimsy house.

And scratching whatever was in the beams overhead.

Scratch, scratch, scratch.

Getting up, she pulled on her clothes. Impossible to stay inside after the dream. The only place that she could breathe would be outside. Glancing about, she took in the dim shapes of the cottage. All she could afford now that the last of the Haltby Road money had gone. Still, no matter.

She went out of the house into the dark. The unkempt hedge of the garden was whipping about. She heard the sea roaring. All winter the coast had been cold and quiet, and the week after Easter had been beautiful, but it was making up for it now.

She went out on to the narrow beach track. The noise was no less here. She went through the gate and started hurrying, head down. She knew that after a while her body would be lulled into the rhythm of the walk, and her heart would stop the irregular thudding in her chest.

For the first few hundred yards her mother rose up out of that long-ago room, screaming. But by the time that Alice got to the tarmac road, she had vanished.

She crossed the road and went through another gate. The land was more open here, with a lone giant beech tree guarding the beginning of the fields. There were sheep out there somewhere in the dark, but she couldn't see them. She walked even faster, despite the gradient, until she came out at the chalky route to the top: the cliff that overlooked the bay.

Now she could see the clouds racing across the sky: grey ocean-going clippers in a roiling sea. The wind almost took her breath away as she rounded the point and saw the English Channel far below. White rollers, but still no rain. Just the wind tearing at the coast.

She sat down on the chalk just a few feet from the edge.

It would be easy, the work of a moment, to fall. All she had to do was roll. Or stand up again and take three or four paces. That would be all that it would take. No one would miss her for weeks. Sooner or later someone would see the open door of the cottage and realise that she was not in the house. They'd come in and look around themselves and say, 'How does anyone live like this?'

Alice put her hands to her face and covered her stinging eyes.

The truth was that no one *did* live like this. Not really live. She was hanging by a single thread.

And that thread was one desire that had never abated in more than ten years.

It was the determination to see Thomas Maitland dead.

14

THE DRIVE UP TO BUTTERMERE was one that Liz Lord had made many times before: the slate-lined road over the Honister Pass that eventually dropped down towards the lake was so familiar that it felt like part of her DNA.

She drove past the postbox at the Gatesgarth farm where she used to leave Mike and John for their day-long walks. She drove on now until she could see Buttermere. Here, she pulled in for a few moments on a scrap of viewpoint on double yellow lines, and looked up the long valley towards the village.

Twenty years ago, this place had become a bit of a family joke. For John, anyway. 'My freedom pass,' he used to call it. Invariably, Mike would glance apologetically at her as they got out of the car and pulled their walking gear out after them. He would shrug. Or sometimes he'd put his head back in the car and whisper to her, 'He doesn't mean it. He talks about you all day.' Later, when they were married, Mike's tone would become softer. 'Sorry, Liz.' Once – only once – he had said in the house, when he had been home from an orchestra tour and was helping her with the washing up, 'Why did you marry him?' And he had put an arm around her shoulder.

The lies that she told herself, the fantasy that she had allowed herself to believe. She would always tell Mike that it was all right. To ride out storms and to make it good. To stitch it together so that the rips didn't show. It became a thing of pride to her. She feared that one day someone would realise what a weak person she had been. Stuck in this marriage she had been ground to ice particles. There were words for it now – disempowerment. Coercion. There'd been no words then. She'd got on with it, proud in a sick way of her resilience. She would beat it. He would bend. He would change. He would see the unfairness of it. That's what she told herself long after she knew that it was utter crap to believe it.

She had worked odd shifts then as a cleaner for the holiday cottages, scraping to make ends meet while John found his feet. He hadn't wanted her to capitalise on her A-Levels. 'What am I going to do if you're away at college?' he'd asked her. He used a little wheedling child's voice when he said such things, and he would pout like a baby. Over and over he would say 'Let's get married, we have to get married' in the darkness of a car parked way out in Eskdale. Or just the two of them huddled on the ground together on the beckside in the Langdales. The places he took her. They were both 17.

One free agent. One tied slave. She'd begun to think of it more and more that way. She couldn't even remember that rush of love that fuelled the dedication. He'd erased it all, drop by slow drop: sly insults in company, grinning remarks to friends.

'I love you,' she would tell him. More out of desperation as the years went on. Because he could be good. He was funny and tender when life was going right for him. She would see the person he could be, and she would try to hold on to it. At first it was for her own sanity, then it was for the girls. She had for years had the feeling that if all the cards fell right, in some sort of pattern that she couldn't perceive but felt that she ought to understand – if all those cards fell right then they would be happy. He would be happy. Her faith had been deep. His, fragile. Yet he told her time and again that she was the reason that he went on living.

She'd formed a barrier for the girls. 'You dad doesn't mean it,' she'd tell them. 'Your dad is busy today.' School concerts. Sports days. 'I'm taking a picture so that your dad can see.' Eventually they wouldn't pose for those images anymore. They knew him and they kept out of his way. He shouted at them the same way that he shouted at her, and then came to them all for cuddles, for hugs, for kisses. He would ask them. 'Kiss me.' As six- or seven-year-olds, the girls would delightedly obey. Later, they would refuse.

When Christie followed Mae to uni at Durham, Liz at long last took up where she'd left off years before. She'd been waiting too long. That had sparked the biggest row. He had come raging at her. She'd been standing in the centre of the kitchen, trying to find a TV channel to keep her company while she cooked. He snatched the remote, yelling. 'Where are you going?'

'I'm only going to Skelton College.'

'It's hours away!'

'I'll come home at weekends.'

He'd gone red and started breathing heavily, panting. He'd been drinking for hours. 'You'll not go at all,' he warned her. 'How long have you been planning this behind my back?'

'I've been for an interview,' she told him calmly. 'I'm going, John.'

That was when he hit her with the remote and cracked her cheekbone. She rang a friend, and reported him to the police. He came to the hospital crying and begging forgiveness. He actually went down on his knees in A&E.

She started part-time that autumn, working in a little shop nearby to get extra income and pay her rent, and eventually she got her degree.

And when she came home, they were still together. But the marriage was over.

*

She got to Sally Latham's house at nine.

Sally opened the door and stared at her, shaking her head. 'Jesus holy Christ, look at you.' She opened the door wider, and ushered Liz in, touching her arm in the hallway with a brief stroking motion.

They sat outside in the fresh morning. To Liz, it felt better than being inside. She was afraid that if she got warm, comfortable, she wouldn't be able to think straight. They each nursed a cup of tea and looked up at the sky, half cloud and half sun, pushing sequences of racing shadows across the fells. 'Summer's coming,' Sally murmured.

Liz lit a cigarette and nodded.

'What are you going to do about him?' Sally asked. She leaned forward. 'Don't tell me you're sticking with it again. For Chrissake, don't tell me that.'

Liz started to smile at her concerned face, but soon gave up. 'I've come out to give him space to pack his things and go.'

'He's worse than usual. Will he really leave?'

'To tell you the truth, I don't know. Maybe.'

'Okay,' Sally murmured, scrutinising her. 'So how long are you going to give him?'

'All day.'

'Where are the girls?'

'They've gone back to Durham.' Mae worked in a lab in the city; Christie was in a new accounting job. 'They wanted me to go with them.'

'Everyone is frightened for you, Liz. When you turned up yesterday...'

'I know.'

'You should have let me call the police.'

'Not at his brother's wake.'

'But what will you do if he doesn't go?'

Liz said nothing. She shook her head slowly, took a deep drag of the cigarette and then pinched it out.

'Come and stay with us,' Sally told her.

Liz smiled briefly. 'Thanks. But it would take me eighty minutes to drive to school every day.'

'Get a flat in Kendal, then.' Sally held Liz's hand. 'Just go, Liz.'

'The house would have to be sold in a divorce.'

'So what?'

'It's the girls' home, Sally.'

'Do you think that'll matter to them? Living in Kendal you'll be a few miles closer to Durham anyhow.' Sally rocked back in her chair. 'Listen to me. If you get home and his car's still in the drive, come back here. Don't look at me like that. Take a week off school and plead sick, and we'll go together and find you a flat. I'll come with you to the house and stand guard while you get your stuff.'

Liz put her cup on the table, and briefly covered her eyes with her hands. 'All right.'

Sally nodded, satisfied. 'He might have gone anyway. If he has, change the locks. I mean it!'

Liz put down her hands and sighed.

'What happened when you got home last night?'

'He said that he would go.'

'What, no argument?'

'No argument. He said it as soon as we were in the house.'

There was a silence. Sally let it lengthen, thinking all the while that she would have to clear out her spare room. She couldn't imagine John leaving his house, even after he had arrived at his own brother's funeral wake with a wife whose face was darkening with a bruise.

He had sat himself down in a corner while Liz had tried to make the best of it, listening intently while the musicians played. Albinoni's *Adagio* had broken her, however. It had broken everybody. Only when they began playing Cumbrian melodies had the mood lightened and the conversation increased. But through it all, John had sat with his clasped hands hanging between his knees, and spoken to no one.

Liz reached down into the bag at her side. 'I haven't just come for tea and sympathy. I want to ask you something,' she said. She unfolded a sheet of paper. It was a copy of a newspaper cutting. 'When he was on the south coast, he met a woman.'

'Oh yes?'

'Not like that. At least... I don't think so. He'd gone to the police station to complain about this man who drove the van in the road accident, and he was sitting in the town afterwards and a woman came up to him. This woman. John said her name was Alice Hauser.'

She handed the piece of paper to Sally, who held it up to the light, frowning. There was a grainy image of a woman getting into a car, and beside it an article about the disappearance of another.

'Who is she?'

'It's ten years old. I got it from the internet. The article says that her partner – a woman – had disappeared, and that the police had questioned her.'

'And?'

'What would you do if you wanted to know who somebody was?'

'Google them.'

'Right,' Liz said. 'So that's what I did. If you search the name Alice Hauser, loads of stuff comes up from ten years ago. Not just this page, but masses of it. Her partner was never found. Never a trace.'

'So did John tell you what she said to him?'

'She asked John what he was doing in the police station, and he told her, and she said that she knew the other man in the accident.'

'What, the man who collided with Mike's car?'

'Yes. She said he was an ex-police officer, and he'd investigated this disappearance. The disappearance of her partner ten years ago.'

'But... I don't get it. What's that to do with John?'

'The police have told him that this man – his name's Maitland, Thomas Maitland – wasn't at fault. That Mike's car went into him. That they think Mike was getting something from the floor of the car – a CD – and inadvertently pulled on the wheel, and veered across the road straight into Maitland's van.'

'But I thought John told you that another witness said it was the van's fault.'

'Yes, that's why he's got so fixated on Maitland.'

'And that witness was wrong?'

'Apparently, yes. The van swerved a tiny fraction but slammed on the brakes and the impact was in the same second. Maitland saw Mike coming towards him and braked, but Mike's speed was too fast.'

Sally sighed. 'Oh God, I can imagine how John's taken that.'

'I don't think he'll ever accept it.'

'He'll have to one day, Liz.'

Liz pushed back her hair and leaned forward, pointing at the photograph. 'But that's just it, you see? This woman's told him that Maitland was to blame for her partner going missing. She's told John that Maitland was having an affair with her. *She* made a complaint, just like John is doing. And got nowhere, because she says that the police covered it up. Protected their own. She absolutely hates them.'

'But what was she accusing Maitland of exactly, besides knowing the woman who went missing?'

'She says that Maitland was responsible. That he killed her.'

Sally stared at her in astonishment. 'The police wouldn't cover up a thing like that, Liz.'

'John thinks so.'

'Oh Jesus.' Sally was looking abstractedly at the paper. 'And John's got himself wound up with all this speculation, in his state of mind?' She thought for a moment, confused. 'But how did this woman – Alice Hauser, is it? – how did she know who John was?'

'She'd gone to the station to ask where Maitland was – she'd lost track of him, we're talking ten years ago after all – she sees John coming out looking annoyed – and later on she sees John sitting in the town and she comes up to him and tells him straight out that the police won't help him.'

'Because...'

'Because they didn't help her.'

'Bloody hell.' There was a long silence. Eventually, Sally made a face. 'You want my opinion, Liz?'

'Yes, I do.'

'She sounds deranged.' She waved the paper that Liz had given her. 'She's still harping on about it after ten years? What does she do, stand outside that police station and randomly grab angry-looking people who come out and start ranting on about herself?'

Liz ignored the question. She pointed to the photograph. 'Look at her again.'

Sally dutifully scanned the picture and the article. 'What am I looking for?'

'Doesn't she look familiar?'

Sally got up and moved to the light of the window, retrieving her glasses from the kitchen table and scrutinising the image. 'No.'

'Alice Craig.'

'What!' Sally started shaking her head. Then she laughed outright. 'You have to be kidding me!'

'Look at her height next to that car.'

'So what? She's small. A lot of people are.'

'Remember they used to say how small Alice Craig was, how little, as if she was defenceless?'

'Yes.' Sally came back to the table and sat down slowly. 'You're sounding like John, Liz. You've made a hell of a leap here. Listen, it's nonsense, all right? How the hell would you come to that conclusion?"

'John said she had a northern accent.'

'A Cumbrian accent?'

'I don't know.'

'Liz…'

'Where did Alice Craig go, Sal? Do you know?'

'No, I don't.' Sally had crossed her arms in a gesture of exasperation. 'When they're eighteen they move out of our jurisdiction. You know that.'

'But it was your case.'

'No, it wasn't. It was on our team. But it wasn't mine.'

'Well, whose was it?'

Sally started shaking her head slowly, frowning. 'I can't remember. It was, what, fifteen years ago? Do you know how many cases I've had in that time? How many families? How many girls like Alice Craig?' Sally paused, thinking. 'It was Catherine Derby's case. She was in charge. But it's not relevant now.'

Liz took the paper back and re-folded it. 'You remember what Alice Craig and her brother did.'

'It's hardly anything I would forget,' Sally replied softly. 'She helped her brother bury their mother after he had killed her.'

'In their own garden. Without telling the police. Without telling anyone.'

'Yes.'

'Her brother was younger than her. He had the IQ of a baby. Childhood degenerative disorder.'

'That's right.'

'And when people started searching for the mother, Alice Craig told them that the brother had attacked the mother and killed her. And was so distraught that she tried to cover it up. They buried her in that wasteland of a garden and told everyone in the village that she had gone away.'

'Yes.'

'And she was believed.'

Sally eyed her speculatively. 'She was believed because her brother admitted it. These two kids were poor little buggers all their lives, Liz. Dragged up with no love. Beaten. Locked in cupboards. Half drowned in cold water.'

'But never taken into care.'

Sally took a deep breath. 'Don't start on that, Liz.'

'I'm not accusing anyone,' Liz replied. 'But that's a fact. They were never taken into care.'

'They were visited regularly. The mother struggled, but whenever she was visited the house looked reasonable. There was food in the fridge. The boy went to day care, the girl to school. There were no bruises, no complaints.'

'But you believed her afterwards.'

'Look Liz, what is this, the third degree?'

'No. No.'

'It sounds like it.'

'I'm sorry... but the girl was believed, and the boy admitted the murder, and it was... well, not accepted, that's not the right word. But it was understood, when she finally said what had been happening.'

'They buried the mother to protect the boy,' Sally replied. She put a hand to her forehead, pressed the palm against her skin in a gesture of frustration. 'It was one of those cases – once in a lifetime. But they buried their mother to protect the lad, and that was their deluded way of looking at it. They were innocents. They had no concept of the outside world and how it worked. They clung to each other when he was put in secure accommodation. I remember that all right. I remember Catherine telling me. It was a horrible scene, apparently. So much grief from the boy. Screaming and crying.'

'And the girl... what happened to her?'

'Like I say, for any detail you'll have to ask Catherine.' Sally regarded her friend for some moments, an anxious expression on her face. 'You need to take a step back, Liz. This is the last thing that you need at the moment. That photo is not Alice Craig.'

'But it's definitely Alice Hauser,' Liz responded. 'There's no doubt about that. It says so there in black and white. It's the woman who approached John about Maitland.'

'But it is *not* Alice Craig.'

'They've even got the same Christian name. Don't you think that's significant?'

'Not remotely!' Sally retorted. 'If you wanted to change your *whole* life, you'd change your *whole* name, wouldn't you?'

Liz scrambled to pull out another cutting from her bag. She took the first one back from Sally, and then held them both up side by side. 'This one is Alice Hauser, right? This one – this older one, with William's picture too, is Alice Craig. You don't think there's something about her, some likeness?'

'No, Liz.'

Liz dropped her hands and stared at the two photographs in her lap. 'They have each other's phone number now, Sally. John and Alice Hauser. John told me. She's keeping tabs on Maitland for him.'

'Oh God. This is crazy.'

Liz looked up at her. 'And I found other stuff about Alice Hauser online. She was brought in for questioning herself about the disappearance. She was a suspect.'

'But…'

'What if she murdered her partner, Sally?'

Sally flung up her hands briefly, horrified. 'Now you listen to me,' she said firmly. 'Don't get involved in this. You don't know anything about that disappearance, or why she was questioned, let alone thinking she murdered the woman. I mean—' She gave an exhalation of dismay. 'Just because one woman looks a bit like another woman? Maybe. And that's stretching a point. You're adding two and two and making five.'

'They look very similar to me.'

'And that's it,' Sally said. 'Because of the situation you're in, because you're under stress, because you're living with a man who has rapidly – and wrongly, don't forget! – decided the guilt of another person, you're in danger of doing the same. It's not the same person.'

'That's not the way I see it.'

'Of course it isn't. You're not in a position to be objective.'

Liz regarded her steadily for a second or two and then sighed, putting the cuttings away.

Sally seemed as if she was counting to ten. She rearranged herself on her chair, and gave Liz a sympathetic half smile. 'Look,' she murmured quietly. 'They're both grieving, Liz. Both John, and this woman by the sound of it. Sometimes grief does take years, you know. It looks like this woman – this Alice Hauser – is still searching for someone to blame. She's lost the person she loves and she's stuck in that angry accusing phase. She's like a… a sodding guided missile. Except it's not guided at all. It's *mis*guided, randomly veering about trying to find a target. Any target. Anyone who'll listen for more than two seconds put together. I'd think it highly likely that she needs help.'

'I just think…'

'Well, don't. Don't think,' Sally told her firmly. 'Let it go, it's not your issue. I've seen fury like hers time and again. You tie it up with John's anger, *his* way of grieving right now, and it's trouble.'

'I know that. That's why I'm worried.'

'Frankly, *your* safety is what I'm concerned with right now. And it's the only thing that you should be concerned about too,' Sally replied briskly, standing up as she spoke. 'I'm coming back with you and we'll see if John has gone, and if he has, we'll call a locksmith.'

'But…'

'Forget Alice Hauser. Forget Alice Craig. Forget John for the time being. Don't get in the way of the rage, Liz. And don't get involved in John's fantasies. Because that's all they are.' She walked to the hallway, grabbed her coat and came back into the kitchen. 'Did you tell John that you thought it was Alice Craig?'

'No.'

'Good. Because it isn't. Let's go.'

15

THREE DAYS AFTER HELEN MCALLISTER had disappeared, Thomas Maitland and Richard Ellis went to her house in Bloxley. It was the day after Thomas had interviewed Alice. And it couldn't have been more of a contrast to Alice Hauser's rundown home.

The searches of the ridgeway and the tangled paths down to the beach had turned up nothing. No trace of Helen. Now it was house-to-house questioning in the village beyond the ridge.

Helen's house was a new build in a quiet cul-de-sac, not more than two or three years old. Set back from the street, all of the half-dozen houses had a wide front garden, a garage alongside and a path leading to an attractive front door. Helen's garden had been professionally landscaped with semi-mature trees, neat flower beds and a stone sculpture in the middle with a terraced mound built around it.

'Very nice,' Thomas observed.

The place had evidently been cleaned up after the tenants. There was a pungent smell of new paint and floral air freshener. Thomas and Richard walked into a large living-room that ran the length of the house from front to back and ended in French doors to the rear garden. The room was tasteful, and the furniture looked expensive. Thomas looked at the two paintings critically. They were not the kind of thing that Fran liked, but he did. He used to be quite decent at art at school, and even now he would read about artists, and would often wonder if he could take it up when he retired.

The back walls near the French doors were filled floor-to-ceiling with bookcases, craftsman-built to fit the space. He glanced over the titles. Ravilious. Keats. Medieval history. Biographies.

'There's no TV,' Ellis said.

'She liked books better,' Thomas said, indicating the bookshelves with a nod of his head. 'She had wide tastes.'

'Educated.'

Thomas was thinking *Open-minded. Restless.*

'She likes books,' Ellis murmured.

'That's what I just said.'

'No, sir,' he told him. 'You put her in the past tense.'

Thomas smiled briefly. 'Quite right, Richard.'

They both looked out into the back garden. It was as beautifully done as the front. There was an entertainment space, with lighting set into the pavement and the walls; a lawn, a hedge of copper beech.

'Must have cost a packet,' Ellis remarked.

'She works at a private school,' Thomas said. 'Probably earning a fair wage. She's not frugal like Alice Hauser. Alice who lives in a dump. Alice who never had a key.' Momentarily, he chewed on his thumbnail, frowning.

'They don't fit together,' Ellis said. 'Her and Alice.'

'No, they don't.'

'Alice Hauser told us the day before yesterday that they were everything to each other. Partners. Life partners.'

'Perhaps in Alice Hauser's mind. But not in Helen McAllister's.'

'She wasn't next of kin at the school, either. They'd never heard of her.'

Thomas nodded. He went through to the kitchen. Everything was just as immaculate there. They went up the stairs, and the upper floor told the same story. Everything was good quality: the linen on the bed, the furnishings, the Arts and Crafts dressing-table, the clothes hanging in the wardrobe.

'It's very organised.'

'It's too organised. The tenants only left days ago and all her things are in the wardrobe. Coffee by the machine. Book on the bedside table. It's like a stage set.'

'For whose benefit?'

Thomas turned full circle, trying to collect his impressions. 'She brought everything back here, things that must have been in storage. But she hasn't lived here.' He went into the ensuite bathroom. There was a strong smell of cleaning materials again. He lifted the toilet lid and saw the blue liquid skirting the rim. 'No shampoo, make-up... She hasn't even used the toilet, or stayed a single night.'

'So you think that Alice Hauser stopped her? That she knew Helen was intending to be here, and she couldn't stand it?'

Thomas was slowly shaking his head. 'It must have taken a while to bring her things here – the clothes, the food downstairs. If she was going to come here on the day she disappeared she must have been carrying some things with her. But there's nothing in the car.'

'Must be at Alice Hauser's place then.'

'There's something wrong,' Thomas said. 'Something askew somehow. Too clean, too neat. Would she have had time to do it all?'

'With Alice watching her? How?'

'Maybe it was all done for her, then. Bringing stuff out of storage. Getting food in. Cleaning. The full monty. There are firms that do that for people.'

They walked back into the bedroom. On the table by the bed was a framed photograph. Ellis picked it up. It was of Helen herself sitting at a restaurant table, smiling broadly, and holding a glass of wine up to the camera. The setting obviously wasn't England. He stayed looking at it for some time, wondering who had brought it there and why. Why that photo in particular.

'Foreign. Tall towers in the background,' Ellis said. 'Venice?'

'I know this place,' Thomas told him. 'It's San Gimignano in Tuscany.'

'Very nice.'

They went back downstairs and stood in the hall.

'There's somewhere else,' Thomas decided. 'Not at Alice Hauser's. Somewhere else she belongs.'

'Where?'

'I don't know. It's just a feeling.'

*

They were back at the station by noon.

Chloe Donne was waiting for them. When she had first been posted to Brimham, Thomas had asked what subject she had taken at uni and been told that she was a mathematician who didn't want to teach or research. He was glad of her; she had a nice clean logic in the dispassionate way that she looked at things.

'Helen McAllister has a very limited presence on social media,' she told them. 'Only a Facebook page, and very little on that.'

Thomas looked at the page that Chloe had found. There was what looked like an old picture of the coast, rather blurred. There was not much in the profile details either: only her location as being in the county.

'She doesn't post. Not on Facebook, and she doesn't have Instagram or Twitter either. No normal culprits.'

'How unusual is that?'

'One of my friends calls social media the devil's work. He's a solicitor.'

'Legally not a good idea then?' They all knew this.

'Maybe it's because she's a teacher. Doesn't want the pupils seeing. Maybe that's a school instruction.'

'What about Alice Hauser?'

'Nothing at all. Has she got a laptop?'

'I don't know,' Thomas replied. 'I didn't see one when I was in her house.'

'The two of them must have internet connection somewhere,' Ellis said.

'I found Helen McAllister on someone else's Facebook page, though.' Chloe told them. They went to her desk. She brought up the Facebook page for the school.

'Prizegiving for a science event,' Chloe said. 'Young Inventors. It's a national competition.' She pointed to a photograph of a group of adults smiling broadly with five or six sixth-formers. There was a tag line to explain the event. Helen McAllister stood far left, dressed in a dark suit and with a sombre expression on her face.

'The only one who isn't smiling,' Chloe said.

'She certainly looks pissed off about something,' Ellis observed, over Thomas's shoulder.

'Further down the page, there's a photo where Helen is tagged again, with a woman called Alexandra Wilson.'

This image seemed to be a large gathering in someone's garden, and was dated a year previously.

'A third party posted it, and tagged them both. Alexandra has her own page.' She switched to it.

Thomas could see that Alexandra Wilson was a dark-haired woman of about 35 or 40. Her profile picture was of her on a sailboat on a bright blue sea. In the garden photograph, Helen was standing alongside her, looking as if she had just told a joke. Alexandra's face was turned towards her. All three of them silently considered the image for a while.

'Does it say how she knows Helen?'

'She's a school governor. This is a social event, a thank you to a donor, Pressham Brewery.' Chloe pointed to some text under the photograph. 'This has been shared from Presshams,' she said. 'They tagged half a dozen people in the photo, the great and the good. Probably a bit of PR to show how well connected and generous they are.'

She started scrolling down Alexandra Wilson's page. There were plenty of posts. 'She's married... two early teenage boys... husband an ENT consultant... house in France...'

The page projected a moneyed, charmed existence. Alexandra Wilson stared back at him with assurance. Entitlement, even. She had that wind-tunnel look of the heavily Botoxed. In every photograph she was immaculate, even the ones where she was on holiday. When he and Fran were away, they gave up on looking smart. They liked to let their hair down. But this woman looked as if that would be a horror for her. Perfect make-up, perfect varnished nails.

Chloe was evidently thinking the same thing. 'Women like her give me the creeps,' she muttered.

And there was the husband, wearing the same kind of smug smile, sitting in the shade, dressed in a Hawaiian shirt, his feet up on the chair opposite him. Thomas felt a sudden and irresistible urge to ease the scratchy collar of his shirt from his own neck. He didn't like the look of Alexandra Wilson, nor the husband. And he didn't like St George's on principle, with its manicured lawns and its £35,000 a year school fees.

'You bloody old socialist,' he imagined Fran saying.

'Those kind of people fit with Helen McAllister's house,' Ellis remarked.

'Hardly,' Chloe told him. 'They wouldn't be seen dead in a new build, however exclusive. This is their house.'

Another image showed a Georgian rectory set back in another wonderful garden, sheltered by a copse of trees, with a curving drive. 'It's in Nether Hinton. Last Good Move posting was fifteen years ago. Even then it was worth over a million.'

The three of them looked at the screen, and then at each other. Ellis whistled between his teeth. 'And Helen McAllister lives with Alice Hauser for nearly a year,' he said. 'In that dump in Asham Ferry.'

'I bet nobody at the school knew that, especially not Alexandra Wilson.'

The two men walked back to Thomas's office.

'What do you think has happened?' Ellis asked.

Thomas sat down, and gazed out of the window. 'There's only a limited number of reasons why someone goes missing,' he said almost to himself. He counted them off on his fingers. 'They've committed suicide somewhere outside the home, outside their usual routes. Or they're running away because of debt, or love, or fear.'

'Helen McAllister didn't look like she was in debt.'

'She wasn't in love with Alice Hauser either, and I can't think why she'd be afraid of her.'

'Unless she had some sort of hold over her.'

'What kind of thing would that be?'

'I don't know.' Ellis shrugged. 'If Helen had committed some crime?'

'Or if there was a sexual hold of some kind. Some perversion or private taste that only Hauser could supply.'

'Really?'

'Anything's possible.'

'Would that make her afraid? Afraid enough to commit suicide?'

'We haven't found a body yet. She may have walked further inland though.'

'She looks so composed in those photos.'

'Yes,' Thomas agreed. 'The house, the school, the job, all belong to someone competent and organised. Alice Hauser said they had argued, but I don't see Helen McAllister clinging to the edge of life, suicidally depressed. I see her here as someone with contacts. A life away from Alice even when they were supposedly together.'

'People cover up depression.'

Thomas smiled at him. 'Yes, I took that course too,' he told him. He tapped his finger briefly on his chest above his heart.

'Just a feeling. We need to go through Bloxley and see if she's taken her passport. We need the phone records to see if she's made any arrangements – email. Bookings. Ferry. Plane, whatever.'

'She took her bag and phone though, didn't she?'

When Ellis had gone, Thomas continued gazing out of the window.

*

He had been in this job for 25 years. When he had started out there had been no mobile phones, no internet, no DNA analysis to rely on. At 46 he was running to keep up. He knew that. He sometimes felt like a dinosaur, though Fran regularly chided him for it.

However, people didn't change. The essentials were still the same. They still did the same things for more or less the same reasons. They cheated and stole. They killed and injured. They drank, they gambled. They loved and lusted. They coerced and bullied and raged. Or they kept silent, dangerously silent, nursing a grievance until it turned inwards on them and made a cancer in their soul and destroyed them. Or else, they let it out and the rage randomly flew at someone else and brought them down. Strangers killed on a roadside by a drunk driver. Loved ones smothered for no apparent reason in plain sight on a sunny day.

Events could take you by surprise, knock even sane people right out of their world in an instant. This thought made Thomas close his eyes briefly, frowning.

There was always a reason.

Always a reason.

He knew that he was thought of as a plodder by some. He was well aware of it. Probably to someone like Chloe he was unutterably old. But detail was everything. He had never been a hothead, never jumped to conclusions. He was an old warhorse even at 46 with his polished shoes and his notebook and the pressed handkerchief that he always carried in his pocket. He was steady. He was just like his father.

His dad sprang into his mind unbidden. He had worked on the railways all his life, for Great Western. Thomas had a vivid memory of a day out, a treat that his father had taken him on when he was eight or nine. It had been on a train that was being decommissioned and on its last journey; one that his father had driven. Suddenly he had a lump in his throat. His father had been dead since 1971; he had gone into work as usual one morning and died of a massive stroke.

What had made him think of that now?

The missing, the loved.

The ones that never came back.

He still could conjure the feeling of that eight-year-old self: of how inexplicable his father's death had been to him, how chokingly unfair. And how relevant it was now.

*

After he had spoken to his boss to bring him up to date, Thomas went out to his car.

The heat was heavy now, the late afternoon air cloying and still. It smelled as if thunder was coming, and the sky over the coast was threateningly dark.

Thomas got into his car and opened the glove box. He took out the plastic pocket that held his insurance documents. Unfolding them, he came to a small booklet wedged inside, something that he and Fran had once picked up at a garden centre. *The Rules of Rose Cultivation.*

He took out the photo that he had hidden in there.

Helen McAllister in the town square of San Gimignano, holding up a glass to the camera, smiling.

He tore it into four pieces and put the fragments in his pocket.

16

JOHN WAS WOKEN BY RAIN on the roof.

There were a few precious seconds when he couldn't remember where he was, or why he was there. Then it came thundering back: the funeral, the bruise on Liz's face. The hostile looks of people at the wake.

He lay on his back and looked up at the plasterboard ceiling of the Portakabin. In the dawn light, dark gradually became grey. He was half-lying, half-crouched on the hard two-seater sofa between the two desks in the transport office, and he was cold. He uncranked himself to put his feet on the floor, rubbing his shoulders and neck.

He'd been dreaming about Mike, thinking that his brother was standing out in the yard in the rain, holding the viola in one hand and staring towards him with an expression of sadness on his face. In the dream, John had yanked open the office door and shouted at him to come inside. But Mike had only shaken his head. And without his brother touching the strings, a melody had come from the viola and filled the yard, one of the songs played at the grave side.

John groaned to himself now, head in hands, and then rubbed his eyes ferociously. God, it stank in here, he thought. It stank of him, and the bottle of Scotch that he'd brought with him. His stomach gave a lazy flip, and bile rose in his throat.

He jumped up, flung open the door, ran behind the Portakabin, and threw up on the grass.

For a moment, he thought that Mike was still standing in the yard.

'Don't look at me, Mike,' he muttered. 'Don't look at me, kiddo.'

He straightened up, and wiped his face with the back of his hand. It was Saturday: there were no deliveries today. But anyway, he'd stopped work three days before. He'd sent the drivers home and handled the phone calls. Predictably, he'd found himself shouting down the phone about his brother dying. About the customers having no patience and no respect. He'd probably lost a few because of that. But what did it matter? The business was going to the wall sometime this year. He couldn't find it in his heart to care, no matter how many times Liz had nagged him over it. She'd even come to the yard and tried to sort out the creditors and debts, and what little they were owed.

'You'll have to declare yourself bankrupt,' she had warned him. 'You'll have to see Geoff Kendrick.'

'I'll see him then,' he told her. She made him an appointment with the accountant, but he didn't keep it.

It was all going to shit long before Mike's accident. That was the truth of it. Or *he* was. *He* was going to shit. He'd loved this place once, ten years ago when his dad left it to him. He used to like coming in of a morning. He had been proud. He'd worked hard in the beginning. But then he didn't have whatever it was that had kept his father at it for 30 years. He'd lost drivers, hired others, not bothering to follow up references. He reckoned that half of them must have stolen from him, deliveries and money. At least that was what Liz had decided.

'I don't like that new one,' she'd tell him. 'Dave Curtis.'

'You don't like anyone. He's a good bloke.'

'He's a good bloke down the pub, you mean.'

'Yeah, he's a good bloke down the pub.'

Her hand on his shoulder. 'What is it that's getting to you, John?'

'Me? Why is it my fault? It's business. Up and down. It'll come right again soon,' he'd told her.

'Not if you keep losing customers.'

'Well, if they don't like it, they can fuck off.'

She'd dropped her hand from his shoulder, stared at the floor as if trying to control her temper. 'You sound like the kids in school,' she murmured. 'But I'm not talking about the business. I'm talking about you.' She'd tutted with impatience, which drove him crazy. What did she care, anyway? They were only married in name. She had her own income. If he fell down, she'd still flourish. 'Why don't you see someone?' she'd persisted. 'Why not have a word with Doctor O'Neill?'

'What for? There's nothing wrong with me.'

He looked around the yard now in the driving rain.

Of course, he knew what was wrong with him. When it was at its worst, it was like a blanketing fog. Some people talked about feeling as if they'd dropped down a black hole, something that opened suddenly in front of your feet. But it wasn't like that for him. It was much slower. It was like driving down from Keswick in the evening and seeing fog in the basin where Grasmere lay. And then realising that the peaks above were shrouded in the same creeping greyness, until by the time that he had gone another few miles he was in a thick all-enshrouding blanket that pressed up against him.

That was why he walked. Out of the office. At a pace. Grinding down the miles. Climbing up as fast as he could go, until the breath scoured his lungs, until his joints ached, until he could get his head out of the grey.

Sometimes it worked. He'd come back in a better mood. 'Just needed a breath of air.' That was it. If he could just climb up and breathe. Just force himself up into the sunlight. He didn't need a doctor. He could solve it himself.

The thing was, Mike never had it. Never had rage. Mike was

kind and patient and understanding. He'd been content to walk it out with him and not speak for miles on end. But it wasn't fair, was it? Him not having the same thing. Not sharing that with him. They were twins, after all. People always said that Mike had a sunny personality. Some woman had said once at a concert that the sweetness of his character came pouring out in his music. She had called his own brother a sweet soul to his face, like an accusation. Of course, it wasn't an accusation. She didn't know him. She only knew Mike. Maybe she thought they were the same because they were twins, and she was paying him some sort of compliment. 'You're the brother, so you must be cut from the same cloth.'

He laughed to himself now, sour at the memory. Same cloth? He'd like to think so, but no. Maybe until they were 11 or 12. Then Mike got the scholarship and all the talk in the house was of how talented Mike was, and he'd been pleased for him, really pleased. But he was left behind. Not by Mike himself but by those outside the family. He was the also-ran, the ordinary one. Fair enough. This bloody musical genius had somehow skipped over him. Fair enough. 'You've got other talents, John,' his dad would say. 'You've got a good head on your shoulders, you're clever.'

But was he clever? He doubted it. That was something that Dad said to encourage him. 'He's the musical one, you're the clever one.' He'd passed his exams but never wanted university. He'd met Liz by then. She lightened the grey. He had lived for years off her optimistic nature.

He held his face up to the rain, then walked back to the Portakabin. And for years now she was gone from him. Living under the same roof, but absent. She tried to help, but like you would help a sick dog, out of a kind of gentle, objective pity.

Inside the cabin, he cleared away the blanket and righted the couple of cushions. He opened the window to get rid of the smell. He picked up one or two papers from the desk, scanning them in an effort to make sense of them. Then he filled the kettle and made himself coffee. He unzipped the holdall that he'd packed and got out a fresh shirt. He went into the tiny loo and washed himself at the hand basin that was hardly big enough for a cup of water. He mopped the floor of the water that he spilled. He took out the electric razor and shaved, and he looked at himself in the speckled mirror.

He felt like cutting his throat.

'Jesus H Christ,' he muttered. He went back into the main room and drank the coffee, rolling the bitter taste around on his tongue. Then he sat down at the desk and fired up the laptop.

He'd seen it before, but he wanted to see it again. He had time now, he had the space. He typed Alice Hauser's name into the search engine, and was looking at a photograph in the news article that had run when her partner had disappeared.

The headline read 'Local teacher missing'. The largest image was of Helen McAllister herself, one in which she looked very formal. It said that she was a tutor at a school called St George's. A wry smile came to his face. No 'teachers' here. It was 'tutors', like at university.

It had a brief pen portrait of Helen's life: her Master's degree, her involvement in school life. Her year's sabbatical in the USA. Her age, 30. The fact that she was unmarried. Nosy fuckers, journalists. His fist unconsciously clenched. They'd come round to the house after Mike's death. Thank God he'd been down south and Liz had dealt with them, because he probably would have had an assault charge for real by now.

And it looked to be the same here: they'd gone either to Alice's work or her house, and they'd photographed her getting into her car. Her face was averted, in profile. She hadn't changed much in ten years. She looked upset, as well you might when someone you loved had just vanished.

Helen McAllister had gone away as quickly, as irrevocably it seemed, as Mike. The newspaper article said that her car had been found on the coast road. It confirmed most of the things that Alice had told him, although in a bit more detail.

Poor kid. Because she *was* only a kid then – 22. He tried to imagine dealing with Mike's loss if he had been 22 years old and nobody to help him, no wife and no family. He couldn't imagine coping even as badly as he was now, let alone at that age.

It said that the school were deeply distressed at news of Helen McAllister's disappearance and the mystery of it. 'Miss McAllister is an extremely reliable and valued member of staff.' That was the headmaster. A photo of him, your typical poncy-looking git with half-moon glasses and a full three-piece suit, his thumb tucked in a waistcoat pocket like some sort of Victorian patriarch. He could imagine that there would have been fireworks between Helen McAllister, the way that Alice had described her, and a man like him.

That first article was fairly short. John scrolled down for the next one. It was a repeat of the same by another source. But the one after that was three or four days later. And here he was. Thomas Maitland, by God.

They'd held a televised appeal. There was a link through the article to the TV footage via YouTube. The camerawork was pretty shoddy – surely some reporter, not official – and it scudded about for a few seconds, then focused on Maitland's statement.

'We are concerned for the safety of Helen McAllister, who was last seen…'

John leaned forward and concentrated on him.

He ran the film several times. Maitland did look a lot younger, and he didn't look weary. Those intervening ten years had aged him a lot. He'd lost a lot of hair for a start. He didn't look defeated. He wore an expression of professional concern, and at moments he seemed slightly anxious, consulting the papers in front of him. But his voice had a kind of fatherly assurance, with a 'we'll find her' tone. Not dismissive, just… Well, what was he? Kindly. That was it. He was kindly.

John sat back in the chair with a sarcastic grunt.

According to Alice, at this point Maitland knew Helen McAllister a damned sight better than he was letting on. And his treatment of her had not been kindly or fatherly. He'd dumped her. If you believed Alice. But there he sat, everyone deferring to him, in control. Somebody in the audience asked him if the police had any theories.

'We're pursuing several lines of enquiry,' he said.

John switched off the film. He went back to the search and found another item. It was Maitland giving out prizes at a school. Not St George's. And other cases. Some murder or other, a drowning on a beach. And another on a pebbly stretch of coast with a greyish cliff above him. 'Police warn of cliff falls.' A man walking his dog had been caught in a sudden downslide of ashy-coloured rock.

John chewed on his thumb distractedly. Helen McAllister couldn't have had an accident like that, could she? No, he decided. They would have known straightaway. Was there stuff like old mineshafts or anything round there? He knew that there were some in Cornwall. Where did someone come by an accident? Had she jumped? Thrown herself into the sea? Had she just walked away into the countryside and lay down exhausted somewhere, and died? Had she been ill?

He rubbed at the frown that now seemed to be a permanent feature of his face. He could feel the furrow lines in his forehead. The answer to all those questions was the same. She would have been found. Even country areas aren't unpopulated. And a body would wash up somewhere from the sea, wouldn't it? There would have been something fairly quickly, certainly within ten years.

She had taken her bag, keys and phone. The newspaper article said so. Had they ever found her phone or the bag? And what did her phone records say? Had she phoned Maitland, had he phoned her? Was there evidence of them meeting in the weeks before she went?

There were so many questions that he needed to ask Alice

Hauser. Facts to back up her story, for a start. He'd swallowed it whole, but did she have any evidence? When she went to the police she said that they'd rebuffed her. That nothing had happened. But surely they would have investigated. They would have been frightened that she would go to the press, point the finger. They must have been sure of themselves, but why?

He was still scrolling down the search page, vaguely following links to Maitland. One more result caught his eye, and he opened it.

'Hundreds attend funeral of local woman'. And the name under a photograph of the beautiful Frances Maitland.

'The funeral was held today at St Cuthbert's Church, Pennybridge...'

That was where he'd gone to find Maitland. He lived just outside that village.

'... of Frances Mary Maitland, wife of Inspector Thomas Maitland...'

It was only two years ago.

John hunched forward, closer to the screen.

So maybe that accounted for the way Maitland looked. It said that she died of ovarian cancer. He tried to imagine how terrible that might be, finding out that something was incurable and nursing her through it. It was called the silent killer, wasn't it? He knew that much. Frances Maitland looked as if she'd been a popular and respected person.

So that was Maitland's life. The man was alone. Alone in that studio in that garden. Ageing beyond his years. Looking 66, not 56. Grey under the artificial light at that easel.

John was glad.

Glad that he'd lost her.

Glad that he had no one.

'Did you tell your wife about Helen McAllister?' John said, out loud.

17

Ten years ago, under the morning sun.

From the ridge, Alice could see along the coast in both directions: west, the beginning of the curve of the shallow bay of Asham Ferry. To the east, the long line of shingle, hazy in the heat. It was already 70 degrees, and it wasn't quite 9 o'clock.

She sat with her phone in her hands, her legs splayed in front of her. The ground fell sharply away into pasture. She sat just below the well-worn path so as not to obstruct any walkers. On either side of her, leaning on her hands, she could feel the chalk and tufts of grass.

She was very good at waiting. She'd waited for weeks after her mother had died, patiently looking after William. Biding her time for the right moment. Waiting in the dark every night at their back door, hearing him snoring, the sound carrying down from his open window, while all the time she expected to see her mother rise up out of the grave. The mountain outlined against the sky, the col in its side like a scooped wound that had healed, a darker grey. Waiting during the day for the time that would come when people started asking questions. Knowing what she'd say at first. Knowing what she'd say when they didn't believe her. Rehearsing in her mind how she would confess, little by little, what William had done. Rehearsing the tears.

Waiting afterwards for what they would do with him. Waiting to be 18. Waiting at the train station in Lancaster, and on the platform in Carnforth, with the address in her pocket of a hostel in Manchester.

And now she saw Helen's car come up the hill from the village that lay on the other side of the ridge. She saw it pull sharply in to the lay-by. She saw Helen get out and stand, shielding her eyes, trying to find her in the landscape. She didn't raise her hand. Eventually, Helen spotted her. She seemed to stare in exasperation, then grabbed her bag from the passenger seat, slammed the door of the car and started towards her.

It took her five minutes to climb the hill.

'What the fuck are you playing at, Alice?'

'I want to talk to you.'

'And threatening God knows what.'

'It worked, didn't it?'

Helen shook her head. She gave a sigh. 'Look, love.' She glanced down at the coast, then spread her hands. 'It's something you have to get your head around.'

'I don't want to.'

'Listen…'

'I don't want to. I just want you to come home.'

The sun beat down and the grass around them gave off a faint odour of sheep dung and chalk. From above, Alice thought, they would look like a cameo: white figures on a green backdrop.

Helen bit her lip. She looked as if she were weighing up her options. Whether to hit her. Whether to turn and go. 'This is life, you know?' she said eventually. 'Some things are great, and then they fade. It's no one's fault.'

'It hasn't faded, though!'

'It's… Look, Alice, I know it's shit. I'm sorry. I really am.' But she didn't look sorry as she towered over her, face averted, gazing out at the sea. Helen shrugged as she tucked a strand of hair behind her ear. She glanced back down at Alice. 'What more can I say?' she asked.

'You've got to let me go.' She glanced back down to the lay-by below. 'Where's your car? Don't tell me you walked here.'

'It's in the village. I was coming after you. Then I thought maybe you wouldn't want me at the school.'

'You're damned right I don't want you at the school. Threatening to come there, for God's sake. Making me turn round.'

'You've got to come back.'

'No, Alice, there's no "got to". There's no "have to". We've been through all this.' Helen raised her arms and then dropped them abruptly, in a gesture of frustration and impatience. 'Jesus, you're like a limpet, aren't you?'

'If I've done something wrong, you can tell me,' Alice replied. 'Just tell me what it is. I can change.'

Helen gave a long frustrated sigh. 'Look, love. What good would that do? I'm not staying, Alice. Not. Staying. I'm leaving.' She turned to go, then looked back. Alice was sitting with her fists balled at her temples, knocking either side of her head.

'Whatever you want, I can be that,' Alice whimpered.

'Why? Why would you change?' Helen demanded. 'For me? But I don't want you, so what would be the use of that?'

Alice's mouth opened in a little gape of shock. She dropped her fists from her face. It was something new, something she hadn't heard in so many words. *I don't want you.* Her lower lip trembled.

'My darling girl,' Helen said. 'You've really got to grow up.'

'You did last year.' Alice dropped her hands, breathing heavily. 'You wanted me last year.'

'Last summer.'

'And you had people in your house and you came and lived with me. And you liked it.' Alice was shaking, tremors plainly running up and down her throat like a landed fish gasping for air. 'It was…' She stopped and drew breath with difficulty.

'Yes, all right. For fuck's sake, okay. Whatever you want.' Helen regarded Alice for a long time. 'You really are a bit peculiar, aren't you?'

Alice looked up at her with such a hopeful expression, a pitiful expression, the thought telegraphing plainly across her face that she was good for something, entertaining at least. 'I love you,' she whispered.

Helen's face was stony. 'Get up.'

Alice sprang to her feet immediately. She grabbed at Helen's hand. 'Are you coming home?'

Helen looked down at their clasped fingers; then, very slowly, she disengaged herself. 'Let's get your bloody car,' she said. 'Where in the village is it?'

'On the first bend, before the pink house.'

Helen knew the place. 'I didn't see it.'

'Right by the house.'

'Why there? Why not up on the coast road?'

'Because that's when I phoned you. I thought you'd see it and park opposite me.'

'*God almighty*,' Helen complained.

Alice started to cry. Sobs grunted out of her despite herself. 'I wasn't thinking.'

'Ludicrous,' Helen hissed. 'You are just ludicrous. If I leave you to it, you'll let it stay there all day, won't you? You'd let it get towed away, wouldn't you, while you sat here feeling sorry for yourself. I know you. Come on. Let me see you get it. You can give me a lift back to mine, too.'

'But you're coming home?'

'I have work, remember?'

The village was busy, a single file road, a lane in the centre leading to a big National Trust property. It was always choked with traffic because the only legal place to park was on the other side, and visitors baulked at paying the parking fees. So cars littered every spare few inches of road and made progress all but impossible in the summer months. 'You'll be popular leaving it there. Come on.'

They went over the ridge, following the footpath down. Halfway along, when the village came into sight, the path split. They took the lesser one, knowing that it crossed a field and came out at the back of the lane by the pink house at the corner.

Alice trotted after Helen like a dog. At the field gate by the road, there was a moment of fumbling because it was a kissing gate and in months past they had always made a joke of it: that you weren't allowed through the gate unless you gave a kiss. And now Alice tried to kiss Helen in a groping way, a way that made Helen flinch in disgust. For a second, Alice gazed after her, rebuffed, unbelieving. Then she followed.

It was much steeper here. The roofs of the village below were a pattern of thatch and red tile.

'Listen,' Alice said. Helen slowed, but didn't stop. 'I could come with you to Bloxley. Maybe you'll feel better about us in your own place.'

Helen finally stopped. 'You're not coming into my house, Alice.'

'But you came into mine.'

Helen looked at the ground for a few moments. Then she looked at Alice, shaking her head from side to side. Flies buzzed around them. She swiped one away from her face. 'When I came back from the US, that stupid agent had let my house again,' she said slowly, as if explaining herself to a child. 'You remember that, don't you?'

'Yes.'

'And you remember that I was going to rent somewhere else.'

'Yes.'

'I was going to rent the flat near the school.'

'Yes.'

'And what happened then?'

'What happened?' Alice repeated, confused. 'Then you met me.'

'That's right,' Helen said exaggeratedly, as if Alice had come up with a brilliant revelation. 'Spot on, Alice. Well done.'

'It was a nice flat,' Helen continued in the same slow tone with a sarcastic edge. 'Don't you think that I would have liked to live there?'

'I don't know…'

'Yes you do. I showed you the details. I was sitting in your own bloody café reading them and you asked me if I was going to move here, near Asham.'

Alice had become red in the face. She would never forget that morning. It had been like a bolt of lightning. Helen had been sitting at the table outside, reading the file in front of her. And then she had turned and raised her head to beckon Alice over.

'Can I get a mocha?' Helen had asked.

And when she brought it to her, Alice did what she *never* did. She made conversation. She asked a question about the house details, and Helen had showed her the page.

'Lovely,' Alice had said.

'I don't know,' Helen had replied. 'It's so expensive. The annoying thing is, I have a rubbish bloody agent who re-let my own house. Can you believe that? Greedy bastard. Now I can't get in my own place.'

'He ought to pay your rent,' Alice had said.

Helen had grinned. 'You know, you're right?' she replied, smiling broadly. 'But wish me good luck with that all the same.' Then she'd turned and looked at the sea. 'Do you know what I'm going to do?' she said. 'I'm going for a swim.'

And Alice had watched her. Helen went down to the water's edge and took off her clothes in the kind of way that she expected everyone to be looking and admiring her. Which everyone usually was.

Two days later, she'd taken off her clothes in Alice's bedroom.

And that was the beginning and the end of everything. The start and the end of the world. Alice had been loved and now she realised that it was only ever going to have been for a few months. In a flash she saw that Helen had been too lazy to care what she had said. The plans and pictures had never been real.

They were just things that she made up on the spot routinely, for her own amusement, to see what reaction they would get. It had been a kind of game, one that had thrilled Helen in a cruel way, playing Alice along, seeing how happy she could make her before she got bored.

'We went to the abbey and you talked about getting married,' Alice whispered now, her voice lisping with the horror of it, the word 'married' coming out something like 'madded'. Wasn't that an old way of saying maddened, to make angry? The useless definition trembled inside her skull as if some kind of metal grille was being dragged down in her brain. Madded. Made angry. Infuriated.

'What?' Helen demanded.

'The abbey.'

'Oh,' Helen replied. She turned away and started down the hill at a hell of a pace. Then she stopped again abruptly, and turned. 'But listen to me. I told you I was going to get a flat last year, and what did you say? What did you say, what did you beg me to do?'

'Stay with me instead.'

Helen nodded. 'Stay with you instead. Begged me. It wasn't my idea, was it, Alice? I did what you nagged me to do.'

'But it saved you a lot of money.'

'Oh, did it? I had to keep my furniture in storage. Have you forgotten that?'

'But you would have had to do that anyway.'

Helen grabbed her by the left arm, and the grip of her fingers hurt. 'What you don't seem to realise, Alice,' she muttered, 'is that I did *you* the favour. And no thanks for it. That's the sort of person you are.'

Alice stared after her, the sun beating on her back, the sweat prickling in her scalp, and her hands clasped in front of her like a prayer.

She would never forget the sight of Helen's back and the movement of her body as she walked: that springy step. Helen was wearing a patterned pink top and a knee-length linen skirt, and her legs and arms were brown, and her hair looked almost white in the sunshine. A cross-body bag bounced at her hip.

She looked free. The walk said so. It said *I'm walking away, and I'm happy about it.* And all the time that metal grille, that clamping down of despair, rattled in Alice's mind, and there was a wrenching, pulling sensation in her chest.

She started after her at a run. Helen heard her coming and stopped, looking at the ground and shaking her head.

'It's him, isn't it?' Alice demanded.

Helen put her hand to her head in a gesture of *you're crazy*. She put the heel of her hand on her forehead. 'Who?'

'The policeman. Maitland. You talked about him at Christmas. You said he rang you up. Asked you out. More than once.'

Helen started to smile, but pinched it back. 'Yeah, okay.'

'That's the man, isn't it? The one you won't tell me about whenever I ask. You're still seeing him.'

'Whenever you fucking nag me endlessly about it, you mean.'

'It's him, isn't it?'

'Jesus Christ. Look, if you like. Whatever, Alice.'

'Since when?'

'It doesn't matter if I'm seeing him, or a dozen others, does it? I'm leaving because I don't want to be with you. That's it. That's all.'

'But why him?'

'There isn't a why, okay? I'm just leaving. *Leaving*, Alice!'

She started walking again, much faster. They were soon at the top of the lane at the back of the house, and Alice's dusty blue Ford could be seen half on and half off the pavement. As they drew level with the garden, an old man standing by the wall asked if it was their car.

'Talk to her,' Helen told him, hooking a thumb behind her in Alice's direction. 'And don't go mouthing off at me, you bloody old fool. Why don't you mind your own moronic business? She was the idiot that left it there.'

Alice half ran, half walked, feeling for the car key in the pocket of her jeans.

'You're not leaving me,' she said.

Helen was already too far away to hear.

18

THREE DAYS AFTER HE HAD first come to her house, Maitland was back.

It was 8 o'clock in the morning. Alice opened the door and there were people standing there in a group, Maitland at the front. The man alongside him said they had a warrant to search the house.

As soon as she had opened the door, a wash of salt-heavy heat rolled in from the beach. She'd kept the windows closed, too the curtains, for days.

There was no alternative but to let them in. Maitland stayed behind and looked at her.

'What do you want?' she said. 'She's not here.'

'Where is she then, Alice? Do you know?'

'Of course I don't know. I reported her missing. Me.' She stabbed her chest with her forefinger.

'I wish you had come to the press conference, Alice.'

'You can't make me.'

'No. That's perfectly true. But just the same.'

'I don't want people looking at me.'

She walked away from him and sat on the breezeblock wall that edged the patch of scrubby grass in front of the house. Almost at once, she stood up again, wringing her hands and looking at the house with an anguished expression.

People were already coming to the beach, walking down from the car park at the top. A couple of families passed with their spades and beach tents, staring at the police cars.

Strangers didn't know that there was only an inch of sand by the waves, and would grumble in the café afterwards. They never read the signs at the top, either. Cars would come down, realise there was nowhere to park, and go back up again with a grinding of gears.

A woman carrying a cool box looked inquisitively at Alice and Maitland. Alice turned and shielded her face with her hand.

'Tell me about the argument again.' Maitland was smiling encouragingly as if the commotion in the house were nothing to do with him.

'It was nothing. She was coming back here with me.'

'What, that morning?'

'Yes. No,' she corrected herself. 'She was coming back again that night.'

'Was it a fight?'

She squinted up at him in the sunshine. 'A fight?'

'Did she hit you? Did you hit her?'

'No, of course not.'

He sat down on the wall, three or four feet away from her. 'People do lose their tempers,' he observed mildly. 'It does happen.'

'Well, it didn't happen with us.'

Moments slid by in silence.

'What did you mean the other day,' he said eventually, 'about me?'

'I think,' she said, 'that you know what I mean. She told me things, do you realise that? She spoke to me.'

'But what exactly did she say, Alice?'

'She told me that you came to the school.'

'I did come to the school,' he said. 'I gave a talk one morning. It was two years ago.' Alice stared down at her bare feet. 'Alice… Miss Hauser…'

'You went for a drink, and you saw her after that.'

'No.'

'And slept with her.'

Maitland was watching her carefully. 'Tell me about that conversation. Tell me exactly what Helen said to you.'

'She told me at Christmas,' she replied.

'This Christmas just past?'

'Yes.'

'And when was this supposed to have happened with Helen? Then? Or before that? Before you met?'

Alice stood up abruptly, and stepped towards him. 'Why are you asking? You know already.'

'Helen told you that she and I knew each other. She told you this at Christmas? Perhaps she got it wrong,' he said. 'Misremembered. Confused me with another person.'

'How can you confuse someone you've slept with!'

Maitland glanced back towards the house, and lowered his voice. 'I didn't sleep with Helen,' he said. 'And I don't think she actually said that to you, did she?'

Colour had rushed to Alice's face. 'I gave her a game. A game like a puzzle box. She couldn't do it. She said that it would take a detective. She threw it across the room. And I said she ought to take it to you. She said that she would.'

'She threw it. Threw it across the room, or at you?'

There was no reply.

Maitland shifted a little, so that he could look properly at her. 'You've been crying,' he said.

She shrugged, as if to say *So what*.

'And you have a bruise.' He nodded towards her left arm. Since he had last seen her its redness had blossomed into an ugly blue. It ran from wrist to elbow. 'How did you do that?'

She glanced at it as if it didn't matter. As if she had only just noticed it herself. 'I bumped into the door taking the rubbish out. It swung back on me.'

'When was this?'

'Yesterday.'

Maitland frowned at her, then got to his feet. He walked over to the house and talked quietly for a few seconds to Richard Ellis. Ellis made no attempt to acknowledge her, even though she had spoken to him first about Helen. She sat in the heat seething at his rudeness. The rudeness of everyone going through her home.

Let them look. They'd find nothing, because Helen had never come back here, and Helen had taken almost everything she owned out of the house last weekend.

She watched as they both walked towards her.

'Alice, where are your rubbish bins? The waste bins?'

She inclined her head towards the large skips behind the café. 'Over there,' she said.

'But you have your own?'

'They're all there.'

Ellis walked away with a constable in tow.

Maitland smiled at her. 'There's an unusual smell in the house,' he said.

'There isn't,' she retorted. 'I clean every day.'

'*Every* day?'

She stood up. '*Every* day.'

'Is that something you have to do?'

'What do you mean?'

'In the way of needing to. A compulsion.'

She knew where this was going. She had heard it before long ago. A woman and a man standing in Haltby Road paying her a compliment that wasn't actually a compliment, because it had another meaning. 'Do you feel a need to clean, Alice?' And she'd told them yes, she felt a need to clean. *I feel a need to clean after my mother.* She'd said that, and they had nodded, because they thought that it was a reaction to her mother's well-known slovenliness. A natural reaction. Maybe even a doctor, a social worker, had said the same thing. That it was normal in the circumstances.

'Things have to be clean,' she told Maitland. 'Or where are you?'

'Oh yes,' he said, seeming to agree. 'Is Helen clean like that?'

'Helen?' she smiled. 'No.'

'That's strange,' he murmured. 'We were in Bloxley yesterday. It was beautifully clean. But maybe that was professional cleaners, was it? Did she get cleaners in after the tenants?'

Blood buzzed in Alice's brain. A gasp rose in her throat, and she made a concerted effort to swallow it, to keep her mouth clamped shut. She looked at this man who was telling her that he'd been where Helen had told her she could not go.

'Was it you who cleaned Helen's house, Alice? Did you go back there with her the other day?'

'No!'

'A very nice house,' he added. 'A beautiful garden.'

And he glanced around, just a fraction of a glance. At the scratchy grass that wasn't really a lawn in anyone's estimate. At the chalk soil poking through the threads of green. At the breezeblock wall and the litter around it: cigarette butts and pieces of plastic wrapping that had been long shredded by the sun and rain. His glance illustrated what he did not say: that this place was a tip, an eyesore. And that Helen's house was an almost unbelievable contrast.

'She kept her two lives separate, didn't she?'

'She didn't have two lives,' Alice blurted out. 'She had only one life. With me.'

'Oh,' he said. 'That's not true, Alice. You said so yourself.'

'What?' she asked, stung. 'I never said that.'

'Yes,' he told her. 'The first time I came here – just a day or two ago – you said "She hasn't wanted to stay here lately". Or words to that effect.'

Alice said nothing.

'Isn't that right? And so, if she hasn't always stayed here lately, where else does she stay?' Maitland put his hands in his pockets. He veered away from the remark as if the answer didn't matter in the least. 'I'm not much of a gardener myself,' he told her. 'My wife's the one for all that.'

It was the first time that she had heard anything about him being married. Helen's averted face came back to her, looking out of her own car window while she had manoeuvred the car at the top of the village. Helen saying, 'Let's not get into that again for Christ's sake'.

'Your wife?' she echoed.

'Yes,' he said. 'Some people have a knack for living things, don't they?'

There was a noise over at the café. They were dragging out the rubbish bins.

'Helen got a gardener in, did she?' he asked.

'I don't know.'

'Was it all done before you met her, the landscaping?'

'I don't know. She never told me anything about her house.'

'Really?' He affected a kind of wounded surprise on her behalf. 'You don't know anything at all?'

'No.'

'You met her after she came back from the States,' he said.

'Yes.'

'Had she liked it there?'

'She didn't say.'

'Was she planning to go back?'

'I don't know.'

'Did she like St George's?'

'She came back to it, didn't she? Afterwards. After the States.'

'But she didn't tell you why? Not that she'd missed it? Or that she felt an obligation, perhaps?'

'I don't know,' she repeated.

He put his head on one side, regarding her with an expression of sympathy. 'But you said that Helen told you everything. That there were no secrets.'

The pounding in her head was threatening a migraine. She was trying to grasp what he had said – the bit about Helen having two lives. He meant with him, didn't he? He had been in the Bloxley house, and before yesterday. He had been there already, maybe two years ago, just before Helen went to the USA on her sabbatical. That would have been the summer too. Did they have an affair that year, in the rosy, cloying heat of the same season as this? Did he stand in that garden when it was just done, did he have a say in the design? Did he sleep in the bed there? He was trying to tell her that he had a prior claim to Helen. She'd tried to get the truth from Helen over and over. Asking her the same questions, gnawing away at the pain of it. 'Leave it alone about Maitland,' Helen had told her. 'It was nothing. It was a joke. Don't you understand a joke when you hear one?'

What kind of joke? She didn't understand. Was the affair with this man so important that she hated having let the secret out, or was it really meaningless? It had started in the abbey that day. Helen had said that there were details about a man she'd known. She'd smirked all that day as if she were laughing to herself at Alice's uneasiness.

Alice stared at him now. The tell-tale migraine indicators jumped in the left-hand side of her vision.

'Which way did you drive when you drove away from the village, after leaving the ridge?' Maitland asked.

'What?'

'You said the other day that you left Helen on the ridge, and walked back down to your own car in the opposite direction, down to the village.'

'I did.'

'Even though you'd called her back in the first place, made her turn around instead of going into school, you left her there.'

'Yes.'

'And you supposed that she'd gone to the school after that.'

'Yes…'

'Which she didn't. So which way did you drive out of the village?'

'Away from the coast, towards town.'

'Not back home?'

'No.'

'Because if you'd turned your car towards home, you'd have passed Helen coming the opposite way.'

'My car was pointing in the direction towards town. You can't turn around until the other side of the village, and when I got that far, I just kept driving.'

'Was it because you didn't want to see Helen coming back from the coast, you didn't want to pass her again?'

'No. I wasn't thinking. I was upset. I just drove.'

'But you wouldn't have seen Helen passing you, as it happened, would you?'

Alice put a hand to her thudding, aching head. 'Why not?'

Maitland smiled again in his quiet, fatherly way. 'Because Helen never got back to her car. It stayed where it was all that day and all night. She never got to the car. She never got to the school. She never came home to you. Where is she, Alice?'

At that moment, Richard Ellis came striding quickly back from the bin store behind the café. He was carrying an evidence bag in one hand, and he called Maitland's name.

Alice watched Maitland stand up and turn his back to her, his hands still in his pockets. She felt a visceral, absolute rage.

'This was in Miss Hauser's bin,' Ellis said.

And in the bright sunlight, he held up the bag with the vegetable knife inside it, tinged with a brownish residue along its blade.

19

THE MORNING LIGHT WOKE THOMAS.

He sat up in bed, and then swung his legs over the side and rested his head in his hands, looking obliquely at the alarm clock. Ten past six. Six hours' sleep. With a sigh, he got up and went to the bathroom.

It was amazing how quickly the dawn came now. Only a couple of months ago he had got up in the dark. Now the garden below him was bright. The green of the trees was amazing; he felt glad of it, another year, another season. And from this angle he could see where he'd been working for the last few days. The scrubby area of grass at the bottom of the garden beyond the workshop had already been half dug over.

He leaned both hands on the windowsill. It was a good house. A good position. He would never leave it, never want to. It was safe, somewhere the whole nasty business of Helen McAllister and Alice Hauser, and all that came with them, couldn't touch him anymore.

Newly retired, he and Fran had spent a year changing the house around, refurbishing it and bringing it up to date. Building the studio too. For him, it was to scour out the past. Fran understood that. He could still see her painting the landing, splattered with cream emulsion and laughing at herself. Still see her putting up the paintings and the photographs of their holidays. He tried not to look at them usually; but today he turned around and looked through the open door and smiled at the image of them on a clipper ship in New Zealand two years after he'd left work. They had been in the Bay of Islands. They'd really tried to make a go of things. He'd tried to repair everything he could think of: house, garden, marriage. Sometimes Fran, with that easy slow smile of hers, would even say that he was trying too hard.

Lovely time that had been. Lovely. All the grime from his years of work had gradually sifted out of his head, and he had started buying equipment for the studio and attending art courses. Gradually, he had even managed to put that miserable house in Asham Ferry and the lasting mystery of Helen out of his mind.

Or he had until lately.

He dressed in what came to hand, without considering it: the muddied old jeans, and a faded T-shirt. It had been Fran who had made him relinquish the shirts that he used to wear for gardening. The T-shirt that he put on now had a photograph of Fleetwood Mac on the front, the image from the front cover of *Rumours*.

That dated him. He'd been 12 years old when that was released, but it had hit him straightaway, and he'd saved up his pocket money and bought it. His parents had got sick of the sound of the music coming from his room, and had told him so. He'd told Fran the story when they had first met.

On his 50th birthday she'd bought him 50 presents – not big stuff. Not all of it. Some of it was silly – biros in different colours, his favourite chocolate bar. That kind of thing. And the T-shirt *Rumours*. He put it on now and looked at himself in the mirror, a 12-year-old boy grown old, with 30-odd years in the police force sandwiched in between. He looked harder at himself. He was losing weight; his face had deep contours.

He went downstairs and out into the garden.

He stood on the slope, looking at the field beyond. The only sound that he could hear was a couple of blackbirds trying to outdo each other in the hedges. He took a deep breath, looking around. Perhaps he ought to get another dog, he thought. He missed Fish in a deep, quiet way. He'd stopped himself from actually loving the dog, because loving and missing, with that awful visceral ache, belonged only to Fran. But he had to admit that Fish's absence caught at him often.

He didn't have to live with sadness all the time, he told himself now. He had a choice in the matter. Grieving had become a habit. He wondered if he could come out the other side: get another dog, feel life was worth living, take pleasure again. Occasionally he even wondered if he'd ever fall in love again, but always dismissed the idea. His heart had been mashed to a pulp, and he'd be a pain in the neck for any woman, he told himself. About the only thing that he liked was painting. In the circumstances, he felt that in itself was a bloody miracle.

Thinking of Fish, he wondered again where the dog was. He'd asked the police, but nobody knew, or could remember the kind girl who had taken Fish from him before he got into the ambulance. 'Fish,' she had said to him. 'Cool name'. And he'd given the still-warm body over to her, holding up the dog's head until she got a proper hold. She had looked like a horsey kind of person: practical, scruffy. Or perhaps she worked in a kennels, or at a vet's. He ought to ask around: ring local kennels and so on. He felt a little stab of guilt that he had abandoned Fran's beloved dog to a stranger.

The spade was lying where he had left it last night. He'd stopped when it was too dark to see, and now he wondered what he had eaten last night when he'd finally gone inside. He might have thawed out one of Christine's shepherd's pies, but he couldn't remember. For a moment, he leaned on the spade and cursed his lack of concentration. It wasn't right to let his mind wander like this, he told himself. But he knew the cause.

He was distracted by the thought that Alice Hauser was back. Or could be back. She went around and around in his mind. Had he really seen her? If not, why had she sprung so clearly into his mind, like some sort of phantom materialising out of the past?

The last thing on his mind before he went to sleep last night was Alice Hauser's complaint about his conduct investigating the disappearance of Helen McAllister. She had told the story about him sleeping with the missing woman. And more. It had caused such a bloody horrible lot of grief for so many reasons.

'For God's sake,' he muttered to himself.

He began to dig. With the rhythm of the work, he finally relaxed. He was double digging so that he could make a vegetable patch; it seemed a waste not to make use of this stretch of good earth. It was coming up lovely: rich, untouched and a beautiful dark colour. There was a patch further down where it had once been dug, and by making a vegetable garden, he would eradicate the odd colour of that area.

Once, he and Fran had gone to the local records office and looked at an old tithe map of this stretch of road; there had been a brickfield on one side, but this garden had been all apple orchards. He glanced over his shoulder: there was only one tree now, and it produced huge cooking apples that for the past two years he had let rot on the ground. He'd let Christine take them this year, he thought. He might get a few apple pies in return.

He heard the gate: the scratch on the path, and the click of the latch. He looked around.

'You're out early.' As if she'd been summoned by his thoughts, it was Christine herself. She looked pretty much as he did: dishevelled, hair on end. She was swamped in a hand-knitted jersey and corduroy trousers.

'What are you doing?'

When she got close, he swung his hand over the grass and soil by way of explanation. He had stopped digging, and moved so that he was between her and the turned soil.

'What're you going to plant?'

'Veggies.'

'Naw... get away!' She grinned. 'I'd gathered that much.'

'I haven't thought about it. Potatoes. Beans.'

She smiled at him. 'I haven't seen you in ages.'

'No,' he said. 'I thought I'd take a break from the studio. I've been out walking, mostly.'

'Anywhere nice?'

'The coast.'

She nodded. 'Do you want any breakfast, Thomas? I got a meat delivery yesterday. The bacon's really nice.'

He hadn't realised he was hungry until they both heard his stomach rumble.

She laughed. 'I'll take that as a yes. See you in ten minutes.'

*

Breakfast over, they lingered over their tea.

'Where on the coast did you walk?' Christine asked.

He was going to make up something: one of the cliff walks maybe, or a long hike that took him out of the village to the far west of the county, and down towards a nice stretch of deserted beach. In actual fact, he'd nearly done that one and had actually planned it – down the long hill towards the sea, among the spring lambs, over the earthworks of an Iron Age hillfort, part corroded by time. But in the end he told Christine the truth.

'I went to Asham Ferry.'

'Oh,' Christine responded. 'It's a bit dull, isn't it? Or has it changed?'

'No. It's just the same. More rundown, if anything.'

'There used to be a café…'

'It's still there.' He put down his cup. 'I had a case there ten years ago,' he said. 'A missing woman. Maybe you remember it?'

'No. I don't read the papers much,' she replied off-handedly. 'Did you go to Asham because of the case?'

'Yes.'

Christine said nothing, but she was looking at him questioningly, expecting him to elaborate.

'It was a teacher at St George's. She had a partner, another woman, who lived in Asham Ferry. One day she went missing. Her car was found on the coast road.'

'Did you find her?'

He paused, lining up the knife and fork on his empty plate. 'No, never.'

'What do you think happened to her?'

He sat back in his chair. 'Her partner said that they'd had an argument that morning. They'd met on the ridgeway, then gone their separate ways. The partner – this other woman – walked down to the village on the other side of the ridge. The missing woman walked back to her car, in the opposite direction. Or so she said.'

Christine was concentrating, arms folded on the kitchen table.

'We found the car. We questioned her partner, more than once. We searched her house.'

'And?'

Thomas sighed. 'At one point we found a discarded knife, but it had been used to cut up meat.'

'Did you think that the missing woman had been murdered then? When you found the knife?'

'For about a day and a half. We took her partner in for questioning.'

'What did she say?'

An image crashed into his mind: Alice Hauser in an interview room steadily crying, without much noise, her solicitor beside her.

'Nothing, really.'

'Literally, nothing?

'She just repeated what she'd already said. That she left Helen McAllister on the ridgeway, and that was the last that she'd seen of her. Helen must have gone somewhere on foot, away from the road. She wasn't seen in the village below, either. She didn't hire a cab. The last phone signal was in the area that day. She wasn't seen walking. There was just no evidence of her.'

'Vanished, just like that?'

'Yes, vanished.'

There was a short silence while Christine digested this. She was chewing on her lip. 'What happened next?'

'We searched her car. We took it in for forensics.' Thomas ran a finger round the rim of his empty cup. 'I thought we had her then, because there was a smell of cleaning in that car. She admitted that she *had* cleaned it.'

'And you didn't find anything?'

'We found evidence of Helen having been in the car, yes.'

'Well then!'

'No. Alice Hauser made the point that Helen had been in the car dozens of times. There was no sign of a struggle or foul play.'

Christine frowned. 'But you'd arrested her?'

'No, we didn't arrest her. She just came in for interview. She maintained all along that she was as confused as any of us. We pressed her pretty hard, but other than slightly changing her story in the beginning, she kept to the same one after that.'

'But you pressured her, you say?'

Thomas sat back and sighed. He glanced at Christine, then back at the tabletop. 'And that…' he shrugged. 'That backfired somewhat.'

'Did it? How?'

He looked back up. 'She made a formal complaint,' he replied. 'She said that I had killed Helen McAllister.'

20

JOHN WAS DRIVING DOWN THE M6.

The last time that he had done this journey he had been coming down because of the accident. He sighed to himself, and rubbed his eyes. Sleeping on the hard little sofa in the Portakabin was getting to him, making his whole body ache, and he struggled with the feeling, the increasing conviction really, that it was unfair.

He knew that he had always been something of a bastard to Liz – how could he not, when everyone was telling him so? – but it rankled deep in his soul that he was suffering. And those people who claimed that depression wasn't suffering were talking out of their arses. He knew he was more sick than he had ever been, and yet there was Liz sleeping in a bed in a house and he was… Well, what was he? A cast-off, beyond the pale.

It was raining as he went through Stoke and Stafford. He stopped once, running through the pelting rain to grab an apple and a coffee. God, how he hated these families getting in the way. The stink of overcooked food and the look of boredom on people's faces. Waiting in line, he watched the couples sitting in Costa and the people with their Big Meal lunches with an air of busy-busy-busy-ness on laptops. Imagine a life emailing from a table in Burger King. He guffawed to himself as he walked out. He hated humanity.

It was 4 o'clock in the afternoon when he pulled into the services at Gloucester.

He sat in his car for a while on one of the higher parking ranks. This was one of the better service areas. It was fairly new, landscaped and spacious. He sat staring at the cars as they arrived and departed. Alice had said that she had a blue Fiesta, an old car.

At last he got out and wandered down to the building. He saw her sitting on a bench. For a second or two, he couldn't decide if it was her, and then she stood up and waved at him. He went over to her.

'So you came,' she said.

'As agreed.'

'I wondered if you would change your mind.'

'Let's go inside,' he said. The rain had followed him, and was threatening in the blustery sky.

They took their drinks to a table near a large plate glass window that looked out onto a pond and a garden.

'You wanted to see me,' she said.

'Yes...'

'And I wanted to see you.'

He glanced up at her. She had bought a scone and jam, and was methodically unwrapping the butter and spreading it. She seemed disconnected, oddly calm.

'What for?' he asked.

'The same reason. Maitland. Have you got any further with him?'

'They say it wasn't his fault.'

She smiled. She bit into the scone and chewed for some time. He felt irritation mounting as he looked at her. Did she think that this was some sort of entertainment? She seemed amused. 'They would say that, wouldn't they?'

'I made a complaint,' he told her.

'So did I, once. Get anywhere with it?'

He sat back, grimacing. 'They've recorded it. It's up to the local force.'

'Oh yes,' she murmured, wiping her mouth. 'They'll do that. It's not serious to them. Not enough to go before the Independent Police Complaints.'

'It's not called that now. It's the Independent Office for Police Conduct.'

'Is it?' she intoned, seemingly unimpressed. 'Well, it's a matter for them. Not the local plod. Don't you think that? This is someone with *two* accusations of murdering someone now.'

'He's not in the police anymore.'

'Yes,' she said. 'He resigned.'

'Over you?'

'You see,' she murmured. 'I wouldn't let it go. I just—' she paused. 'Would not, would *not* let it go.'

'But it ended the same.'

'Yes, he was not involved.' And she laughed a little and then made a disgusted face at him. 'It's a phrase, isn't it?' she asked him. 'Getting away with murder. It's not often that it actually means that someone did.'

And for the first time he saw that she was close to tears. His heart gave a little skip; he understood that. He understood just going on trying to keep that horrible feeling of rank injustice at bay. It was under the surface all the time.

'The last time I saw you, you said that you didn't think he murdered Helen—'

'I didn't say that.'

'I asked you if you thought that he'd done something to Helen, and you shook your head.'

'I did not.'

John paused, frowning. 'You did shake your head, Alice.'

She suddenly leaned forward. 'I might have been shaking my head at the thought of it, but I didn't mean that he didn't do it. I told you that she was meeting Maitland that day.'

'All right,' he conceded. 'But this is what's been getting to me. I can't figure out what you mean.' He sat forward, determined to get to the bottom of it. 'You said that Helen had told you that he made all the running, that he bullied her, and you said that it had all been over by the Christmas before she vanished. Five or six months before, right?'

'Yes.'

'So when did they have this affair? Was it going on while you were together?'

'No,' she said. 'At least I don't think so. I think it was the year before.'

'You don't *know*?'

'No,' she retorted angrily. 'Does anyone ever really know the truth about what their partner does? She mentioned Maitland not long after we met, she said – she implied – that they'd seen each other a year before. Then, for a long time, she used to tease me about it. She knew that the idea hurt me, and she thought that was funny.'

John thought to himself, *I was right. This Helen woman was a really cruel bitch.*

'Then when we had the argument at Christmas, it was because she'd mention him… I mean she would be sly about it, she would just refer to him, and then claim she had never said a word about him, you know? It was back and forth, I never got to the bottom of the timings because… she was like that…'

'Like what?'

Alice glanced away, out to the pond where the rain was now dancing on the surface of the water. 'She liked to say one thing and then deny it…'

'Gaslighting?'

'I don't know what you'd call it.'

'So the affair happened? Or it didn't happen? Which is it?'

'Oh, it happened.'

'Just because she told you it had? I mean, it sounds like she had you under her thumb, told you whatever to get you jealous, get you going, provoke an argument…'

Alice was silent for some moments. He saw a flush of colour creep over the flesh of her neck. 'Yes,' she murmured, eyes downcast. 'She did that.'

'Abuse, then. Coercion.' And he felt sick all of a sudden. He knew what it was, because he had done it himself. He'd bullied Liz in that way, forced her to do stuff that she didn't want to do. He had liked feeling her bend under pressure.

He couldn't look Alice in the eye when she suddenly raised her gaze to him.

'I loved her,' she said. 'There was nothing wrong in the relationship. There really wasn't. We lived together. She wanted to be with me.'

He pushed his cup away from him. The sight of the dregs of the drink made him feel worse. He wished that someone would come and take their plates away. 'But you said that you thought she was meeting Maitland the day she disappeared. You said that in the abbey last time.'

'I think she did meet him,' she said.

'But you can't prove it.'

'No, I can't,' she said. 'But...' And she stopped. She stopped with a stricken look on her face, and she rocked backwards and forwards. 'Look,' she said, 'I didn't tell you everything. I haven't told you quite the right story.'

'Oh Jesus,' he muttered. 'Great.'

'We weren't happy that day,' she said. 'We'd had an argument. She had a house in a town nearer where she worked. We argued about it, and she said she was going. I... I went after her, and told her to come back, and I climbed a place near the coast called the ridgeway where we always used to walk, and she came back and she met me there.'

He said nothing. He was trying to decide if she was sane or not, or living in her own distorted world, a world where she was still going over and over the loss of the person she loved, and probably would do all her life. She would be an old woman and still agonising over it, he realised. And he'd be the same

– old and bitter over Mike's death. Both thinking of Thomas Maitland and how powerless they were.

'We argued some more, she said that she was determined to go. She said that it was over.' Real tears had formed in Alice's eyes now, and were brimming over. 'I know she didn't mean it,' she continued hurriedly. 'It was the sort of thing she said, you see? And then she'd come back and deny she'd ever said it, or she'd say that we should forget it, and everything would be all right. She *always* said that kind of thing, you see? It was *always* like that. I could stand in front of her, like this, just a few inches from her, and she would listen while I said something, and not react, and then when I asked her again she'd say that I hadn't spoken at all. You see? You see?'

'Yes,' he whispered, guilty.

'So I thought that this was the same. She was cruel that morning, she was in a mood, perhaps it was school, perhaps it was Maitland... I'm sure it was Maitland...'

'But you've got no proof.'

'I know... I know.'

She didn't know for a fact, but she felt it. Which was more important to her. He got that.

'You've only got Helen's word that they had an affair.'

She wiped her face. 'What?'

'You've only got Helen's word,' he repeated. 'She said that there was an affair just to wind you up. You only guessed at them meeting that morning. You grabbed at the idea of it being Maitland because it was the nearest thing you know to making sense.'

She gave a half-smile. Very bitter, it was. Almost as cruel as the stories of Helen. 'I can prove that affair,' she said. 'I've got evidence.' She opened the bag on the chair next to her, took out a book and opened it. A photograph was wedged between the pages, which she handed to him. 'There's the proof.'

It was a photograph of Thomas Maitland and Helen McAllister sitting at a café table. In the background were tall stone towers. It was evening, and there was a bottle of wine on the table, and they were both smiling. They looked pretty drunk.

'Here's another,' she said. This one was of Helen alone, holding a glass of wine up to the camera. 'Maitland took that photo,' Alice said.

John held it up to the light from the window. Rain was running down it in rivulets. 'Where is it?'

'Italy.' She pointed at the detail. 'He's holding her hand,' she said. He'd already noticed that. Clasped hands on the table top. Very cosy. 'They went there two summers before we met. City break. Four days.'

He lowered the photograph. 'She told you this?'

'Yes. And gave me those photos, just to rub it in.'

'Have you got anything else?'

'No. Just them. Isn't that enough?'

'It could be any time. It could be years before.'

'It could, but it isn't,' she insisted. 'Helen lived in Cardiff before she came here fourteen years ago. So he couldn't have known her until, at the latest, three years before I met her.'

John gave her back the photograph. 'He was married then,' he said.

'Yes. Nice man, eh?'

He shook his head slowly from side to side. 'You still don't know that he met her on the day she disappeared.'

'I *do* know, because she always came back. That night I thought she'd come back and say something like "The house is ready now and we can move in". Her house, I mean.'

'But she told you the opposite.'

Alice swayed, frowning, clasping her hands in front of her. 'But that's what she did. Don't you see? It's the kind of thing she did. I thought she'd come home and say "Pack your bags, love". Because it was a surprise, you see? Helen never did anything straight, it was all in circles. She came at you from the side. She liked the dance. But she wanted me with her.'

Oh God, he thought. *She fell for it all. Everything this bitch Helen handed out, she took.*

'And you still think that she loved you?' he asked slowly. 'Surely you can't still think that, the way she treated you?'

Alice had plunged her head in her hands, leaning her elbows on the table. The tears ran unchecked. 'It's the only explanation why she didn't come back to me.'

He bit his lip briefly. 'There's any number of explanations,' he told her, quietly. Not unkindly. He started picking up the plates and cups. 'Look, do you want anything else?' He was thinking, *Maitland's a bloody chancer, and you're more than a bit crazy, love.* But he couldn't tell her that.

'Another tea,' she said, without looking at him.

As he joined the queue, he looked back at her. She was wiping her face again with the heel of her hand. She looked a bit ravaged. He'd noticed the frayed edge of the cloth bag and her bitten nails. She was a lost soul, and now he was stuck with her. But all the same, the thought of Maitland, smug in his expensive house having extricated himself from any kind of blame for the misery he had brought, made him order the tea and bring it back to Alice.

'Thank you,' she murmured.

'I can't be much longer,' he said. 'I have to get back.'

'To your wife and daughters.'

He couldn't help but laugh. 'Not really. She threw me out.' He allowed himself this tiny bit of fiction. He'd walked out, but the point was academic. To his satisfaction, Alice looked at him soft with sympathy.

'But your brother just died!' she said.

'Yes. Good, isn't it?'

She stared at him a moment longer, then poured her tea and stirred sugar into it. 'I've been alone most of my life,' she said. 'The only time I had anyone was Helen.'

'Where do you come from? I can hear the north in your voice.'

'Oh,' she said, lifting the tea. 'Yorkshire.'

'Whereabouts?'

'Near Skipton.'

'I know Skipton.'

'You do?'

'Our firm delivers over that side all the time.'

'Well, it's not really Skipton actually,' she said. 'It's a small place in the Dales, north of there. Anyway,' she added, 'I wasn't there long. My mother died and I was put into care in Bradford. And then when I was eighteen, I went to Manchester.'

'How long did you live in Manchester?'

'Not long. I've moved about. After Helen disappeared, I did the same thing. Moved.'

'But you've gone back to the place where the two of you lived, you and Helen.'

'I've bought a house nearby,' she said. 'Well. Not a house. More of a shack. It took the last of my money.'

'Don't you work?'

She set her mouth in a straight line before she replied. 'I can't work,' she told him. 'Because of Maitland.'

'He's not stopping you, is he?'

'Yes,' she said. 'He's stopping me. Because I want to repay him. I've lived ten years in this nightmare. I've tried to escape it, but I can't. Do you know that soon it's the ten-year anniversary of her going missing? I can't let it go another ten years. I have to do something.'

'For what?'

'For Helen.'

He looked at her as she drank the tea and looked into the garden. The rain was heavy. Eventually, she put down the cup.

'Well,' she murmured, turning the spoon over and over in the saucer. 'Well.'

'You'll never let go of this,' he said.

She looked up at him. 'Will you?'

It was a good question. It wasn't as if he could see any kind of future; all he could really concentrate on was Maitland, and the thought that Mike's body was rotting away in that muddy field by the estuary, and that Maitland had put him there. He didn't care what the accident report said. It *would* say that. They would always cover their own. He knew that Alice was watching him closely now, waiting for an answer, and he just couldn't articulate the rage that he felt, that he carried with him, that burned a hole inside him. It was like Maitland had stepped forward into that blaze, stood himself centre stage, offered himself up as a target.

Alice leaned forward, elbows on the tabletop. 'Will you ever think that he didn't kill your brother?'

'No.'

'Then we're the same.'

'Yes,' he conceded. 'We're the same.'

'And you're just going to leave it, are you?'

He couldn't. He knew that he never would.

They got up and walked through the café and out into the glass-roofed concourse. By the doors, they stood looking out at the rain and the dark sky. It's going to be fun driving back through this, he thought.

'Where's your car?' he asked.

'Not here,' she said.

He turned to her. 'What do you mean, not here?'

She gave a wry smile. 'It's in Tewkesbury. It broke down.'

'When, today?'

'Yes, as I was coming up the motorway it was making this grinding noise. Actually, it's been making it for ages. I took the exit and it broke down on the slip road. Just stopped at the roundabout.' She shrugged. 'Lucky, really. Not to be on the motorway.'

'What's happened to it?'

'I called out a roadside rescue and they said it needed a garage, and it got towed. It's sitting in somewhere called Dave's Spares.'

'Jesus. What have they said?'

'Nothing yet.'

'What time was this?'

'Late this morning.' She sighed, and started putting on her jacket. 'I'll ring for a taxi and go back there. A taxi brought me here. I'll call the same man.' She got out her phone. 'Though he charged me stupid money. It's only fifteen miles.'

'But what if it can't be sorted?' he asked. 'What if it's something major?'

'It will be,' she told him, resigned. 'It's a wreck. I shouldn't think it'll be worth repairing.'

'But how will you get home?'

Again, she gave a shrug and a sigh. 'Train to Bristol, then another...'

'What, just leave it?'

'For scrap, yes.'

'God, I'm sorry. It's a bugger to be without a car.'

'I've had it twelve years. Chose its day, didn't it? But it wasn't new when I got it.' She was scrolling for the number of the taxi.

He put his hand over hers. 'I'll give you a lift,' he told her.

*

Dave's Spares was shut.

Alice tried ringing and only got a voicemail.

'That's charming,' he said. 'Could at least answer you.' He cupped his hands and looked through the filthy window of the office. The garage doors themselves were locked down with a steel shutter. He could see a counter, and a plastic shelf of chocolate and bags of sweets that looked as if they hadn't been touched in months. Dust was everywhere. He turned back to Alice. 'You're sure that they brought it here?'

'I saw it put in the garage bay,' she said, hooking her thumb in the direction of the bolted door. 'Maybe he ripped it to pieces already and he's avoiding me.' She smiled to show that this was a joke of sorts.

'I bet he would, too,' he agreed. 'Looks a dead and alive hole to me.'

It was past 6 o'clock, and growing dark. As they stood there, the streetlights flickered on as if to underline the fact. She shuffled her feet in the puddles on the tarmac. 'Thanks for bringing me back here, anyway.'

'What are you going to do? There won't be a connection to the coast now.'

'There might be. It's not late,' she said. 'Go on, I'll be all right. The station isn't far. We passed it.'

'But if there isn't a train, what then?'

She shook her head, and laughed at him. It was the first time that he had heard anything like real humour out of her. It struck him as sad. Not the laughing, but the fact that she seemed so irrevocably down that the simple fact of her laughing surprised and touched him. They were living in the same dark place, he thought, echoing what he had felt earlier.

'What's funny?' he asked.

'Oh. You,' she said. 'It's not the end of the world is it, a train?'

'If you don't get a connection tonight, it'll be a bloody task tomorrow,' he told her. 'I don't know about your part of the world, but where I come from, they do engineering on Sundays and you can't get anywhere fast. Replacement bus service taking twice the time, for all you know.'

She pulled her bag over her shoulder so that it hung across her body. 'You'd better go,' she said. 'You've got nearly two hundred miles ahead of you.' She held out her hand. 'Thanks for coming down,' she added. 'Though I don't know what it achieved, do you?'

It took only seconds to make the decision.

'We passed a Best Night Inn,' he said. 'Let's go back to it.'

21

THE HOT WEATHER CONTINUED IN the days after Helen disappeared.

Forty-eight hours after he and Richard Ellis had been to inspect Helen's house, Thomas drove to see Alexandra Wilson.

'You had better be quick if you want to see me,' she had told him over the phone the night before. 'We're leaving for France tomorrow.'

It was one of his pet hates: the imperious attitude of entitlement in the well-off and well connected. He'd researched the Wilson woman before he set up the meeting. Besides being married to the ENT consultant, who had a lucrative private practice as well as his National Health Service job, Alexandra Wilson was from county stock. Her father owned an agricultural estate near Salisbury, and her uncle was an MP. Thomas could find nothing particularly interesting in the father's background but Uncle Theodore was your typical dead-eyed Tory, full of prejudice. He was anti everything: abortion, refugees, you name it.

'Lovely bloke,' Thomas had muttered to himself, making a few notes about Alexandra the night before.

The house looked just as sublime in reality as it had done in the Good Move page: very pretty in the morning sun, wisteria on the walls, and a rose bed on either side of the front door.

In the driveway, a Range Rover was parked outside the front door, the boot open.

He stopped his car and got out; noticed that a teenage boy was slumped in the back, feet up on the seat in front, earbuds in. He turned his head slowly in Thomas's direction but didn't respond to his wave.

Alexandra stepped out of the front door and came down the shallow stone steps to the gravel, registering him only at the last moment. She was carrying two suitcases.

'Who are you?' she asked. She stowed the cases in the back of her car.

He showed her the warrant and said his name, but she was leaning into the Range Rover. 'Seb, for Christ's sake, give Jonno a hand,' she ordered.

He couldn't hear Seb's response.

'Yes, you fucking well will,' Alexandra retorted.

The boy got out, slamming the passenger door after him. He was rangy – well over Thomas's height. He went into the house at a slouch.

Alexandra turned back to Thomas. 'What do you want?'

'I can see you're busy.'

'Yes, I am.'

'I rang last night.'

She looked him up and down. 'You're Inspector Maitland?' she asked.

'That's right.'

'*Thomas* Maitland?'

'Yes.'

She bit her lip, looked down, and put her hands on her hips.

'It's concerning Helen McAllister's disappearance.'

'I realise that, obviously. Since you said so last night.' She looked up, then tilted her chin. 'But I can't for the life of me think why it should concern me.'

'It's something that came up on the school's Facebook page. We're chasing up everything that we can.'

She began to laugh. 'Facebook? I don't use it anymore.'

'Two, three years ago?'

'Heavens. Ancient history.' Thomas looked closely at her face. She was now about 40, slightly overweight, broad-faced, what this mother would have called 'well-preserved'. She had very thick, shiny dark hair, and arched eyebrows that gave her an imperious questioning expression. In the sunlight, he could see that her foundation had been thickly applied.

'The brewery tagged Helen McAllister in a photograph. The two of you were standing together,' he continued.

'Well, since you've looked at the page in such forensic detail, it may have registered with you that I don't post on it.' She looked up at the house impatiently. In profile, he saw the slight hint of a sagging jaw. *That'll be fixed soon*, he thought.

'The page is current.'

She looked back at him, and smiled. 'With no recent posts from me. You did see that?' Perhaps in response to his scrutiny, she put on a pair of sunglasses.

'We saw that.'

'When I was first on the school's Board of Governors, I would copy photographs of sponsors or social events. Fundraisers. I simply can't be bothered with it anymore, however.' Her hand fluttered mid-air as if swatting away a fly. 'One doesn't, if one has a life. Don't you agree?'

'I don't use social media.'

'Very wise.'

The teenage boy reappeared with almost a clone of himself, but three inches shorter. This evidently was Jonno, clutching a bag of books.

'Ma, he's bringing all this shit,' Seb complained.

'Get in the car, both of you,' his mother retorted.

She turned back to Thomas. 'As I told you last night, we're going to France today,' she said. 'I have a very long drive ahead of me with these two idiot children, so you'll excuse me if I refrain from any more conversation.' She took a set of keys out of her pocket. 'Why don't you talk to the school about Miss McAllister? They'll know far more about her than I do.'

'I've been there,' Thomas said. It had been a fruitless visit. The Head had shrugged and admitted that he knew very little – in fact, nothing – about her private life.

'Well then. I really can't see what more I can add. She's probably gone on holiday, since it is summer. It seems extraordinary to me that you would bother. She's only been missing… what? Four days?'

'Five.'

'I would bet any money at all that she's sunning herself somewhere.' She waved her hand at the Range Rover. 'As people do, you know. If they're not obstructed from doing so.'

'There's been no use of her credit cards or phone. She left her car parked on the coast road.'

Alexandra hesitated at that. She started to walk to the driver's door. She turned back briefly. 'I'm sorry to be rude,' she conceded. 'It's rather fraught trying to get these two shoehorned into enjoying themselves with their embarrassing parent. You see my predicament.'

'Your husband isn't going with you?'

'No,' she said. 'He's very busy. He may join us later.'

'No one to share the drive.'

A voice – Jonno's – piped up from inside. 'I don't want to go!' he shouted. 'I want to go to Jack's football party! I said I would!'

'Shut up,' Seb told him.

Alexandra looked through the window at Jonno, frowning, but said nothing to him. She glanced back at Thomas. 'I have to go.'

'Did you ever meet Miss McAllister's partner, Alice Hauser?' He thought he saw a momentary flicker in her face: some expression that was hard to categorise. Recognition? Disdain?

'No,' she said.

'Did she ever speak about her?'

'We didn't have any personal conversation like that.'

'You seem to be having a conversation in the photograph. A joke, perhaps.'

'I doubt that very much.'

'The evening was for Presshams Brewery.'

'There you are, then. Those people have children at the school. But I've never found them exhilarating company.'

'So the joke was about Presshams?'

She shrugged, looking at him with exasperation. 'How on earth am I supposed to remember that?'

'I'm sorry,' he said. 'It's just that we seem to have so little information about Miss McAllister. Her friends, contacts. Have you been to her house at Bloxley?'

'Of course not.'

'She didn't throw any parties herself, for colleagues at the school, or the governors? She had a nice entertaining space at her home, out in the garden. Perfect for a party.'

'God in heaven,' Alexandra said. 'What teacher throws parties for school governors? She'd be out of her mind.' She shook her head, smiling. 'I wouldn't want to go to such a thing.'

'Why not?'

'That should be obvious.'

'Not to me.'

She put her head on one side. 'No, I suppose not,' she said. 'We simply wouldn't.'

He realised that it was a class thing. Her father from the landed gentry; her uncle the braying backbencher. And a husband with a well-heeled clientele at his private hospital – the smug man in the Hawaiian shirt in the photograph.

Thomas smiled back at her. 'You did say last night that you were catching the overnight ferry. That you'd be here until mid-afternoon.'

She hesitated. The car keys rattled in her hand as she tapped her hand against her thigh in apparent irritation. 'I changed my mind.'

Thomas stepped back. 'Safe journey,' he said.

She said nothing, got in the car and started it up. There was some conversation inside for a minute or two. More raised voices. More whining from Seb, it seemed. Jonno looked out at Thomas and stuck up his middle finger. Sunny little soul. Thomas waved at him. What hell he's in for, Thomas thought. All uphill work through school, taunted by an elder brother, a mother trying hard to crawl even further up the social classes, a father who didn't care too much.

He watched the Range Rover pull away. He watched it all the way down the drive until it turned into the road beyond.

Thomas looked back at the house. A woman, cleaning rag in hand, was polishing the brass door knocker and trying very hard not to notice him.

'Good morning. Lovely day,' he said.

She nodded at him. She wasn't very old: maybe thirty. He took a folded piece of paper out of his pocket. It was a photograph of Helen McAllister arm in arm with Alice Hauser. He had taken it from Alice Hauser's home; it had been in the drawer of the cheap bedside table when they searched her house. At the time, he had thought how sad it was that Alice had a picture of her and Helen together by her bed, but Helen only had a picture of herself next to hers. The picture he knew all too well.

'I wonder if you know either of these two women?' he asked.

The cleaner looked at the image. 'No, I don't,' she told him.

'Take your time.'

'No,' she repeated, louder and firmer this time. 'I don't know them.'

'Okay,' he said. 'Thanks anyway.'

He got in his car and drove down to the road. He went a mile or so before he pulled into a lay-by and turned off the engine. All around him the beautiful country rolled away in shallow hills, green on green. He thought of how hot the journey would be all the way to Paris, and beyond. He thought of Jonno's face at the car window. He thought of Helen McAllister and a trip to Italy that had ended in such acrimony; of rage and silence.

He thought about Alexandra Wilson hauling her children out of the country without her husband, and he wondered if that was the norm for that family every summer. He thought about the cleaner who didn't want to get involved.

And he thought that – for all the make-up – Alexandra Wilson looked as if she hadn't slept.

After a while, he started the car and drove to Brimham.

22

'S TOP THE CAR.'
The first opportunity to turn the car around in the village had been missed. And the second. Then they were almost out, and were passing the big car park by the open fields.

Alice carried on driving. Furious, Helen slammed her hand on the dashboard. 'Stop the car!'

Alice glanced at her. 'No,' she murmured. 'I don't think so.'

They passed the village sign, and the marker to show there was now a national speed limit. Alice put her foot on the accelerator.

'So help me, Alice, I'll open the bloody door.'

Alice just smiled. 'No you won't.'

'Won't 1? Won't I?'

But, at 60 miles an hour, she didn't.

They got to the junction of Stone Hill, and Alice took the turn at speed. The hill rose up out of the green fields of the coast and the white rippled backbone of the ridge, up into a limestone land that looked bled dry, no fields and no grazing, only flat areas of gorse and bramble between the rock.

There was a viewpoint: a bald flat circle of gravel. And only here, two miles from the nearest house, did Alice do as Helen wanted and stopped the car.

Helen's face was flushed. She sat in silence, her fists balled in her lap. Then, 'You bitch,' she said. She was still holding her phone, and eventually she opened the cover and tapped a number. Halfway through, she stopped the call. 'What am I going to say to them?' she asked.

'Who?'

'The school, Alice!'

'Ah,' Alice murmured.

'You're crazy,' Helen retorted. 'That is what you are.'

'Maybe.'

Alice saw how her calm took the wind out of Helen's sails. She sat gawking at Alice in surprise.

'The signal up here is rubbish,' Alice told her. 'It's one of those dead spots, remember?'

Helen threw the phone on the floor, into the footwell. 'Look,' she said, 'what do you want?'

Alice seemed utterly impassive, a shocking contrast to her earlier weeping and objections. 'Oh, I don't know,' she said. 'Let's see, what do I want? I want you to shut up, for a start.'

There was a little gasp, almost comical, from Helen. She opened her mouth, and then rapidly closed it again.

Alice was tapping the steering wheel with one finger. 'I don't like things that are unfair,' she said. 'And this is what you are. You, and this whole thing. Unfair.'

In frustration, Helen looked out of the car window. She was disconcerted, but there was something more than that. She was sitting in a car with a sudden stranger, and she had lost control of that newly revealed person. There was nowhere to go up here. There was no one else parked on the white-stone strip. It wasn't as if she could get out of the car and go over to someone and say, 'Excuse me, but could you give me a lift?'

She rolled down the window on her side of the car. The hot breeze blew in, carrying dust with it. The coast showed only as a hazy line shimmering in the heat. She knew that there was a walk that would take her down through woods and past

Bronze Age barrows. But it was a long way back to her car. She tried to figure it out, tried to remember the way that the path went. Where did it go after the wood? After the barrows? She couldn't fix it in her mind. But it would probably take two or three hours, back down to the baking hot road to the village, and out the other side to her own car on the coast road.

She could have cheerfully hit Alice, shaken her. Grabbed the car keys from the ignition, perhaps. Insisted on taking them back. But one look at Alice's face told her that it might be the wrong move to get out of the car, walk around to the driver's side, and try to open the door.

The feeling of fear rose up again. She didn't like the sensation of things unravelling. She thought that she knew Alice through and through: her insecurities and her fumbling affection. Now she saw something else: an unfathomability. Helen picked up her phone from the footwell and turned it over and over in her hands. 'So crazy,' she whispered to herself. 'Just insane.'

Alice said nothing.

Helen squirmed sideways in her seat to face her. 'Look,' she said. She didn't understand how they had got to this. Usually, she would let people's angst flow past her. She couldn't bear conflict not because it worried her, but because it bored her and revolted her. It was weak. And yet from time to time she liked to dip herself, like a sort of baptism, into the disgusting waters of the loving, the passionate, the committed.

Alice's profile was unreadable. Helen waited another few seconds for her expression to soften. For the lips to tremble, the prelude to Alice's crying. But nothing happened. Alice seemed mesmerised by the view in the way that someone's gaze could fasten on a random object and not leave it.

Helen decided on a way to get out of the situation. She settled on an apology that she didn't feel. 'You're right,' she told Alice. 'I've been unfair.'

There was no reply.

'I mean,' Helen continued in a cajoling voice, smiling now,

'to live with you, and say all that about marriage.' In the silence, she still turned her phone over in her hands. 'But you know, at the time I meant it.'

Alice's gaze flickered towards her, then back to the view of the coast through the windscreen.

'Alice,' she said, more quietly, 'you've got to understand that you're better off without me. So much better. You'll see that soon. I'll never stick to anything much. A job. People.' She gave a self-deprecating shrug that was meant to indicate how hopeless she was. 'I get bored, you know? I get something and then I don't actually want it. It's not very nice of me. I see that. I'm sorry and all that. But a country, even. I could leave a country out of boredom.'

This time, Alice looked directly at her. 'You're leaving the country again?'

'No, no.' But then she shrugged. 'I might. Who knows?'

'You didn't like America.'

'Not much, but there's more than one country in the world.'

'Like where?'

'God knows. Australia? I've never been there.'

'You'd go there?'

'I don't know. But why not?'

'Without me?'

'Alice...'

'And you've had this in your head – that you might even go there, and leave me behind?'

'Look... I'm sorry. What else can I say? And how many bloody times do you want me to say it?'

'Is this what you do?'

'What do you mean?'

'Do you love people and then just leave?'

'I didn't intend to hurt you. Can't we leave it at that?'

'No,' Alice said. 'Tell me if you've done this before.'

'What would be the use of that?'

'So that I know.'

Helen sighed. 'Maybe.'

'With that man, Maitland?'

'Alice, I'm not going over everything. It's pointless.'

'But you told me that he was bad to you. You told me…'

Helen pushed her hair back, stared up at the roof of the car for a second, and then looked back at her. 'Forget him. Another place, another time.'

'Wasn't that true?'

'It doesn't matter.'

'Yes, it does.'

'Oh God,' Helen raised her voice. 'All right then. Before I went to the States, we had an affair. Satisfied?'

'A proper, real affair?'

'Yes, yes. All right? Happy now? Are you going to repeat everything I say? We met at the school and we saw each other for two or three months. We went away together, too. We went to Italy.'

'But you said…'

Helen threw up her hands. 'You know, you've got to stop believing everything that people tell you. I could have said that he was an axe murderer and you'd have lapped it up, wouldn't you?'

'But…' Alice frowned. 'Why would you tell me that if it wasn't true? Was he bad to you or not?'

'I liked him for a while.' Helen looked away from her. 'But he was a bastard like all men are,' she muttered.

Alice was shaking her head a little, like a child trying to shake away a fact that they didn't like. 'So it's not… it's men and women…'

Helen gave another deep, exasperated sigh. 'Bingo,' she told her. 'Life is short, Alice,' she said. 'Got to take what you can.'

Alice looked away again. Her face reverted to the curious disconnected stare that she had had since she drove out of the village.

Life is short.
Alice was thinking of another place.

*

The mountain in the evening, half-lit by the setting sun.

Half dark with the oncoming evening.

The garden already in shadow and the dead-end lane that ran past it obscured by overgrown hedges and self-seeded trees. That time, dusk, when any colour was more subtly deeper and more vibrant for 20 minutes or half an hour before it was eaten up by darkness.

They were in that time. She and William. Dew was coming down across the grass behind them. Alice looked back towards the house. The concrete posts that held the washing line. The low grey roof with its slipped slates. Insects were buzzing across the unmown lawn. A rambler rose, too ancient to be productive, lay over the garden wall holding its two or three flowers up to the last moments of the day. A musky pink among the green and the blight of rose rust.

'I can't move her on my own, William.'

He was sitting among the stalks of last winter's sprouts and cabbages, whole yellowed rows of them. Sitting on the ground cross-legged and with his arms crossed too. A picture of resistance.

They had got their mother's body down the stairs wrapped in the pale green candlewick bedspread. Bumped it down. After the initial two or three steps William thought it was a joke. He looked at her with a lopsided, slack smile. Close to the bottom, William lost his grip and the corpse had slithered of its own accord, and ended in a crumpled heap on the hail floor.

'We have to go into the garden,' Alice said.

'Garden?'

Alice had sat on the last step, breathing heavily. 'We have to bury it.'

He had frowned, puzzled. 'What, for good?'

'Yes, for always.'

'Not always.'

Still, he helped her carry the bundle out of the door and down into the garden, along the path until they were almost at the end.

'William,' she had prompted softly again. 'We have to make a hole and put this in it.'

'But how will she get out?' he asked, and saw her face. 'Not for always. Not for good.'

She went over to him, avoiding the wrapped bundle at her feet and stepping through the waste of the plot, among the detritus of the year. She grabbed him by the arms and tried to haul him to his feet.

'Not for always,' he whispered, half standing and half leaning on her. The darkness a little more dense with every long minute that they stayed that way, clasped in each other's arms while the day ran off the mountain and the lane became full of shadows and the house stayed unlit. 'Not for always, no, not for always,' he told her.

*

She turned back and looked at Helen.

'Is it for always?' she asked. 'Is it for good?'

23

A SHAM FERRY WAS NOT QUITE as Thomas remembered it. It still had that slightly down-at-heel air, but the house that Alice Hauser had lived in wasn't there anymore, nor the others that had been alongside it. Thomas stood looking at the space under the chalk rise and the scrubby cliff face, and thought back to the searches that they had made of her home. Nothing found. No blood traces, nothing of Helen McAllister's. It wasn't often that a search came up almost sterile, but that was what Alice's place had been. The cleanest and most depressing living space that he could remember. Sad, really. Sad to have so little, or to think that you were worth so little. He recalled Alice in her living-room when it was all over. Just a little speck of a woman, really. Five foot three of nothing, like a breath of air. Pale and insubstantial.

'You won't find her, because she isn't here,' she had told him when he went back to interview her again after the knife results had come up as animal blood.

She had opened the door to him, but he hadn't stepped over the threshold. 'Then where is she, Alice?'

'I don't know.'

Round and round they went, round and round.

They never did find Helen's phone. But they knew that she had called Alice. Alice's own number confirmed it.

'She came back,' Alice said. 'I asked her to.'

Round and round and round.

Nothing of Helen McAllister was ever found. No body, no further calls, no trace at the school except her desk, which was full of school business and nothing personal. No colleagues could give a clue.

Standing here now, with a bitter wind belying the fact that it was June, he thought of he and Helen getting the flight from Exeter one June day 13 years ago. Fran had been at a local government conference in York. It was coming to the end of the school year for Helen. As he had driven down the A30, he had expected to feel a rush of guilt, because it was the same route that he and Fran drove to Cornwall for the summer. Always the same little beach, always the same two weeks in August. And he was driving the same car that they filled with their cases and boards and cool boxes. They liked their picnics and walks and swimming in the sea, and close to their usual cottage was a café that served the best fish and chips in Cornwall. They'd been going there for ever.

He'd told Helen, and she'd laughed. 'Jesus Christ,' she'd told him. 'Don't you get bored?'

And he'd thought, *Yes, I'm bored* but he knew it wasn't true. The lie had kept him going because Helen wanted to see Italy, and they were going to Siena and San Gimignano. All a rush. A rush to organise and a rush to an early morning flight and a rush to see everywhere and a rush to their room. It had been just one conversation in the school assembly hall, a kind of *Where do you like to go on holiday?* sort of aimless, drifting talk while they waited for any student who had questions. He had been holding a clipboard tight to his chest, thinking of going home soon, when Helen had asked. 'Where do you like to go on holiday?' 'I've always wanted to go to Italy,' he had heard himself say. And then ten days later there they were, in a room overlooking the valley outside San Gimignano's city walls.

'Let's have a picture,' Helen had said on the first night, handing her camera to the waiter. 'Cuddle up, Tom.' She'd raised her glass, and held his hand tight. She was like a fire burning. Sitting at that table, grinning for the camera, it didn't seem to matter. It was just a few days out of his life. It would pass. It meant nothing at all. He felt binge-drunk.

He used to think about their conversations, and it made him wonder what drug he must have been on.

She'd been putting on make-up on the first morning. 'I don't know that I've ever liked working,' she said to him. 'Most people are inadequate. You must see that in what you do.'

'I see a lot of poverty-driven crime,' he said. 'Drugs. Violence. Alcohol-related.'

'There you go then,' she replied. 'Inadequates.'

He sat on the side of the bed and watched her in the mirror. 'What kind of home did you grow up in, Helen?'

'Nice enough.'

'What did your parents do?'

She'd turned on the dressing-table seat and laughed. 'What is this, a police interview? You should read me my rights.'

He had smiled. 'Just interested.'

'We lived in Essex.'

'I don't hear an accent.'

'Nah, got rid of it, mate,' she joked. She put the mascara down on the dressing-table and looked back at him. 'Both my parents are dead. Both of them were only children. I have no siblings. Anything else?'

He thought for a few seconds about the implications of her being alone. It could be a hard road to follow. He was an only child too, with parents and two uncles dead, and cousins that he hadn't seen in 30 years who lived in Canada.

'Have you got any children, Thomas?'

It was shocking to think that she didn't know this, and yet here they were sitting in a hotel bedroom together.

'No children.'

'Choice?'

'Just the way it's turned out.'

'Ambitious wife then?'

This made him laugh out loud. 'No. That's not the reason.'

Perhaps she saw something affectionate in the way he responded. The light in her face went out. She snatched up her bag and stood up. 'Breakfast,' she told him.

That morning, they climbed Torre Grossa. From the top of the tower the Tuscan countryside was spread out beneath them. Its greenness reminded him of home, and he suddenly experienced a terrible vertigo. He felt as if he were falling into the town square below. He leaned against the stone parapet and pretended to line up a photograph, and the camera felt cold on his skin despite the heat of the day. On his phone was Fran's text to him yesterday. He'd told her that he'd probably do the coast walk from Seaton to Charmouth. 'Enjoy your walk,' she'd told him. 'Wish I was with you.'

Helen was leaning out at the other end of the terrace, looking at the view. He had a sudden urge to run away, down the long stairway. The bells were tolling for midday and she was watching the tower opposite. Down in the square was a gathering: a couple had got married in the *municipio* and it was like looking down on a scattering of flowers, bright clothes and white dresses translated to a flush of petals far below. He thought that he might be sick; sweat crawled on his back.

Helen turned around. Seeing the camera, she struck a pose with one hand behind her head. She walked up to him with an exaggerated sway. 'Let's go back to the room,' she said.

Once there, the blinds drawn, she kissed him and took his hand. She was slim, with none of Fran's comfortable curves. He could feel the bones of her hips, even the ribs. Even her jaw was angular. He felt as if his hands were slabs of meat trying to grab her, and he dropped his arms to his sides in an agony of self-consciousness that dated back to being 15. Dim memories of squirming, whispering girls in back streets and bus shelters and late-night drizzle and the smell of the Mecca dance hall and cigarette smoke. Last night, in the first frantic rush, it hadn't seemed to matter. But now it did.

He opened his eyes and looked at Helen; she snapped into focus out of the teenage memory, smiling at him in her sly way. He tried to take off her dress, reached for the zipper, missed it. *Enjoy your walk. I wish I was with you.* And he thought, *I wish you were too.* Helen pushed her body against him, smiling her slightly gap-toothed smile.

He had stepped back, pulled the curtains, pushed at the wooden blinds, and went out on to the balcony. He could hear the rattle of plates and cutlery in the restaurant below. In his pocket, his phone buzzed. He took it out and without seeing who the caller might be, turned it off. All the excitement of yesterday was gone, replaced with that recurrent vertiginous nausea.

He had told Helen that it was over when they were in the Exeter Airport car park when they'd come back. He had said that it had been just a few days out of both their lives, and lied that it had been wonderful, but that it couldn't possibly go on, and was something he wanted to leave behind.

She had gaped at him in disbelief. He remembered that afternoon in acute detail. They were both grubby. Not just with travelling, but he had *felt* grubby. In those few seconds, putting her case into the back of the car, feeling her hand on his neck, pinching and caressing, he'd looked back at her and seen her clearly for what she was.

'We can't do this again,' he'd told her.

'What?' Her hand fell from him, but then caught him halfway down his back in a small punch. 'What, fed up so soon?'

'No, no,' he'd lied. 'But it's not practical, is it?'

'Listen, sweetheart,' she said. 'I leave people. They don't leave me.' And he heard the dangerous edge in her voice. She wasn't joking.

'I can't carry on. I'm sorry.'

Oh,' she said in a voice seething with contempt. 'The little wife.'

He had felt like closing his hands on her neck and watching the air drain out of her.

For a whole year, he had lived in fear of every phone call that came to the house. He lived in fear of his own phone – or Fran's – ringing. He wouldn't have put it past Helen to find Fran's number. He felt utterly sick at himself, and confused in a stupid, clumsy way. He felt that somehow he'd been tricked into being with Helen, and couldn't believe that he had done it, or that it had been so easy to do. He loved Fran. He respected and admired her.

And it disgusted him that he had betrayed Fran's trust. For what? Helen wasn't even a pleasant person. In those four short days, she'd told him about battles she'd had with the people she worked with and how she had always won her argument because she was 'right'. Always right. She'd told him that she didn't even like the students very much. She had no vocation that he could discern; just an ambition to get on, to be listened to, and to be paid more. That stuck in his throat. He'd thought – assumed – that a teacher would be dedicated, a nice person. She looked nice at least. And then it struck him that this was a naïve, crass way to look at women. It made him feel ridiculous. A bad judge, at best misguided and at worst misogynistic. It hit at the heart of his own opinion of himself: a good copper with a straight-up view of the world. He was the careful, methodical one, not prey to passion or mistakes. Helen had taken that from him, held up a mirror to him and showed him as a mid-life cliché.

You bloody deserve it, he told himself, *for being a fool.*

Then he had heard that Helen had gone to the States for a year. He'd sent up a private prayer that she would never come back. But two years later his sergeant told him that a woman called Helen McAllister had gone missing, and showed him the picture that Alice Hauser had brought in. Helen, standing on the beach at Asham Ferry, hands on hips, laughing by the water's edge.

*

He went over to the café.

The woman who had given him a glass of water ten years ago was gone. The place had been painted; the old Formica-topped tables had been replaced with wooden benches of different colours. There was a smoothie bar and an espresso machine, and a boy of about 20, perhaps younger, wiping glasses. There was a blackboard behind the bar listing various sandwiches under a heading 'artisan bread'.

'Good morning,' said the lad. 'What can I get you?'

'Hello,' he said. 'A latte, please.'

'Sure.' He started preparing it. 'Has it got any warmer out there?'

'Not really.'

'Summer, huh?'

'Yes,' he agreed. In the past few years he'd acclimatised himself to coffee. Tea – a proper teapot and two cups, with saucers – was something that belonged to Fran. The pot on the breakfast table, and conversations they would have. On his own, he would just make a mug of tea with a teabag. But maybe soon he'd manage to get the pot out of the cupboard again, like she used to.

'This is a bit of a long shot,' he said to the lad. He took Alice's photograph out of his pocket. 'But do you know this woman?'

The image was scrutinised carefully. 'What's her name?'

'Alice Hauser. Or it was.'

'Yes,' he said, handing it back. 'She comes in here now and again.'

Thomas had been propping himself up at the serving bar, but now he sat down. All the air had gone out of the room. 'She does?'

'Yes, why? What do you want her for?'

What did he want her for? What indeed.

'I knew her about ten years ago. She worked here.'

'Yes, she came in looking for a job. But I haven't got one. It's just me and my brother.'

'How long ago was this?'

'About a month, a bit more.'

So it *had* been her at the fair. Standing looking at him as he closed down the stall. 'Did she leave any kind of address, a phone number?'

The lad paused at this. 'I can't give you that, can I?'

'No. No. Right.'

'You're not family or something?'

'No, not family.'

The door opened and a couple came in. They were walking to Lyme. They took a long time to order their sandwiches, and they sat opposite him while they waited for them to be made. They had London accents, and he sat there wondering where Alice had been all these years. Maybe London. He had a completely irrational urge to show them Alice's photo and ask if they had seen her. He watched them leave, and realised that his stomach was churning.

He delivered his cup back to the counter. 'When did she first come in here?' he asked. 'Was it long ago?'

'Like I say, a month. Maybe two months.'

'So she asked you for a job the first day she came?'

'She said she used to work here. I told her maybe in the summer if we got busy.'

'And what did she say?'

'She said that was fine.'

'So she wasn't just visiting? Not a holidaymaker?'

'No, she lives near here.' And he rolled his eyes as if he shouldn't have said that. 'Look, I can't say any more, can I?'

'No, of course not. But thank you anyway.'

'Shall I say you were asking if she comes in here again?'

He thought about it for a few seconds. 'No,' he said. 'Don't do that.'

The lad narrowed his eyes.

'I want to surprise her,' Thomas explained. 'It's nothing serious. She's not in trouble. I just knew her and... Well, somebody told me she's come back.'

He could see what the lad was thinking. *You're old enough to be her father.*

He said goodbye, and went and sat on the beach.

He tried to put himself in Alice's shoes. He tried to think what she would have done without Helen. Maybe she had gone to college and got herself some qualifications. Maybe she had a job, a business. But if that was the case, why was she here asking about working in the café? He wondered if she was trying to reconstruct a happier time, a time before Helen disappeared. Or perhaps she was still trying to find the answers, and coming back here was a way of rethinking it all.

Or maybe she was after him.

His heart was beating heavily.

She had ruined his life.

He could still see Richard Ellis standing at the door of his office all those years ago, twisting his hands and then putting them self-consciously into his pockets in an agitated fashion.

'What is it, Richard?'

'It's Alice Hauser.'

'Is she here?'

'She was. She asked to see the boss.'

Thomas had frowned. He had got to his feet. 'The boss? Why?'

'She...' Richard was shaking his head, and had an expression on his face that was half-smile, half-grimace. 'She wants to make a complaint about you.'

'Does she? About what?'

'He wants to see you about it,' Richard had told him. 'Now.'

24

IT WAS JUST AFTER MIDNIGHT when John Lord was woken by the buzzing of his phone on the bedside table in the motel room.

He picked it up without turning on the light, and squinted at the blue-lit screen. It was Liz. He thought about not answering because of the text message earlier that had arrived when he was checking into the motel. *It's really important. Ring me.* He hadn't heard from her for over a week, and he hadn't heard from the girls even though he'd tried getting in touch; he was convinced that Liz was using this time to turn his daughters against him. In fact, he could have predicted that because... Well, what was he now? He was the bad guy. He was the bastard and she was the innocent party, because life worked like that, didn't it?

He could still hear rain hitting the window of the room. He turned on the bedside light. He imagined that most of the people he knew now considered him an out and out fucking moron, if they hadn't before. Even though it wasn't like that at all. Life wasn't right over there and wrong over here. There were all the grey areas in between. But try telling that to anyone now. He was the devil out of disguise for the rest of his life. But now – now that she felt like it – she was snapping her fingers and giving him orders, no please or thank you, just *Ring me.*

He looked at the phone now with angry distrust.

But as the phone kept on ringing, his curiosity got the better of him.

'Yes, what?'

'Hello John.'

'Hello.'

'Did you get my text?'

'It's the middle of the night. What do you want?'

There was a pause. 'I have to see you. Where are you?'

'I'm away for a few days.'

'So I gathered. I went down to the yard. Why didn't you tell me you were going away?'

He sighed protractedly. He raised himself from the pillow, sat up, and swung his legs over the side of the bed. 'What do you want?' he repeated.

He heard her take a gasp of breath in frustration, as if she was taking a moment to control her temper. 'There's something I've got to tell you. I've been over to see Catherine in Thirsk.'

'Catherine who?'

'Catherine Derby who used to work with Sally.'

'Hip fucking hooray. You've been to see Catherine whoever-she-is. For Chrissake, what's that to do with me?' He closed his eyes temporarily, and had an image of Liz fading out of his life, draining rapidly away like something out of a film's special effects: fade to grey. Opening his eyes, he laughed softly at himself, at the image. 'I'm hanging up,' he told her.

'No, don't do that,' Liz said. 'This is important. Look, have you seen Alice Hauser again? The woman who spoke to you when you were down south?'

'Why should I?'

'Because… Look, I know this sounds bizarre. But I think she isn't exactly who she says she is.'

'Eh?' His attention had fired up at the mention of Alice's name. But that wasn't the only reason he wanted to listen to her. Her voice was slurred. He thought that she might be drunk.

'I think she's got a peculiar past…'

'How many have you had?'

'What?'

'Drinks.'

'None. I'm tired. I'm exhausted. It's been a very long day. Listen, John. I thought I recognised her. It was one of the cases that stuck in my mind, okay? Because it was never really sorted. It was a big thing in the papers for a week or so. There were always doubts about it with Social Services, apparently. People were suspicious in the village, Catherine said.'

'What village?'

'It's east of Thirsk. There were two children in the house, and a mother who went missing. This is 15, 16 years ago. The girl was 16 and the boy was 13. They said that the mother had gone away with a man, and it was believed because it was the kind of thing that she did, or would do, or had done... Abandoning the children. But the girl was 16 so there was a delay, it wasn't handled properly...'

'For God's sake, Liz. Get to the point.'

'The boy said he'd killed the mother. I mean not right then. It was weeks and they were living like feral kids, they had no idea, the house was...'

'I'm hanging up.'

'John! That girl was Alice – the woman who talked to you. Alice who lived with her brother in that house.'

'So what?' He was shocked, but not as shocked as he might have been six weeks ago or six months ago, before the world went to shit and left him behind.

'The boy said that he'd killed her. Killed the mother, and they'd buried her in the garden, and the girl said – this Alice Craig, Alice Hauser to you – she said that she was trying to protect her brother, hide him, because he was disabled.'

John stared at the sliver of light showing under the curtains. There was a lit courtyard outside. 'Liz...'

'Have you seen her, spoken to her? Has she been back in touch?'

'No,' he lied.

'Don't. Don't speak to her again.'

'Why not?'

'Because it was a strange case. Because they were never really sure.'

He rubbed his forehead. He couldn't make sense of it. 'Sure of what?'

'Of *her*. That she was telling the truth about their mother. About the death.'

'But I thought you said that the boy confessed.'

'He did. But he had a mental age of six or seven, John. He had a lot of problems.'

'So?'

'So how could a boy like that kill someone?'

He snorted. 'Quite easily, I'd say. One blow could do it. That's what they say about death or murder, isn't it? One crack on the head, or she fell, or one wrong push and she slid down the stairs drunk, or whatever... What sort of disabilities?'

'He was very slow in his movements. At first they thought it was foetal alcohol syndrome. But he wasn't properly diagnosed. He was very distressed when he was taken into a secure unit. Catherine told me today that his sister went away. She used to visit him all the time, but then he died and she went away.'

'Died?'

'In care, a year later.'

John waited. Waited for some kind of sense to come into his head. Then he suddenly remembered Sally. 'Just a minute. Let me guess. You got all this from that know-it-all Sally Latham, is that right?'

'No, not really. I went to see her and told her, but she thinks I'm wrong.'

'Sally bloody Latham,' he said. 'She was the one always telling you to leave me. She was the one who spoke to the girls that time.'

'We all went to see her, John.'

'You took them to see her after you'd been in hospital. Sally Latham! Telling you all to get shot of me. And you ring me up in the middle of the night to say that Sally Latham thinks that a woman I know is some kind of headcase, is that it?'

'No, she said—'

'I don't care what she said,' John retorted. 'And I don't know what you're playing at, except to tell me I'm wrong about something, which is pretty much par for the course, isn't it?'

'John—'

'I mean, what the hell is it to do with you now anyway, Liz? We don't live together anymore, do we? That's what you've wanted, isn't it? And I suppose you're well on the way to filing against me for assault and divorce and whatever, so why don't you just stay out of my life, because it's what you've wanted. And it's what you've got.'

He ended the call, threw the phone back on the bedside table, and got up. He went over to the window, parted the curtains and looked down on the courtyard. The sky was pitch black beyond the small lit area. A man in a security uniform was crossing the path towards the car park. He paused to test the doors of the restaurant and glanced up at the big Happy Diner sign above it. John watched him with something like envy. Just a man going about his work, looking relaxed, looking happy, swinging his arms as he went on his way.

Lucky sod.

And he thought about Alice Hauser in the room along the corridor that he had paid for. Thought about the chances of her being the sister of this boy. *Imagine having a brother who killed your mother.* Imagine having a mother who abandoned you. Imagine what she would have gone through, alone like that, knowing what had happened. Imagine carrying that with you for the rest of your life and then you met someone you loved and who loved you, and you had a relationship, and you were together, and then suddenly that person disappeared and you never knew where they had gone, or if they would ever come back, and the years went on and on and they never did come back, and you had a pretty good idea of who had taken them away from you.

If that was the same person... If that was Alice Craig lying by herself in the room nearby, if she had that in her past, in her head, *if it was*...

He stood by the window for a long time.

Then he pulled on his jeans and took the key card from the door, and went out into the corridor. He walked along to Alice's room and he put out his hand and was about to knock.

Instead, he stood there thinking of Alice seeing her brother in a secure unit. That's where they locked them up and... Well, what? Sedated them? He had no idea. But it must have been hell to have your brother murder your mother and then to have to go and see him in a place like that. It would send anyone crazy, wouldn't it? Crazy with unhappiness and fear and frustration. Crazy with powerlessness.

If she was the woman.

The small seed grew in his mind. He didn't know where it was going, and he didn't know how he would handle it – he didn't know what he was going to do with this information, even if it were true.

After a while standing in the corridor barefoot and indecisive, eventually he went back to his own room and lay awake with his ragged and uncertain thoughts.

25

WHEN HE CAME DOWN TO breakfast, Alice was already sitting at a table. John sat down opposite her. She looked scrubbed and clean. Without make-up she looked even younger; she could have easily been mistaken for 18 or 19.

'How did you sleep?' he asked.

'Very well. You?'

He didn't like to say that he hadn't been able to sleep without thinking of her. 'Can I get you anything else?' She already had an empty cereal bowl beside her.

'No thanks.'

He went over to the breakfast buffet. It was all in the price, and normally he would have loaded his plate – waste not, want not – but he didn't like to look greedy in front of Alice. He knew that he had put on weight lately with all the takeaways. And he hadn't climbed a mountain in God knows how many months. It was all beginning to show.

As soon as he sat down again, she spoke up. 'I've rung the garage,' she told him. 'It's not worth collecting.'

'Your car? Why?'

'It'll cost more to repair than it's worth.'

'Sometimes these places have other cars to sell.'

'I haven't got any money,' she said. 'Not that kind of money anyway.'

'Most people haven't. You could buy it on lease.'

She shook her head. 'I'll get the train.'

He ate his breakfast, drank his coffee. She sat drumming her fingers softly on the table. After a while, she got out her phone and scrolled through it. All the time, she wore a blank expression, the one he couldn't fathom. Finally, she poured herself another cup of tea.

She wants to leave, he thought. Impatience.

'Do you know when there's a train?' he asked.

'There's one to Bristol in about an hour.'

'I'll drive you.'

'Thanks. But I'll walk.'

'I don't mean to the station. I mean home.'

She stared at him now. 'Why would you do that?'

'It's not that far.'

'It's 150 miles, John.' She paused. 'I can't pay you. Not in any way.'

He slammed down his cup. 'I'm not after anything.'

'Just so we're clear.'

'You think I'm desperate, do you?'

'Thanks. You're all charm.'

'I didn't mean it like that.'

She gave a short laugh, almost under her breath. He knew that he had blushed; he could feel that his face was on fire. 'I don't know you,' she told him. 'We don't know each other at all. Do we? Except for Maitland, we've got nothing in common.'

'We come from the same part of the world.'

'Oh yes?' she retorted. 'And how do you make that out?'

He hesitated for a moment. Last night, he'd decided that Liz had no right to go scraping around in Alice's life trying to find out things about her. Now, he found himself doing exactly the same thing.

'Look,' he said finally, 'it's none of my business I suppose, but my wife told me something. Or, she guessed something. She thought that you looked familiar.'

Alice sat back in her chair.

'She wanted to know who you were, and she looked up your name online and she saw your photograph.' He paused, trying to gauge her expression. 'Do you know anyone called Craig?'

She didn't reply.

'Did you ever live in a village near the North York Moors?'

She stared at him for some time. Then eventually she answered. 'Yes.'

'You did?'

'Yes.' She hadn't moved a muscle.

'You see, my wife knows a couple of social workers. In our area. But one of them moved to Yorkshire twenty, twenty-five years ago. Yesterday, Liz went to see her.'

Alice gave a slight shrug. He couldn't tell if she were angry or not. She was looking out of the window. 'I'd better start making my way to the station.'

He put a hand across the table. 'Alice, is it you? Are you Alice Craig?'

'Does it matter?'

'Not if you say it doesn't.'

'It doesn't.' She turned her attention back to him. 'But you want to know all the same.'

'It must have been a horrible thing to happen to you.'

'Well. Now you've worked it out, are you happy?'

'No, I…'

She started to pick up her bag, then stopped. 'You've got a clever wife,' she said. 'I changed my name by deed poll. There's no law against it. I hadn't committed a crime.'

'No, of course not.'

She gave him a small smile. 'But you want to know the details, don't you? Be honest.'

All right then. Honesty. He could be honest, and that's what she'd want in return. Probably. She was hard to fathom. But he was intrigued by her: you didn't meet many people who had her history and could sit quietly and discuss it. If the roles were reversed, he would be furious to have had a light shone into his past. But then, fury was his go-to response. He knew that.

'Look,' he said. 'Let's just forget it. Like I say, it's none of my business.'

She was silent for a while, staring down at the table. Then, she looked up at him. 'William and I only had each other. I mean, my mother was technically in the house, but in reality she was rarely there,' she told him. 'We knew what she was like, and it was better when she wasn't home, believe me. It always used to puzzle me looking at other kids and how they behaved around their mothers, because it looked to me as if they had freedoms we never had. Speaking in front of other people, for one. When I first went to school, I soon found out what other people said about us. But to William and me, it was normal. Silence. We used to get visits from social workers – it was a long time before I figured out who *they* were when I was little – and Mum would always say, "Don't tell them lies." And I'd sit there wondering what lies she was talking about. So it was better to say nothing.' She gave him a small, dry smile. 'I remember one of them got down on the floor with me. She had some pens and paper and asked me if I liked drawing. I didn't know what to say to her. She said to my mother that I seemed withdrawn – something like that anyway. I don't know the exact words, but she lowered her voice. After that whenever a social worker came round we locked the door and hid.'

'What was she like, your mother? Was she ill, is that what you're saying?'

'We had a picture of her on the shelf in the kitchen, taken when she was younger. She looked like anyone else looks as a teenager – happy. With friends. When I got older I thought that maybe it was our fault.'

'Whose fault?'

'William's and mine.'

'Why?'

'For being born. I thought that maybe she had postnatal

depression. Or worse. What did they call it? Postpartum psychosis.'

'I don't know what that is.'

'Like depression. But bad. Sometimes she would grab me – this is after William was born – and it was usually at night and she would sit on the floor in the corner of the room and say all kinds of things... that people were coming to get us, murder us...'

'Jesus.'

'Or that she was dying, that her heart was coming out of her chest... She would put my hand on her chest so that I could feel it beating, and it would be, you know, *racing* and I'd think that she was certainly going to die in front of me...'

'Alone there, in the dark with her?'

'Yes. Always at night. She was a bit less frantic during the day. Although she had ways of making us obey her, she had a short temper...'

'Make you obey? Like how?'

'Putting our hands under the hot tap,' she told him in a flat and emotionless voice. 'Or locking us in cupboards for hours. Or she would sometimes go outside and get stones and she'd try to clean our faces with soil and stones...'

John looked at her. He looked at her face and shoulders and body thinking she was a slight little thing and had taken this treatment. God knows that he had sometimes gone for Liz, felt her skin under his hand, felt that the world was closing in and could only be released by shaking her, shaking her, shaking... but this. Stones and soil? *Jesus*.

'Other times she could be lovely,' Alice continued quietly. 'I honestly don't know if it was psychosis or whatever, or if she was just...' She stopped, smiling a little to herself and shaking her head. 'Out of her mind, maybe.' She stopped. 'Do you believe that people are born cruel?'

'I don't know.' It sent a chill down his spine. It was as if she'd read his mind. He'd thought that about himself. He'd thought it as a child. That he was bad. Teasing cats and killing frogs. Nasty little things that boys did. He'd get into bed and a feeling would come crawling over him, a feeling that he was bad, a bad boy. And his mum and dad never saw that. He was always their *good* boy, and he knew how to work it. Hide what he thought he was. The first time that he had given Liz a black eye he'd looked at her and wasn't sorry. He'd gone out that day to work and wondered if that meant that the old convictions he'd had were coming true. He looked at Alice. 'Maybe some people *are* born cruel,' he conceded.

She nodded, then took a sip of her tea. 'Not fashionable to say someone's born evil, is it?'

'You're saying that this was your mother?'

She leaned forward. 'Do you think it's hereditary?'

'What, you?' He laughed. 'No.'

She sat back. 'She'd have phases. She could be ordinary. She'd take us down the village shop. We'd have a huge meal she'd cooked. Or she'd buy plants and she planted a vegetable garden – it really grew when William was a toddler. We would all go out there and dig it together. William was all right until he was about seven or eight. Every weed had to come out… but the garden wasn't like that later. It went to ruin. But she had been okay for three or four years at least. I went to school. There was one in the village.'

'What about your grandparents?'

'Nobody living.'

'So nobody to come and see you?'

'No. And I never knew who my father was, nor did William. I don't think my mother ever told anyone. Perhaps she didn't know.'

'So…she would go and leave you alone?'

'William and I grew close like that. Just us.'

'So you looked after your brother…'

She nodded. 'He went to special school for a while. I mean, intermittently. We didn't have a car and sometimes she didn't get up when the school bus driver knocked on the door. My form teacher asked me about it. I said that Mum had a cold, or… You know, whatever came to mind.' She shrugged. 'But William was happy. He didn't ask much. He was gorgeous in his way. At least at that age.'

John saw her eyes fill with tears suddenly. 'Listen, Alice. We don't have to go on with this. Don't be upset. You don't have to tell me anything else.'

'Helen was the only other person I ever told,' she said. 'People used to say that Helen was difficult. Like people said about my mother. But if you'd known my mother, you'd know what difficult *really* was, and Helen wasn't that.'

'I don't know how you coped with it.'

He was thinking of his own secure childhood. And wondering… *How.* How did William kill their mother? Liz had told him that was what had happened. But he dared not ask. Alice must know that Liz would have told him. After all, that was what it was all about, why it was in the newspaper. But he just couldn't bring himself to say the words, *Tell me how your brother murdered her.*

'Yes, we coped, until…'

Here it was.

But Alice didn't finish the sentence. She pushed the tea cup to one side. 'Do you know what I'd think when I was little?' she asked. 'I'd think sometimes that everyone must be like us inside their houses. That they put on a show when they were outside and with other people, but that when they went home they were just the same. Crazy and afraid of each other like we were. I remember the first time that I was invited to tea with a girl from school, and we all sat around a dining-table. I was just waiting for trouble to start. But nothing happened. They just talked and then the mother washed up and the girl and I played on a swing outside, and then I went home. I walked back along the village street. I was eight or nine. I expected to turn around and see some evidence of that house exploding behind me, combusting, you know? That they'd held it all in for too long and now they were on fire.' She laughed at herself, shaking her head. 'Sounds crazy. But I just didn't know that there was such a thing as normal.'

'Whatever normal is,' he said.

She glanced at him again. 'Yes, whatever normal is.'

A waitress started clearing the table.

When she had gone, John asked, 'So, what will you do about the car?'

'Oh,' she shrugged. 'I think they'll give me some money for its spares.'

'Do you want to go there and sort it out?'

'No,' she told him. 'I've already phoned them.'

They regarded each other for some seconds. 'You want a lift, then?' John asked.

'Yes,' she said finally. 'If it's still on offer. Thank you.'

She followed him out, and went straight up to her room. From her window, she watched John emerge again, go into Reception and come out having paid the bill. He stood by the door waiting for her.

She considered him for some time, biting her lip.

Just as she was leaving the room, her phone pinged a message. *Your car is ready for collection.*

She deleted it.

26

ON THE WAY BACK FROM Asham Ferry, Thomas went into Brimham.

He shopped at the supermarket – this was surely one of the last towns in England to have a supermarket in the centre, he thought – and came out into the high street. He walked down the hill, and all the time he was wondering where Alice Hauser was living.

It was cold, and he pulled his coat tight around him, ambling aimlessly through the pretty medieval part of the town. Finally, on the off chance, he went into an estate agent. He showed them the picture of Alice and got pretty much the same reaction that he'd had in the café. Friendly until he pushed it just a little too far, and then the narrowing of eyes when he admitted that she wasn't a relative.

He came back out and stood on the wind-scoured pavement, indecisive. He thought abstractedly that he ought to go home. If Alice Hauser hadn't contacted him, then it was possible that she was never going to. What her reasons might be for turning up again after so long... Well, there it was. That was the question that was gnawing away at him. He wondered if she thought that he was still a police officer – after all, she had already been gone for a while when he eventually retired. It was possible that she didn't know that he no longer had any kind of influence. If she had come back to try to resolve Helen's disappearance, that is.

He went into a café, ordered himself a bowl of soup, and sat in the far corner away from the street. The atmosphere in the place was hippy-chic, all cushions and dreamcatchers. He looked around. There were CDs for sale – meditation and music. He'd never been spiritual. He liked things in logical sequence. Things that could be proven. That was why a case like Helen McAllister's would never really end. There'd be no closure for Alice Hauser, for him, for anyone. Eventually it had been that angry helplessness, in addition to the allegations and the confession of his time with Helen, that had made him draw a line under his career.

For a while, it had worked. There had been a lot to do in the house. He volunteered at a local National Trust house, enjoying his drive to Wiltshire three times a week. There had been the studio, of course. But sometimes his mind would drift back to Helen McAllister in the same way that he might think about a puzzle that he had no answer to or a name that evaded him in conversation. It would prey on his mind, echoing at the edge of his thoughts.

In his last conversations about the case at work, there had been a 60:40 split of opinion. Some thought that Helen McAllister had deliberately staged a disappearance – had vanished with a lover, or simply taken off somehow under an assumed name. Having known Helen briefly, Thomas himself wouldn't have put this past her. She didn't like her job; Alice was clingy; she had been to the USA before. Although she'd have had a problem there. Her passport was missing from the house, but had not been used outside Europe.

He could imagine her vanishing and re-inventing herself. It sounded far-fetched, but in his experience it happened more than you could think possible. Nearly 200,000 cases in the UK alone, every year. One every 90 seconds.

He had wondered, too, if Helen had committed suicide. She

was outgoing and assertive, seemingly happy with herself – even arrogant; but that sometimes was just a shield. They said that really depressed people suddenly become happier after they've made a decision to end their lives, as if it were a release from the terrible monotony – an answer. Helen could have walked into the sea or thrown herself from a cross-channel ferry or simply walked deep into woodland somewhere remote. A body might never be found in those circumstances. But then his mind would reel back to that house in Bloxley, which looked like a stage set for the next phase of her life. It was so immaculate, so perfect. Unless, of course, someone else had made it look that way.

Back to Alice Hauser. A woman who gave off the vibration of being helpless. A victim. And yet someone who had the strength to be vindictive and file a complaint, a complaint with no evidence. Alice Hauser had been guessing at his affair with Helen. Helen had allowed her to believe it – why? To cause trouble. Because Helen liked to control, and prod, and hurt. Alice had taken the bait. And in so doing she had stirred up a shitstorm in his own life.

*

That summer had been so warm that drought had begun to dry out the garden, and cracks had appeared in the lawn, showing the underlying clay. The previous night, he and Fran had sat out until it was very late, glad of the coolness of the evening. He had watched Fran's bare foot tapping at a fissure in the grass.

They had looked out through the shadowy edge of the garden with its tumble of weeds and blackberry bushes, out to the fields. Stars had begun to show in the sky. It would be their last easy day together.

The following afternoon he drove home slowly. On the way, he stopped in a lay-by near the edge of the river that ran through the centre of the county. There was a long low medieval bridge over the fast-flowing water. He stood for some time looking down at the river and at the fields that were spread around it in every direction. He thought of all the lives that had crossed that bridge, each one of them preoccupied with their own problems. He wondered if anyone else had stood there wondering what had happened to someone they had known, someone who had been in their lives one day and simply vanished the next.

He got back into the car and when he turned into the driveway at home he had a lurch of nausea at what he had to do. He would go in that door and everything that he and Fran had known up to now would be changed.

All because of Helen McAllister.

Fran was cooking dinner. She turned and looked at him as he came in. 'Can you give me one good reason why I'm cooking curry?' she asked.

'No...'

'Neither can I.' She wiped her hands on a tea towel, and kissed him on the cheek. 'How was your day? Mine was rubbish in case you're wondering.'

'Oh? Why?'

'Never mind,' she'd replied. 'Admin. Drove me nuts.' She ran her hands under the cold tap, and pressed her palms against her face in an effort to cool down.

'What have we got to drink?' he asked.

'The usual... Beer. Wine. In the fridge.'

He was on the verge of taking out the bottle of white wine until he saw that it was Italian. Verdicchio. He took out two beers instead and poured them.

'Cheers,' Fran said. She frowned at him, seeing his stricken expression. 'Really?' she asked. 'Was today that bad?'

'It was, yes.'

'Not this disappearance?'

'Sit down,' he said.

Before he could tell her anything, the colour had drained from her face. She knew him so well, perhaps she already realised the awfulness of what was coming. 'What is it?' she murmured.

'I've had a complaint made against me by the partner of the woman who's gone missing.'

'A complaint? Why?'

'She claims that I killed the woman. Helen McAllister.'

Fran laughed. 'What is she, insane?'

'No, I don't think so. Disturbed, perhaps. Very unhappy, certainly.'

'This is the woman whose car was found on the coast road?'

'Yes. Helen McAllister.'

'And who is the one doing the complaining?'

'Alice Hauser.'

'But…' A bit of colour had come back. Fran was shaking her head. 'But that's nonsense.'

'Yes. I can prove where I was for every second of those days, fortunately. I was at a meeting in Bristol. I stayed over.'

'You brought me back my bracelet.' And she held up her arm. She was wearing the slim silver band that he'd bought down on the harbour. She had done ever since he'd given it to her. 'You went on board the SS *Great Britain*,' she added.

'Yes. You've got a good memory.'

She reached across and touched his hand, smiling. 'Only because you were so bloody boring about it.'

He wished he could smile back at her. 'There's something else.'

'Is there?'

'Alice Hauser says that I had an affair with Helen McAllister, and she's right.'

There was a long silence. Several things pinpointed that moment for him even now: the pan bubbling on the stove, the noise of sparrows squabbling in the shrubs by the open window.

When Fran did speak, her voice was low and calm. 'For how long?'

'It was nothing, Fran.'

'Don't be a cliché.'

'We went away for four days. Before that, just a couple of lunches. That was it… I know it's not nothing. I'm sorry. I can't tell you how sorry I am. I don't know why it happened, Fran. I look back now and wonder what the hell I was doing, what I was thinking.'

'When was this four days?'

'You were at a conference in York.'

She hadn't moved. Now she took a drink from her glass. 'Well, well. And where did you go for this lovely four-day break?'

Hearing the sarcasm, he felt his throat close up. Fran wasn't a cynical person. She was always open. She gave others the benefit of the doubt. But he'd never heard her use such a note of scathing contempt.

'Italy,' he told her.

'Italy!'

'Fran, I'm so sorry.'

'Italy,' she repeated. 'How fabulous.'

'If it's any consolation, it was awful.'

'Was it? I'm glad.'

'I'm sorry,' he repeated, fearing that acid tone.

'And there was me toiling away with the great and the good of the local authority system. Keeping the money straight.' She paused. 'Do you know what I thought when you told me that you were going walking on the coast path?'

She remembered the lie, then. 'No.'

'I thought how glad I was that you at least were having a nice time.'

He could feel their decades-old trust draining away. But even so, there was more to say. 'Alice Hauser…' he began.

'Were they together then? Was Helen cheating on her partner too?'

'No.'

'So what happened afterwards? Did she have some sort of revelation after her break away with you? Did she realise that men were shit, and take up with a woman instead?'

'I don't know, Fran.'

'It was such a disaster that you turned her, is that it?'

'It was certainly a disaster.'

She was nodding, tapping her fingers on the table. 'I've heard the stupid male theory that one night with a so-called real man will turn a gay woman but I've never heard it the other way round. Poor Thomas. You must have been lousy. Lousy!' she shouted.

She got up from the table and stood with her back to him, staring into the garden. He sat, smarting at the insult.

'Is it still going on?' she asked.

'No, of course not. She's missing, Fran.'

'And if she weren't?'

'No. I haven't seen her for a long time.'

'Where did you meet her?'

'Does it matter?'

'Where did you *meet her*?'

'She was a teacher at St George's. I went there to give a careers talk.'

Another long silence. Then she abruptly turned around, went back to the stove, and turned off the gas. 'I'm not hungry,' she muttered. 'If you want to eat, cook it yourself.' He didn't move. He watched her as she walked again to the window. 'Where is she?' she asked.

'Who, Helen?'

'Yes, of course Helen. Where is she?'

'I don't know. Nobody does. That's what this investigation is about. I told you.'

'You didn't tell me much. Is she dead?'

'We don't know.'

'So she just vanished? What does this Alice Hauser say? If she claims that you did it, does she say how?'

'She was told that it was impossible. From what I can gather after that, she told them all that Helen had told her, which was basically…' He sighed. 'On the day that she disappeared, Helen said that the affair was still going on, and Alice Hauser assumed that when she vanished, she'd gone to me. And that I killed her. That we got into some sort of argument and I killed her.'

'And did she say why you would kill her? Specifically?'

'To stop you finding out. In a fit of temper. Accidentally. Pick any one from three.' He paused. 'Helen was a hard, volatile person, Fran. Enough to make anyone furious.'

'And where is the body supposed to be?'

'That wasn't gone into since it was obvious I did no such thing. Alice Hauser didn't offer a place or a method.'

Fran sat down again, facing him. She looked at him coldly. 'You might have done.'

'Done what?'

'Helen might have hidden out somewhere, and since then you've killed her.'

'Fran!'

'You might have done.'

'Don't joke about it.'

'I'm not joking. Nobody knows where she went, and since nobody knows where she is, she could be anywhere couldn't she? Dead or alive.'

He stared at her, frightened. 'Fran, do you really think that I'm capable of killing anyone?'

'I bet you wanted to, though.' She held his gaze for another few seconds, then shook her head slowly. 'No, Thomas. I don't think you're capable of that. But then I didn't think you were capable of having an affair, either.'

'I've regretted it every moment. As soon as we were back in this country I told her that it couldn't go on. We were at the airport, and—'

She held up her hand to stop him. 'Enough detail, thanks.'

'I'm so sorry, Fran. So sorry.'

They sat a while longer, each staring down at their feet. He wished he could turn the clock back. He wished to God that he had never met Helen McAllister. Sooner or later every last detail would come out at work about the affair and then they would treat him differently. *The boss shagged some woman a few years back. For a while it was even reckoned he'd killed her. There was a complaint.* It would come out like that, mangled in the way that rumours usually were.

'Is Alice Hauser a suspect?' she asked.

He glanced up. He never brought work home. It was fundamentally wrong to do so. He'd always believed that. But this was different. He owed Fran an answer to any question that she asked.

'Yes. But there's no evidence, except for traces of Helen in her car. Which would be normal. There's no trace of violence. There's nothing at Helen's own house. Nobody saw her or heard from her after Alice Hauser said that she talked to her on the ridge. There's nothing to go on.'

'And nobody else involved?'

'How do you mean?'

'Was Helen having a relationship with someone else, other than you and this Alice woman?'

He thought immediately of Alexandra Wilson. He had already wondered about her and was still wondering. But only today other more pressing cases had come in, and he'd set what meagre resources he had on them instead. Only Ellis had been left to follow up Helen's disappearance.

'Nobody definite. Just a feeling about a woman who's a school governor. But again, no evidence at all.'

'Nothing in her house?'

'No.'

'What about her phone?'

'We can't find the phone. It's turned off.'

Fran had crossed her arms. 'You're screwed, aren't you?'

'Yes,' he said, acknowledging it in more ways than one.

*

He sighed. He got up and paid for his meal at the counter, and then went out into the street.

There was another estate agent at the bottom of the High Street, and he hesitated. It was senseless to keep asking, though. If Alice Hauser had bought a property, or rented somewhere near Asham Ferry she could have done that in a dozen places. Or even online. And there'd be no reason that someone would remember her: for all he knew, she'd been back for a long time, but just never showed her face to him.

He walked back to the car wondering if he'd ever be free of Alice Hauser or Helen McAllister.

27

DRIVING BACK HOME, HE SAW the smoke from a mile away. It bloomed up in the clear afternoon sky, a column of grey and black, pulled this way and that by the wind. Thomas wondered what could be burning. He soon had his answer.

As he came down the hill, he saw the two fire engines drawn up in his driveway. *Oh no,* he thought. *The house.*

He slewed the car on to the verge, and immediately saw Christine. She ran up to him. 'I tried to ring you ten minutes ago,' she said.

'I heard it, but I was driving,' he admitted.

A fire officer was walking towards them.

'This is the owner, Mr Maitland,' Christine explained. Thomas looked closely at her and noticed the smuts in her hair and on her face. She glanced up at him. 'I smelled the smoke and I came down the drive,' she was saying. 'I saw your car was gone. The place was just ablaze. I thought of the garden hose, but… I phoned 999.'

Thomas put an arm around her shoulder. She was shaking. 'Thank you,' he told her.

'It was too far gone to do anything,' she said. 'I honestly didn't hear. I had the telly on. I'm so sorry, Thomas.'

'It's not your fault,' he said. He was worried at the paleness of her face, and held on to her.

Looking down the drive, all he could see was smoke and the fire engine hoses curled like vivid snakes around the front of the house towards the garage.

'What is it?' he asked the officer. 'Is it the house?'

'No, a small building in the garden.'

'Oh, bloody hell,' he muttered.

'Go and get a drink,' he told Christine kindly. 'And pour me one while you're at it.'

He walked with the officer towards the house, and went into the garden. The studio was a ruin, smouldering between the trees, and the garden all around it a sodden trampled mess. He looked at the patch that he had dug over.

'I didn't leave anything burning,' he said. He tried to step forward, and was stopped.

'There'll be an investigation, sir. You can smell the accelerant.'

'Accelerant? What, paraffin or something? I use a paraffin stove in the winter.'

'More probably petrol. What else was in the workshop?'

'Well… all kinds of stuff. Paint and paint thinner and turpentine, varnish…' He stared at the workshop. 'What about the machinery?'

'You'll have to judge for yourself, sir, when it's safe. But I wouldn't hold out a lot of hope.'

'I see.'

Thomas glimpsed a movement to his right, and turned around. Richard Ellis was standing at the gate.

'Hell of a stink,' Ellis commented. He walked forward and shook Thomas's hand.

'I didn't leave anything burning,' Thomas said. 'I didn't leave anything on. Not even a light.'

'No, I know,' Ellis murmured. 'Let's go in the house.'

*

They sat in the kitchen, looking out through the filtered light of the afternoon at the smouldering destruction. Dully, Thomas registered that the apples were getting bigger on the huge tree between the studio and the house.

'Thomas,' Ellis prompted.

'Sorry, what?'

'I asked you if you had any idea who could have done this.'

'I don't know… Somebody *did* then? That's certain?'

'Not much doubt about it.'

Thomas sat shaking his head over the cup of tea that Ellis had made for him. 'Somebody didn't much like my paintings,' he joked quietly, and pulled a face.

Ellis smiled at him briefly. 'Tell me about John Lord.'

'John Lord? The *accident* John Lord? Why?'

'Have you had any more presents in the post?'

'No…'

'Phone calls, texts, anything like that?'

'No.' He paused. 'You don't think that this is him?'

'Can you think of anyone else with a grudge against you?'

'No, of course not. I don't—' He stopped mid-sentence, with a sudden dropping sensation in the pit of his stomach. 'Alice Hauser is back, Richard.'

'Is she indeed?'

'But… no. It can't be her. She wouldn't do something like this, surely. Not after all this time.'

'How do you know she's back?'

'I was at Asham Ferry. The café there. I showed them her picture and the boy told me that she's been coming in there for over a month now. He reckoned that she lived nearby.'

Ellis sat back in his chair with a sigh. 'You showed them her picture?'

'Yes.'

'Why?'

Why? Because he thought that he'd seen her at the fair. Because he regularly thought about her and Helen. Because only today he was remembering telling Fran.

'She was at the fair after you left.'

'Was she indeed? What did she say?'

'Nothing. She was there one moment and gone the next.'

'Has she been in touch?'

'No.'

Ellis considered, head on one side, but didn't venture an opinion.

'Why now?' Thomas wondered out loud. 'It can't be her.'

'Because a woman wouldn't bear a grudge over losing someone she loved. Right,' Ellis replied sceptically.

'It's been ten years.'

Ellis leaned forward, arms on table. 'Don't go around showing her picture,' he said. 'Don't try to find her. Leave that to us.'

'I think the boy in the café knows her address. He just wouldn't tell me.'

'All right. But leave it alone now.' He got up. 'Wait there.'

Thomas watched him go into the garden, walk down the soaked path, speaking on his phone. Call over, he talked to the officers at the studio. All that was standing now were the walls. The roof, with its nice shingles, had collapsed. Ellis was right. There was one hell of a stink, and it was in the house too, in the kitchen where he sat. Probably everywhere else. He put his head in his hands.

'Thomas.' Ellis was back. 'Your neighbour asks if you want a drink? She's standing by the gate with a bottle of Scotch.'

'Let her in.'

Christine's voice, when she came in, betrayed that she'd already started on the whisky. She sat at the table and put down two glasses, both smeared with greyish soot. He didn't care. He took a long swallow of the drink. 'They say someone's done it deliberately, Thomas,' she said.

'I know.'

She slumped backwards, and threw her hands in the air expressively. He saw Ellis grinning momentarily; she presented quite a sight. Cords torn at the knee, a plaid jacket over a T-shirt, matted grey hair, and eyes reddened and smarting from the smoke.

Ellis leaned against the door frame. 'Do you know where John Lord is?' he asked Thomas.

'No. Why would I?'

'He isn't at home. I spoke to his wife yesterday. She said that he moved out a while ago, ten days or more.'

'He can't be down here, can he? Surely? He's got a business to run, hasn't he?'

'Nobody's seen him.'

'Well, I haven't either.'

Christine sat up, eyes wide. 'You think he did *this*?'

'I don't think anything yet. Did you see anybody out in the road or down the drive today?'

'Nobody. But then I can't say that I was really taking any notice because of the TV. I'm sure I didn't hear a car, or voices, or anything like that.' Christine turned to Thomas. 'John Lord. The man whose brother was killed?'

'Yes,' Ellis said.

'But…' She, too, stared down the garden. 'You'd have to be an absolute bloody lunatic.'

Ellis sat down with them. Christine showed him the whisky bottle. He shook his head. 'There's something else,' he murmured. 'John Lord's wife said that when he was down here, he met a woman called Alice Hauser.'

'Oh Christ,' Thomas sighed. 'Oh Christ, no.'

'I need to talk to you about the original investigation.'

'Why?'

'Because she has a theory about Alice Hauser that… Well, all I can say is that it's interesting. Beyond interesting, in fact.'

28

THEY LAY ON THE BEACH and looked at the stars.

When John and Alice had reached her place two days before, she'd said nothing to him. Not even 'Thanks'. She had indicated with a tilt of her head that he should follow her, and down they went under low-hanging trees. He could hear the sea, but couldn't make out the direction. The rain had become a curtain of heavy drizzle, and he could only make his way by keeping close behind her, following in her footsteps.

They got to a gate, a rusty thing in the hedge that complained with a low grind as she opened it. He found himself standing in a large square of waist-high grass. It had gone to seed, and looked luminous in the half light. Alice walked up two shallow steps to the door of a strange-looking kind of chalet, no better in its way than the Portakabin in the lorry yard at home, and probably 100 years older. Dark green corrugated metal and an old asbestos roof, as far as he could make out. He watched her go indoors and switch on a lamp. A low wattage bulb gave little light. He couldn't believe his eyes; it looked like something out of a ghost story, a shadow with the grass shimmering in front of it, the rain reflecting the yellowish flame behind the window.

He walked up the steps, glancing to left and right. A pair of muddy boots. An old wrought iron table. Quartered wood logs stacked on the other side in a line almost as high as the window. He opened the door.

She was standing in the centre of the room.

'This is where you live?' he had asked.

There was a freestanding cupboard, like an old kitchen pantry, on the far wall. Beyond that, only a sink and a wooden worktop and another old cupboard. She took out a blanket and gave it to him. And then without saying anything else, she went to a camp bed in the corner of the room and took off her coat and shoes, and lay down, wrapping a cotton throw around herself and turning her back.

He was gobsmacked. No other word for it. He weighed the blanket in his hands and stared at a chair near the door.

'A cup of tea would be nice,' he said.

There was no reply.

'Right then,' he muttered.

He went out, back into the rain. With the blanket bundled under one arm, he made his way along the narrow path back to his car, and got in.

'Well, this is fucking ridiculous,' he told himself, and started to laugh. What a bloody situation. Look at him here alone in the dark, broke, keeping company with a stranger. If he could have got into bed with her it would have been something – just for warmth, a bit of human contact – though she evidently didn't think so.

It made him laugh more. 'Be honest,' he repeated, out loud. He wiped his eyes and face with his hands. 'Ridiculous.'

He was tired, and his eyes streamed with the concentration of the drive. He couldn't go back tonight. It was 300 miles home. Of all the fucking ludicrous places he'd found himself, this took the biscuit. It really did. Where was he? Somewhere on the coast. The traffic had been terrible around Bristol, the motorway at a standstill after an accident. He'd stopped taking notice of the road signs through the Somerset and Dorset countryside an hour or so back, relying on her murmured instructions.

Alice was weird, there was no getting away from it. But what was he? Weirder still. Coming down here with a woman that his own wife had told him was peculiar, dangerous even. He admitted to himself, staring out of the window at the persistent rain, that he'd given Alice Hauser a lift partly to spite Liz, to show her that she was wrong. He leaned his head against the driver's window, the blanket in his lap. All the bloody petrol money! Nothing to eat since breakfast, except a bag of crisps at the last petrol station. He thought she'd be cooking something once they got here. It was only 7 o'clock. Not even a drink.

And all that way back.

All that way back...

He'd eventually fallen asleep and woken with a crick in his neck and a desperate need for a leak. He'd got out of the car; the sky was getting light. Squinting at his watch, he saw that it was 4.20. The rain had stopped and drops clung to every leaf. Other than the distant sound of the sea, there was not another sound.

He pissed in the hedge, and looked about him.

He didn't know what to do.

He didn't know what she wanted.

But if you had to hide somewhere, this would be the place.

*

And now here they were, at midnight.

In the dark again, the sea a few yards from his feet, the rollers dumping the waves at the shoreline with a thump. She'd told him that the shingle shelved away sharply, and the current ran almost parallel to the land. He listened to the gravelly sucking sound of the water hauling the stones back into the ocean.

The stars were bright, and he was drunker than he'd been for a very long time.

'Alice,' he said. She was sitting up now, staring at the ocean. 'What is it that you want?'

He couldn't hear her reply.

When he'd gone back to the house that morning, the doors and windows had been open. He could hear her moving about. Carrying the blanket, he went inside and saw her making up a fire for the log burner. She looked fresh and clean.

'The place to wash is in the back,' she said.

'I'm not staying,' he told her.

She had stood up. 'It's just a pump. But the water is good. Don't go through the back hedge, though. Fifty yards on there's a two-hundred-foot drop to the beach.'

'I'm not staying…'

'We have work to do,' she had told him.

*

He tried to sit up, but the stars danced about. Slowly, like a waltz. Slowly, like a boat bobbing gently on a current.

'I know the names,' he said. He raised his arm. 'Vega. Altair.' He saluted the arc in the west. 'Jupiter.'

Stars shining bright. He'd liked to name them all when he was a boy. Up on the fells with a star chart and a notebook. When he got older he'd lost track of most of the names of the stars.

It suddenly struck him as unspeakably sad. He'd just given up on his interests, sloughed them off as if they didn't matter, got roped into his father's company even though he didn't want to. Got derailed somewhere. Met up with Liz and wanted to marry her. Suddenly he found that he was crying. Alice was looking down at him with that bland, unreadable expression.

'Stars,' he managed to say.

'Sit up,' she told him.

He did as he was instructed.

'Listen to me, John,' she said. 'The fire was only the beginning.'

'Yes,' he said. 'I know.'

'You're asking me what I want,' she continued. 'And it's that. Torment.'

He didn't know what had happened to him really. That morning. She had been so businesslike about it. She already had it planned. She said she had thought of it for a long time, before even she had moved here. She told him about it slowly and calmly. They had been sitting on the verandah that ran around the chalet; sitting on the back deck eating the breakfast that she had made. It had still been ferociously early, not yet 6 o'clock, the cold water in the pump had taken his breath away and he had sat there feeling scoured cold and calm.

The calm had surprised him. They ate in silence, and he realised for the first time in a very long time that he was in a kind of retreat – a sanctuary, a seclusion. Nobody could get to him. He had turned off his phone while he sat alongside Alice, listening to the distant murmur of the sea and the breeze through the trees.

When they had finished eating, he wouldn't have got back in the car and driven home even if she had asked him to. It was like she never expected him to leave. And somewhere in that half hour – he had wondered why he would go, what there was left to go back to. His girls hated him and his wife was cutting him free. Liz was pushing him out down the street like one of those old hoops that you used to have to whip to get it going. And on and on he was rolling with nothing to bring him back.

It was clean here at least. The shack – let's call it what it was – was bare but grime-free, relentlessly, achingly clean, even the bare metal struts of the roof, no webs or dust anywhere, no wood dust on the floor.

There was nothing – no TV, no radio. Not a rug on the floor. No fridge, no freezer. None of the stuff that was supposed to be essential. Her clothes were in two suitcases on the floor. When he'd remarked on it that morning, she'd said that she didn't need much. That she wasn't staying long.

'Just long enough,' she'd said.

*

He looked at the iron-blue sea. Vaguely, he wondered what Thomas Maitland was doing.

'Everything went up in flames so quickly,' he said.

'I guessed it would. Stands to reason, doesn't it? Plus, I've been there before.'

He looked at her. 'It was me who gave you the address.'

'I'd been there long before that.'

He shuffled on the stones to get a proper look at her face. 'When?'

'Ten years ago, after Helen. Just before I left.'

'What, to see him?'

'That was the idea.'

'And did you? How did you know the address?'

She smiled. 'It was very easy. They were in the telephone directory. Remember those, the yellow directories?'

'Yes.'

'It was… I don't know. Three, four weeks later? The police had stopped tormenting me. They didn't call me in or come around anymore. And I thought, well, he's seen my house often enough, I'll see his. So I drove there.'

'To do what?'

She looked at him, raising an eyebrow. 'What do you mean?'

'See his wife or something? Complain to her?'

She shook her head. 'I don't know. Maybe I would have done. Maybe I'd have hit him.' She paused. 'I used to dream about that.'

'So what happened?'

'Nothing. They weren't in. I knocked on the door and I waited, and then I walked around the back and through the gate, and I walked down the garden. There was no studio then. Just the garden, very neat near the house and untidy down the bottom near a stream. I only figured there must be a studio now because of all the paintings he does.'

'You were right.' John ran a hand over his face. The beach was tilting and turning as he tried to focus on the conversation.

'Helen wanted to go there on the day she disappeared,' Alice murmured. 'We were arguing. She told me to drive to Maitland's house.'

'Huh?' he asked. 'What?'

'She said he'd set the record straight for me. And she said she would tell his wife.'

'But… that's not what you said before,' he protested.

Alice carried on as if she hadn't heard him. 'Because we'd been arguing for a couple of hours. It was hot in the car…' She stared at the sea. 'Helen was angry. She asked if I was ever going to take her back to her car and I said no.'

'But you said…'

'I told everyone I'd left her on the ridge. In the beginning. And then I made a complaint about Maitland, and I kept to the story.'

'But it was a lie.' He sat up straighter, concentrating on her profile in the darkness. 'Leaving her on the ridge was a lie.'

'Helen said that she'd take me to the house and let Maitland tell me himself there was nothing between them anymore. She said that he'd let me know what a bitch she was even if I couldn't see it properly for myself. And she said that would be it, she'd show me she meant business. Leaving me, destroying him and his marriage for being a bastard to her. And Maitland would take her back to her car if I wouldn't, or she'd get a taxi or whatever.' Alice paused, shaking her head. '"I'll give you a showdown," she said. "A nice big fuck-off showdown. You all disgust me".'

John frowned. 'What did you tell her?'

'I said no. I didn't want to see Maitland. I didn't care about him then.'

'What did she do?'

'She slapped me. Hard. And got out of the car.'

'Christ. What then?' He was trying to visualise it.

'We were on Stone Ridge. I watched her walk away. I didn't want to go to Maitland's house. I didn't want her to go anywhere. I didn't want her to leave…'

'So what did you do?'

'I got out of the car and ran after her. I tried to stop her. We were standing right on the edge of the hill just where the woods start, and she got hold of my arm and told me that if I ever tried to see her again, she'd kill me. I was so shocked.'

John wondered if this was the real story. He'd heard all these versions… Her voice was so low that he could hardly hear it. This woman that Alice loved so much was leaving, and Helen had threatened her life. He tried to think what he might do in the same situation. He tried to reason his way through it, but it was no use. He knew exactly what he'd have done in Alice's situation. He'd have done anything at all to stop the woman walking away.

He got to his feet unsteadily. The tide was inching up the beach and, by Jesus, it was bloody cold for an early summer night. It was as cold as winter. The sea must be icy. He shivered involuntarily. He turned around to look at Alice.

'Did you stop her?' he asked.

'No.'

'You just let her say that, and walk away?'

'Yes.'

He judged it. Helen was taller, stronger, fitter. Added to all that, she was a vicious bloody freak from what he could gather. And there was Alice, five feet nothing, just spit and bone. Loser from day one. Loser later. Loser now.

They were two members in a bloody exclusive club, he thought.

'What happened to her, Alice?'

'She got to Maitland somehow. That day, in that mood.'

'Did you go back and tell the police this different story?'

Alice made a hissing sound through her teeth that was barely a laugh. 'Yeah, so they'd believe me?' she asked. 'I was half out of my mind. I just didn't want anyone to know she'd left me. That was why I started out saying that I didn't know what had happened. Then I got it into my head that the only explanation was Maitland. I was already thinking that the very first day that he came to see me at my house. She hadn't come back – I was even thinking she'd turn up suddenly after I'd reported her missing, I was sure she was coming back, you see? Sure of it.' She shook her head. 'Then when she didn't come, I reported Maitland. I reported the affair and I said that he'd killed her. It's the only thing that makes sense.'

'But they didn't believe you.'

'Of course they didn't. What would be the use of saying where I'd last seen her then? The village or the ridge or wherever wouldn't change the fact that Maitland had a lot to lose. I still think that she would have come back to me. But he must have stopped her.'

John looked down at her sorrowfully. *Oh, you poor fucking fool,* he thought. *She was never going to come back.*

'They thought that I was a liar anyway,' Alice added. 'Someone who didn't function right. I could tell. The day after I made the complaint they rang me and said Maitland had been somewhere else that day.' Alice sat in a rigid, hunched-up posture, her arms crossed over her knees. 'I think of that day all the time,' she murmured. 'I think of that argument that went on and on.' She looked across at him. 'Have you ever had an argument like that?'

'Yes,' he conceded.

'And that's exactly what it's been. A nightmare that started that day and has never finished. Answers I'll never find.'

'But you think Maitland has those answers?'

'She never went back to her car, never went back to her house, never contacted anyone ever again that I know of, that I've heard. She never used her phone again, or her bank.'

'Alice,' he said quietly. 'She must be dead.'

The sea rolled, dumped its gravel and sand, and drew it back. He watched it for some time, thinking that she wasn't going to reply. She seemed to be considering something, perhaps if she could trust him. Then she said, 'I think she could have gone to the school'.

'The school? What school?'

'St George's. Where she worked. It was only three miles away from where we were parked. I think she could have crossed the fields and then got out somehow on to the road and then crossed the deer park. There's a place where they hold a fair once a year, I've been there. There's public footpaths running through the land. It comes out by the house – a big Regency house – she could have gone in there and asked for help, or she just carried on another mile. St George's backs on to the estate.'

He began vaguely to see it, the possibility. 'And would she have been able to get in? Wasn't it the end of term?'

'There's always boarders who don't get picked up exactly on time. But there'd been a meeting that morning. Probably some staff would have still been there. She could have used a phone there and rung Maitland.'

'She could have rung anyone, Alice. A taxi, for instance. Like you said.'

She shook her head firmly. 'No. I think she wanted to punish me. Stay missing for a day or two. Drive me crazy. She was good at that. She'd have found it funny.'

'And you're sure it would be Maitland she'd rung?'

'What do you mean?'

'I mean… Maybe there was another person, Alice.'

'No.'

'You can't know that.'

She gave him a smile. Her face was drawn in black and white in the darkness. 'I do know that, John. Because if there'd been anyone else she'd have tortured me with it. Like she tortured me over Maitland. She wouldn't have been able to resist it. She'd have given me every detail that day. She'd have told me.'

'I dunno,' he said, full of doubt.

'That's because you don't know her.'

'All right,' he conceded grudgingly. 'Say she phoned Maitland and he came out to her that afternoon. Came back from wherever he was.'

'An evening meeting in Bristol. Only fifty miles, so he had the time. It would have been about four in the afternoon by then. His wife would still have been at work.'

'All right. So he came back and he picked her up. Why would he do that?'

'To stop his wife finding out. Even at the deer park or the school, she was still fairly close to the house. Helen could have said that if he didn't come, she'd walk back again and tell his wife everything.'

'Okay, he comes to get her. What then?'

Alice rocked back and forth, still clutching her knees. She stared back at the sea.

'That's when you think he murdered her,' he said.

'Yes,' she said. 'I've had ten years to think about it, to work it out. That's when I think he murdered her. That's what happened to her.'

John sighed. Did it make sense? Would Maitland have returned for her? Would he have killed Helen to shut her up, to save his marriage, maybe even his career? Maybe. It was possible. People killed for a lot less than that.

But one thing was for sure. Maitland did kill Mike.

John looked down again at Alice. 'We could go to the police again tomorrow.'

'What?'

'Tell them what you've told me.'

'I tried!'

'But not the real way it happened. Just to straighten it. Maitland's retired now. There'd be other people in charge. They do cold cases, don't they? Chase them up and everything. No reason not to look at it again.'

She scrambled to her feet now. 'And what if they found out what your wife knows? What if they find out that I'm Alice Craig?'

He spread his hands. 'What difference would it make?'

'The difference that it always would make.'

'But it wasn't your fault, what happened to you.'

'No, but how does it look? Why do you think that I changed my name? There's a taint.'

'You're not tainted as far as I'm concerned,' he told her. 'You're a victim.'

She shook her head vigorously. 'Then you're the exception, John. Because most people think like your wife. Raised like that, they think I must be peculiar, in some way affected even if I'm the victim. A crazed mother and murdering brother. A partner who disappears. I mean, *I'd* be suspicious. Helen was.'

He looked at her. 'You told Helen that you were Alice Craig?'

She bit her lip. 'Yes. And the police would be the same. Suspicious all of sudden'. She paused. 'Why aren't you?'

He thought about it for a moment. 'Bad luck follows some people.'

'That's not good enough.'

'You've got caught in the slipstream of what other people do. That doesn't make you a bad person.' He was looking at her, but in reality he was talking in a self-pitying way about himself.

'The police already know I lied to them. They already know that I accused Maitland. I never told them who I was, and they never found out because they were all so bloody slipshod. Small town mentality. Maitland being the respected father-in-residence type thing. They all looked at me like I was out of my mind, peculiar, crazy, so there's no way I was going to confirm it by telling them who I'd once been.'

John made a disparaging noise in his throat, a dismissive noise. 'You've made yourself an outcast.'

'And haven't you?'

She had a point.

'And being here now with me, you're making it worse.'

He laughed. 'Alice, it couldn't get worse.'

They stood there, solemnly regarding each other. He tried not to consider the look in her eyes, that odd blank look. Like you could travel right down deep inside her and never reach any kind of ground. She was either a bottomless pit or just a mirror reflecting back at you. Either way, it made you stop in your tracks and wonder.

'John,' she said. 'Did Maitland kill Mike?'

'Yes,' he told her. That was the one thing that he was absolutely sure about.

'And you believe that, despite the accident report, the investigation?'

'Yes,' looking away now, unable to hold her frozen gaze.

'And you'd stand by that, whatever anyone else said, whatever reasons they gave you that he was innocent?'

'Yes,' he said. 'I would. I do.'

Alice suddenly took hold of his hand and turned him to face her. 'If I'm a victim, so are you,' she said. 'And you know what? No one is going to help us.'

He looked along the coast, biting his lip, feeling that long-accustomed surge of angry self-pity. Far in the distance, where the single-track road came down to Asham Ferry, he could see a light that gave a yellow flicker at the end of the road near the café. Above it and further on along the shore, the ashy black cliffs streamed away in shadows. Far out across the bay he could see where the coast came to a point, and the sky rose above it in a black vault.

It wasn't the old comfortable feeling that he'd had as a boy when he looked up at the constellations. It wasn't like that anymore – the feeling of being part of a whole, some kind of miracle. It had all changed. He really had no place anywhere. He'd fucked up his life and had it fucked up for him. For a few seconds he had a sense of drifting into the sky which over looked his head, like a speck of nothing being washed away in a current. He looked back at her, feeling dizzy and drunk and sick, and saw Alice looking back at him as if he were the answer to her prayers.

'Jesus, why are you looking at me like that?' he said.

'It's on us,' she said.

He'd seen that expression before. He'd seen it today. All lit up brighter than the fire that they set. Lit up, wired up, fizzing. She'd even talked about Maitland being in the studio. How they could leave him there in the flames. And he'd silently thanked God that Maitland had been absent. The studio door unlocked, paints set out ready as if he'd been thinking of starting work but had changed his mind.

'It's our job,' Alice told him.

'What is?'

'Maitland,' she said. 'For Helen and Mike. And we haven't got long.'

29

IN THE YEARS AFTERWARDS, THOMAS thought that it was like the morning of the crash. He looked back at the day and it felt like a re-run of horrors. Two images: the red car turning mid-air and the moment that he stood at Alexandra's door and the realisation swept over him. Something irrevocable and strange and still.

He had got up at 5 o'clock unable to sleep. The stink of the fire was in the house. He opened the windows at the front, the ones that faced the drive, but the smell remained. All the roses that he had trained that distant morning in April were now in flower below those same windows, but their scent couldn't overwhelm the smoke. It clung to the house and his skin and clothes.

He had got up and looked out on to the garden. He guessed that the fire was just a tryout for Alice Hauser and John Lord, like disturbed children who torture and kill animals before they go out into the world to assault human beings.

He thought about John Lord while he stood in the kitchen, a mug of coffee in his hand. Abusive, in financial trouble and alone, without the moderating influence of his wife or family. A loose cannon rolling around. He thought of John Lord in the studio just a day or two after the accident: agitated, furious.

And Alice Hauser. Or Craig. Whoever she was. They'd never

discovered that ten years ago; they had slipped up in the daily grind of other cases. A drowning along the beach, a robbery in a village close to the Devon border. As he recalled, a woman had died of a heart attack in the Post Office robbery and they had had another grieving, angry partner to deal with in the shape of her husband. Sadly, it was the usual things.

He remembered the feeling of helplessness. The village and the coast were quiet places. There was only one CCTV at the village store, and that had faced its own small car park, not the road. The phone records for both Alice and Helen backed up what they already knew – or didn't know – about them both. Helen's curiously selfish life was a conundrum from start to finish, because she didn't act as others did, more or less predictably. She had little spiteful vendettas of her own, never really committing, always causing anxiety or confusion. From what he remembered from his conversation with the Head, Helen wasn't liked at the school: regarded as solitary, organised, and, from what he could glean from reading between the lines, bullying.

Unpredictable too, Alice Hauser did not fit the template of abandoned partner: she didn't weep, she didn't beg, she didn't offer any explanation. She was like a solid brick of resistance, angry at him. Jealous. Cold. And this thing with her mother and brother... the things that Ellis had now told him. Involuntarily, Thomas shuddered. Terrible lives some people led, he thought. Terrible memories to keep inside you. He saw again Alice's rigidity, her clasped hands, her habitual rocking motion. Hard to know what images were behind that confusingly expressionless face, that slight build. What memories and what torment. It answered some questions. But it also raised some.

He looked back to the ruin of the studio and knew that he couldn't spend the day in the house.

He grabbed his jacket and his car keys.

*

It wasn't a sociable time to appear at anyone's door.

Alexandra Wilson said so. 'What's going on? It's only seven thirty.' Then, she scrutinised his face. 'Oh my good God, it's you,' she said.

She stood full square in the doorway of her beautiful house, above the same wide steps and facing the same sweeping drive. But not everything was the same, far from it. The old air of entitlement had gone. As they faced each other, ten years rolled away.

'I supposed that one day you might come back,' she admitted. 'But not as late as this, after all this time.' She stepped back. 'You'd better come in.'

She was already dressed, but not in the way that she had been ten years before. As she walked ahead, he noticed the T-shirt and jeans, the rumpled hair, the slopping sound of the unbuckled sandals. Without turning back to him, she made coffee and eventually put a cup in front of him. Then she sat down opposite him at the table.

There was no make-up on her face, no varnish on her fingernails, no expensive cut to her hair. She gazed at him with a kind of wry smile, as if reading his mind.

'Things change, don't they?' she said.

'They tend to.'

'You don't look happy, Mr Maitland.'

'Don't I? But then I can't remember when I was.'

'I'm sorry to hear it – but snap,' she said, and clinked his coffee cup with her own. They drank, each eyeing the other. 'The boys and I were going to France when I last saw you,' she said. 'If I remember right.'

'You do.'

She looked around her. 'Do you think that this room looks empty?'

He hadn't thought about it, but looked now. 'Is there something missing?'

'A lot,' she said. 'You should see the rest of the place.'

'What happened?'

'Oh,' she said, and waved her hand. 'The usual stuff. Husband left. One boy in the City, the other at uni.'

'Which uni?'

'As far away as he could get and still be in the country,' she told him. 'St Andrews.'

'They say it's a lovely area,' he observed. 'The coastline and the history.'

'I wouldn't know,' she replied. 'He doesn't want me to visit. He sides with his father.'

'Does he?'

She gave him a sad, slow smile. 'My husband had two mistresses that I know of,' she told him. 'But when it came to my affair, the shit hit the fan. It was his excuse to throw up his hands in horror. Seb went to live with him in London. Jonno stayed here until his father decided he'd be better off at his old school. Paid for them, you see? He sold the house in France and left me with this one, minus most of the furnishings, which he kindly sold.'

Thomas watched her. After a while, she met his gaze. 'When did you know about Helen and me?' she asked.

'Not until now.'

Her mouth gaped open in surprise. 'You're kidding me.'

'Not for sure. You've preyed on my mind.'

'But no proof.'

'That's right.'

'Because Alice Hauser never knew about me, and neither did anyone else.'

The truth of it hung between them in the silence. Past her shoulder, he could see the back garden. It looked very green but unkempt; the windows were opaque with dust.

'We sold off the land beyond the fence,' she said, following his gaze. 'I'm just sitting here like a fat woman in a tiny dress – massive house and drive and a handkerchief-sized bit of land.' She sighed. 'You're lucky to find me, actually,' she said. 'I'm selling it.'

'Where will you go?'

'I don't know. Anywhere.' Her shoulders slumped.

'How did your husband find out?'

'Because I' – she put her hand over her heart, patting her chest as if to accentuate that it was her responsibility – 'because I told him. Not clever. But you know… Sooner or later we'd have separated. And at the time, when Helen vanished… it was too much. It was a nightmare. I blurted it out one evening, and…' She paused, shook her head. 'We lived different lives anyway. He was rarely here. He just sent money. So this thing with Helen was the excuse he needed to move on and paint himself as the victim in the process. But he didn't give a shit about us anyway. He didn't care whether she'd lived or died, and wouldn't sully himself telling the police. Far too important and busy.' She gave a little sighing gasp, trying to laugh and not succeeding.

'Was Helen named in the divorce?'

'No. Irreconcilable differences.' And she glanced up at him. 'That was true enough. But he told the boys. He told them what a faithful husband he'd been and how devastated and shocked he was at my deceit and years of lying, and… etcetera etcetera.' She smiled faintly as she drank the last of the coffee. 'Jonno was a little sweetie, held Mummy's hand and all that, bless him. But he changed when he went away to school. He comes back in the holidays and he's not little Jonno anymore. He's more like his father and brother.'

Thomas remembered the boy's face looking out at him from the back window of the car as they had driven away.

'He had a football match, didn't he?'

'That Saturday? Yes,' she said. 'A football party, for someone's birthday. He cried about it on the ferry.'

They both sat in silence for a while. At first, he was thinking, *Ten years isn't a very long time.* But of course, it was. Both his world and Alexandra's had changed considerably. There was no more Helen and there was no more Fran, and there was no more marriage for either of them.

'You were right about the photo online,' she murmured at last. 'I couldn't delete it because it wasn't my account. It was the school's.'

'How long had it been going on?'

'Our relationship? Since Helen first came to the school. We'd tried to end it once'.

'She went to the USA.'

'You're very perceptive. Yes.'

'And then came back…'

'And I wanted to take it up where we'd left it. She – well, she was difficult, Helen, when she wanted to be—'

'I know.'

'Ah,' she murmured, looking at him frankly. 'You would.'

He didn't reply.

'Forgive me, Mr Maitland,' she said. 'But you were something to taunt me with. That's all it was.'

'You, not Alice Hauser?'

Alexandra sat back in her chair with a sigh, looking out of the window at the untidy, overgrown garden. Then she looked back at him. 'Helen was… What's the word? Capricious?' She thought for a second. 'No,' she decided. 'She was much worse than that. She played horrible games. She became very angry if she was thwarted. She couldn't make a decision herself, but she punished you if *you* made it for her. She was wilful.' Another pause. 'And she was wonderful.'

'She lived with Alice Hauser for a year.'

'And I lived here. We met up when we could, two or three times a month. We both lied to the people we were living with, and we both hurt people. But that was Helen and her games. Back and forth, promising one thing one week, and something else the next.'

'She promised Alice that they would get married.'

Alexandra burst out laughing. 'I know.' She covered her face then briefly with her hands. 'She was *bloody* wicked to that girl.'

'Alice has never forgotten her. She's come back to the area.'

An expression crossed Alexandra's face that he had not seen before. Fear. 'Why?' she asked.

He thought of the fire in the studio. 'I dread to think.'

'Thank God she never knew about us.'

'I wouldn't put anything past her, Mrs Wilson.'

'Oh.' She flinched. 'Did you tell her about me?'

'No.'

'Nothing, no hint?'

'I didn't know for sure until this very moment.' He scrutinised her face. 'Why?' She gave a quick exhalation of breath.

'Because that woman is dangerous.'

'You think so?' A sensation crawled up his spine – something akin to vertigo. Similar to the feeling that he had had when he and Helen were in San Gimignano. He found himself holding on to the edge of the table, noticed his own hands, and carefully removed them. But Alexandra had seen his reaction.

'Do you know who she is?'

'I heard just recently. Heard a rumour of sorts. It's being investigated now, today.'

She gave a short, exasperated laugh. 'Only today?' she said. 'Don't you think you're ten years too late?'

'Everything about her name, her background, checked out.'

'On the surface, yes.'

He had to admit it. 'Yes. But there was really no reason to doubt her. Driving licence, credit cards, bank…'

'God save me from country policemen,' she muttered.

'That's not very fair.'

'Isn't it? She told Helen who she was. And Helen never told you?'

'No, never. We didn't have a close relationship. Four days is hardly…'

'Hardly enough time? No, I guess not. But let me tell you it mattered to Helen. She'd taken up with this little wraith of a thing… She struck you that way, I suppose, Alice Hauser?'

'Yes.' Although now he was thinking of the blankness of her, the occasional flashes of anger.

'She told Helen the Christmas before Helen left. Why do you think Helen was covering her tracks? Why do you think we never revealed our affair? We were afraid she'd come after us.'

Thomas thought suddenly that he could smell the rank odour of his own home now, the bitter smell of the smoke. 'She's come after me,' he murmured. 'Part of my house was set on fire yesterday.'

'Jesus, you have my sympathy,' Alexandra said. She narrowed her eyes as she looked at him. 'And that's why you're here today. To check out a theory. Well done at last, Mr Maitland.' And she gave him a cynical smile.

'It might have helped if you'd told me this at the time, Mrs Wilson.'

'Would it?' she demanded. 'I couldn't tell you on the day that you came because Helen and I had an arrangement. Three days after she went missing, we'd agreed to meet at my husband's and my house in France. And neither she nor I had any intention of coming back any time soon.'

'Because of Alice?'

'Because of Alice.'

'And you didn't think to inform the police of this when we were searching for her?'

'We decided against it.'

'Because of…'

'Yes, Alice.'

'You were that afraid of her?'

'Of course we were!'

'Wasting police time.'

'Keeping ourselves from being slaughtered.'

'And you're trying to tell me that you genuinely believed that Alice Hauser – Craig, whatever – was capable of that?'

'We weren't going to take the chance.'

He pursed his lips, nodding. 'You must have been very entertained watching us look for her.'

'I wasn't sodding *entertained,* believe me!'

A silence fell between them for a full minute. Alexandra drained her cup, and sighed. He tried another tack.

'You were taking the boys out of the country, away from their father and their schools?'

Alexandra rested her head on one hand, and drew a circle on the table in front of her. 'We needed to talk about what we'd do, where we'd go once my husband found out. The boys...' She glanced up at him. 'Frankly, I hadn't got that far. But I knew I wanted to keep them from their bloody father when he found out. I wanted to let them get to know Helen, understand what was going on without *his* input. Because I knew how he'd be. How bloody vindictive. I was right about that.'

Thomas continued watching her. He was thinking how selfish love can make a person. Or sex, or passion. Whatever it was. It had made him selfish. It had made Alexandra selfish, using her boys as potential pawns in the coming marital battle.

She glanced up at him now. 'You're wearing a very puritanical expression,' she said.

'She made fools of us both, I think.'

'Yes, she did,' Alexandra replied. 'I went scooting off to the ferry and the house in France, convinced that Alice had threatened something horrible. Enough to make Helen leave early. I had no message, but I thought Helen might be waiting at the ferry port, watching for my car.' She let out a little exhalation of breath, and shrugged. 'I don't know why I thought that. Blind hope maybe. But she wasn't there, and she wasn't at the house.'

'How long did you wait for her?'

'Six weeks.'

'And when you came back, what did you think?'

She gave a dismissive wave of her hand. 'I was too fucking miserable to think.'

'You didn't come to the conclusion then that this dangerous girl had killed Helen?'

'Maybe. But like I say, I didn't think straight at all. And if I accused her and you lot had let her go, she could have come after me.' She paused. 'Which to be fair, you kept doing, didn't you? Had her in for questioning and then let her out.'

'There was nothing that we could hold her on.'

She looked at him steadily. 'Have you ever lost someone that you loved?'

'Yes,' he replied.

'And could you even string a sentence together afterwards?'

'Not really.'

'Imagine that, and then add to it a husband making your life an utter fucking misery.'

He nodded without speaking. Then, 'I think Alice Hauser is with someone else at the moment. A man.'

'A *man*?'

'There's a man who thinks that I killed his brother, in a road accident. I didn't. But he thinks so. He's an unstable person...'

'When was this accident?'

'Not long ago. Earlier this year.'

'So it's fresh in his mind?'

'My ex-colleague has spoken to his wife. He's depressed and supposedly on medication, but I doubt he takes it. The dead man was his twin brother.'

'And this is the person with Alice Hauser now?'

'Yes.'

'Holy shit.'

Thomas tried to even out his breathing. He began to wonder if he ought to go home ever again. He closed his hands around his phone in his pocket. 'I ought to ring and let my colleague know,' he murmured. 'What did Helen tell you, exactly? And why would Alice tell her in the first place anyway?'

'You've already mentioned it,' she replied. 'Alice thought that they would be getting married, and she wanted to tell Helen the truth.' She sighed. 'It was pitiful, really. She said she wanted to start with a clean slate, and she trusted Helen, you see?'

'After all those years of trying to escape it.'

'You haven't heard the worst of it, Mr Maitland.'

He guessed. He'd discussed it briefly with Richard. Richard had rung him after speaking to Elizabeth Lord. 'She and her brother buried their mother after the brother had killed her. There had been years of neglect.' He stopped, staring at Alexandra's face. 'What?' he said. 'Helen didn't say that?'

'Oh, she said that,' Alexandra confirmed. 'But there was more. They buried the mother themselves, without telling anyone?'

'Yes.'

'And Alice fobbed off the Social Services while she tried looking after the brother.'

'Yes.'

'She was sixteen.'

'That's right…'

'And it got too much, and people were talking and she eventually told Social Services and the police what her brother had done, and he was admitted to a secure hospital, and she went to a hostel.'

'I think that's the story.'

'And did you know that she got the proceeds of the house sale? It was a rundown place but it was on the fringes of the North York Moors, and – well, prime holiday cottage stuff – it sold and she got the price.'

'I see.'

'That's what funded her all these years. Not much money, but enough.'

'Okay…'

'It's not the truth, though.'

He sat back in his chair, surprised. 'It isn't?'

'Not the whole truth, anyway. Her brother didn't kill her mother, Mr Maitland. She did.'

There was really not much to say at that moment. He gave a

little laugh, part disbelief, part confusion. Alexandra Wilson continued to look steadily back at him.

'She wouldn't get away with that,' he said.

'But she did.'

'And this is what Helen told you.'

'She said that Alice told her quite calmly. She explained the abuse – that bit was real enough – and she explained that her brother had some sort of degenerative illness, and that he was a big teenager, bigger than her. That he couldn't stand sound, that he was getting worse, and that one afternoon Alice told him that he had smothered their mother even though it was she who had done it. And she realised that she could manipulate him… She said that she told him over and over again that he had done it, and he believed it. It made him cry, she said. "Weep and wail, the full drama." That's how she described it to Helen.'

Alexandra shook her head at the cruelty of it. 'Helen said it was that description that made her blood run cold. This frail-looking little girl had relentlessly gone on telling her brother that he had killed their mother, even though he couldn't bear it. She stood by and watched him driven crazy by it. But to Alice, that was mission accomplished, you see?'

'Yes, I see.'

'She told Helen that it was better for them both that the mother was dead. She said it very calmly as if it was logical. I expect it was. But you understand the problem at the heart of that, don't you? It doesn't really matter actually if she snapped one day and killed the person who'd tormented her for sixteen years. She could have explained that. Maybe got a custodial sentence, but not for long. She'd have been under surveillance of some kind once she was let out, but no one was going to blame her. Duress and abuse. She could have argued that anyone would snap in those circumstances.'

'Yes, she could.'

'But Helen said much the same to her, and Alice told her that wasn't good enough. William – the brother – would need care anyway – she didn't ever want to be responsible for him again, or even be the next of kin for his care, he might live for years, and she wanted out… So she said that it was *William* who killed their mother.'

'So she could be a free person.'

'Yes. So that she could walk away and leave him.'

He nodded slowly. 'Okay… yes.'

'Okay yes?' Alexandra mimicked. 'Have you any idea how Helen felt hearing that? She was living with a murderer. Living in the woman's own house. Sleeping with her.'

'And when was this exactly?'

'Christmas.'

'But she carried on living with her all the same.'

'She tried to get away. She came to meet me in Brimham between Christmas and New Year. The tenants were still in her house. I didn't have money to give her, not without my husband knowing. Beside all his other delightful traits, he controlled our finances. Or, as he called it, *his* money, being the wage earner.'

'But Helen earned a good wage. She could have rented somewhere. Gone to a hotel.'

'That's exactly what she did,' Alexandra told him. 'She booked an hotel – a little place out past Brimham, in the country – and she sat Alice down and told her – told her carefully, mind – that she needed some time away, and Alice seemed to accept it, seemed to acknowledge that it was a lot to understand, and understand that Helen was going away. She was quiet, Helen said, not aggressive or crying, just quiet and listening, and seeming very sensible about it, and she asked for the hotel where Helen was going to be. And I don't know why Helen thought it was going to be all right, I mean I told her, *don't* for Chrissake tell her where you are, but Alice got around her somehow. And it *was* quiet for a week or ten days.'

'Just ten days?'

'Yes. And in that time we planned what we were going to do. We were going to move into Helen's Bloxley house as soon as we could. And I would find a way to weather the storm with my husband and the boys. It was to be measured, calm... You know, "amicable". That ghastly word.'

'And something happened?'

'Oh Christ! Did it ever happen!' Alexandra exclaimed. 'Alice came to Helen's hotel and she stood in the driveway with a knife, and she threatened to cut her wrists. It was eight o'clock in the morning.'

'Good God. What did the hotel do? Did someone ring the police?'

'Are you kidding?' Alexandra said. 'A place like that doesn't need that kind of publicity. It's in the *Luxury Dreams* catalogue. It's been written up in the *Telegraph*. They got Alice inside, and Helen was asked to leave, and she went back to Asham Ferry with Alice.'

'And what then?'

'Alice was as docile as you like. It was as if it had never happened. And Helen got the message that she could never upset her. Never leave and tell her where she was going.'

'But Bloxley...'

'Alice didn't know the exact address. And I thought I could negotiate with my husband and maybe we could go to France for a year or two.' She looked at him, raising an eyebrow. 'And Helen didn't tell you this?'

'We had that affair two years before, Mrs Wilson. Two years before Helen disappeared. What you're telling me now happened two years later.'

'But Helen never came to you and told you what was happening with Alice, then? She didn't ring you up and say, "I've discovered I'm living with someone who needs investigating". Nothing like that?'

'No. Why, did you think that she had?'

'I wondered if she might have gone to you and asked for help.'

'No, she didn't. Helen... Helen struck me as someone who

wouldn't ask something like that, anyway. She seemed to be the sort of person who'd think she could handle it.'

'Yes,' Alexandra murmured, looking down and playing with the empty cup in front of her. 'Yes, she did think we could get around it. I wasn't so sure, I...'

Her voice tailed away. Thomas regarded her acutely, looking at her downturned head, her restless fingers. It was all hearsay. 'Helen did this, Alice said that.' Nothing that Alexandra told him could be proved. Richard Ellis could bring Alice in, of course. He could bring John Lord in, too. Perhaps questioning them could fracture their alliance. But Alice Hauser wasn't the person he had once supposed. She was something quite, quite different. And much, much worse.

'Did Helen come here that day, the day she disappeared?' he asked.

'What? No!'

'Are you sure?'

'Shit, you think that I killed her?' Alexandra cried. 'Haven't you been listening to a word I've said? If you think she was killed, look to Alice Hauser!'

'I'm simply asking you if you saw her.'

Alexandra sighed deeply. 'You saw the house in Bloxley?'

'Yes, I saw the house.'

'I'd spent all week cleaning it. Bringing her things back from storage. I even bought all her cosmetics and perfume and books. I bought them new and put them in the house. It was our new beginning, together.' She paused. 'Took hours and hours.'

'It looked like a stage set.'

'It was. The first act of our little production. She was coming to me after the meeting at the school and then a couple of days later we'd go to France. My husband was away on one of his "work outings" with his assistant, the lovely Barbara.'

'Had Helen told Alice?'

'Of course not! I had the car packed. Do you remember?'

'Yes...' He was hardly likely to forget her air of aggressive superiority that day. Now it occurred to him that it had been something different: panic.

'It had been packed for days. I went to the house and she didn't come. So I drove home. I sat waiting for a call. I saw the item on the news about her car, and I thought that she must have done a bunk. I thought that she might have gone to France.'

'Yes, but… without telling you?'

'Yes. Because that was Helen. Even in her state of mind, she would still have thought that it was a fantastic joke, outwitting everyone. I couldn't see her leaving her phone behind no matter what else she left, so I expected her to ring me sooner or later. You know, even when we got to the house, I expected her to be sitting by the pool saying "What kept you so long?"'

'And was she?'

'No, Mr Maitland. She wasn't.'

'And she never rang?'

'No.'

'What did you do?'

Her eyes filled with tears. 'I waited all that time. And then I came back. And two weeks after that, I told my husband because I was so fucking miserable with it all, and him, and the thought of the future without her. Maybe I had some sort of zoning out, a breakdown, I don't know. But I know that I didn't feel that life was worth living.' She stopped. She was staring down at her once elegant hands. 'And it really isn't,' she whispered.

He sat wondering the same ten-year-old question.

Did anybody know where Helen McAllister was?

Alexandra seemed to read his mind. 'She's got to be dead, hasn't she?' she asked quietly. 'There's just no other explanation.'

He paused, then slowly shook his head.

'You don't think so?' she demanded.

'It seems the likeliest possibility.'

'But?'

'I'm sorry?'

'There's a "but" in your voice.'

He leaned forward, his elbows on the table, and clasped his hands. 'Perhaps there was someone else. Someone she ran to. Someone who none of us knew about.'

Alexandra gaped at him for a second, then straightened up in her seat. 'No, that's not possible.'

'Why?' he asked.

'Because... because I knew her. I knew what she wanted. We... we had it planned...'

'Just as Alice once thought they had it all planned.'

'Helen wouldn't do that to me.'

He spread his hands now in a gesture of *Maybe so, maybe not*.

'If... and it's rather a large *if*, I grant you,' he said, 'we suppose that Alice didn't kill Helen. And contrary to what Alice thinks, I didn't. And you didn't. So let's just go with that idea for a second. Let's suppose that Helen didn't die at all. Let's suppose she did, as you say, know that she had to disappear from Alice and leave no trail. But perhaps she thought about life with you and found some fault with it. The husband taking all your money, for instance. The boys being upset. She doesn't strike me as the sort of woman who'd make a good stepmother.'

Alexandra remained utterly still, staring at him.

'Perhaps she thought it would be quite amusing, in her way, to see us all running around trying to find her.'

'She wouldn't have done that to me.'

'Alice Hauser told me exactly the same thing.'

Alexandra's gaze ranged over his face as if she was trying to see a flaw in this argument. Then her expression hardened. 'No, no,' she told him.

'Someone in this country,' he suggested. 'Somewhere remote. Someone perhaps with money to support them both. She never used her passport. But it's not inconceivable that she found someone to provide her with a new identity.'

'No, no,' Alexandra repeated. 'That's too fantastical to be true. Helen was the only person who knew that Alice had killed her mother, Mr Maitland. And Helen was leaving her.' She crossed her arms, still staring at him. 'Would you say that those were motives?' she asked.

*

He drove away feeling sorry for Alexandra Wilson: someone whom ten years ago he had thought possessed everything – house, children, husband, money – all enhanced by a raging sense of entitlement. Now she had nothing at all except a house that was a poor version of what it had been when he last spoke to her, and wouldn't be hers for much longer. And she had lost something else that he had only guessed she once had – Helen McAllister. Which seemed to be the greatest loss of all.

He found himself driving towards the coast.

The old recurring puzzle was back – the puzzle that had almost driven him crazy, because he tried to look at it objectively, as others would who had not been involved. Nobody simply vanishes in broad daylight, he told himself. And yet he knew that they sometimes did. You only had to look at the thousands of missing persons reports to know that. The theory that he'd given to Alexandra was perfectly logical – Helen could have gone somewhere with someone. She wasn't lying out in the fields and valleys beyond the ridge, unless she had been buried. And even then, in his experience, murderers rarely bury anyone six feet deep if they hadn't got a specific place in mind. If the attack had been on the spur of the moment. On the ridge, for instance, sooner or later an animal would find the body in a shallow grave, most likely a dog being walked along the coast paths bringing back a gruesome souvenir to a horrified owner. Had Alice Hauser had enough time to bury a strong, healthy woman like Helen? Did she have the strength to kill her in the first place? Everyone – those objective observers – would say not.

Within half an hour Thomas was at the lay-by under the

ridge, and pulled the car into the place where Helen had parked. He sat staring out to sea. It was still not yet 9 o'clock.

Alice hadn't killed Helen. For one thing, Alice was in love. When she had been interviewed by Richard Ellis over her accusation that Thomas had murdered Helen, Richard said that she seemed to really believe what she was saying. And he had pointed out that it would have taken an incredible amount of courage to come there with her complaint if she herself had committed the crime.

Of course, nothing was impossible. Helen had betrayed Alice, and stark cold fury could give a person strength, enough strength to put their hands around their throat and fight off their struggles. Alice was used to telling lies. She'd covered up her real identity. And then the shocking revelation that she'd killed her own mother. He himself had seen that blank look in her eyes, and sensed that awful hollowness in her, the echo of horror. It might have been just that emptiness that enabled her to accuse him of something that she herself had done.

He sat there for some time, resting his head on one hand, gazing sightlessly ahead. If they took Alice Hauser into custody now, they could probably make a fair case, body or no body.

Eventually, he got out of the car, locked it, and crossed the road. He went through the gate, climbed the path up the hill, emerging on to the ridge after five minutes. He stopped and looked around him. It was a glorious view, encompassing miles of coastline in either direction. Down behind the ridge was a long slope of fields and, standing with his back to the sea and looking to his right, he could make out the village nestling in the shadow of the ridge.

He began to walk down to it. There was a shop on the main street, and a café. If nothing else he could use the walk, and the promise of a strong coffee was enticing. The path began to slope quickly downwards and where it split, he took the turning towards the nearest houses. At the kissing gate, he walked on with the street now in his sight.

Just before the road, he saw a woman in a back garden. She was weeding the garden and had stopped, hand on hip, to watch him coming along.

'Good morning,' he said.

'Morning,' she replied. 'You're an early one. It's not you parked up on the kerb outside is it?'

'No,' he told her. 'I'm in the lay-by up top.'

She nodded. 'Sorry,' she said, 'I was all ready to have a go at you. It causes so much trouble. People curse us because they think it's our car when it's usually some walker or other.'

'And you get that often?'

She smiled. 'You wouldn't believe. Even though the yellow lines are there, they still park.'

'A nuisance,' he agreed. And he glanced back the way that he had come. 'I don't suppose that you remember everybody, though?'

'We remember the ones who argue,' she told him. 'Why?'

'Did you live here ten years ago?'

'Yes. I came here to look after Dad.' The woman paused. 'He died last year.'

'I'm sorry to hear that,' he said.

'It was ten years ago that he had a stroke. That hot summer.' She paused. 'And it was walkers that caused it, shouting at him one morning,' she added.

'Walkers? Really?'

The woman took off her gardening gloves and walked towards him. 'Two women arguing with him. Well, one was anyway.'

'How do you mean?'

'Over a car parked up on the kerb like there is today. He complained, and the taller one said something about blaming the other. Dad objected, and this woman laughed in his face. She called him something – I don't know what, I was at the kitchen sink and only saw it through the window. By the time I got out there they'd moved on. I went down the path to the road, and they were just getting into the car.'

'Did you speak to them?'

'No, I didn't get the chance. They were arguing between themselves. But I remember it because Dad was upset – he was such a softie, everybody loved him, he never argued with anyone, you know? And that afternoon he fell ill and we had to call the ambulance.' She sighed. 'I was back and forth to the hospital for three weeks.'

'Which direction had they come from?' he asked.

She pointed up at the ridge. 'Up there,' she told him.

'Would you remember them if you were shown a photograph?'

She smiled. 'After ten years?' she said. 'Other than the fact that they were both blonde, not a chance.'

But Thomas didn't need a chance.

He knew exactly who those two people were.

*

He rang Richard Ellis as he climbed the path back to the ridge and his car. He told him what he suspected, and heard Ellis sigh briefly on the other end of the line.

'Tell me where Alice Hauser lives,' Thomas said.

'Are you kidding me?' Ellis retorted. 'No way.'

'Have you been out to her yet?'

'It's early yet, Thomas. We'll go today.'

'Richard,' he said, 'where is she? She's somewhere near Asham Ferry, I know that much.'

'Keep out of it.'

'Normally I would, but if John Lord's with her, he's in danger.'

Ellis didn't reply.

'Is she out towards White Point, up on the coast path? There's three or four houses up there. Remote. There's nowhere for her in Asham itself. There's no houses up the hill out of there and there's only the main road after that. But I know she's nearby.'

'Thomas, we're going out there later today.'

'You'd better go there now.'

'Why, what do you know?'

'I don't know anything. It's instinct, Richard. Today is ten years exactly since Helen McAllister disappeared. I think they're coming after me.'

There was a silence of some seconds.

'Okay, Thomas. We'll go there this morning.'

30

JOHN LORD HAD BEEN AWAKE for hours, sitting in the chair watching Alice Hauser.

It was disturbing how motionlessly she slept. She lay on her back in the camp bed, her arms at her side. She looked as if she might be dead, she was so still. Once, in the dark, he had got up and crept to her side, to check on her. He had had to put his hand close to her mouth to feel the faint breath.

Now, in the morning light, she suddenly turned on her side, opened her eyes, and stared straight at him.

'I'm not going to do it,' he told her.

She slowly got up, swinging her legs out of the bed. 'It's today,' she said. 'It's ten years.'

'I know. But I'm not going to do it. It's your anniversary, not mine.'

She got up. Still in her underwear, she walked over to the sink, splashed her face with cold water and filled the kettle. He sat in a mounting rage with himself at being here in this stupid, mixed-up, bitter situation. All night he'd looked at her and wondered what had brought him here: fury and some kind of misplaced anxiety for her, she who didn't need his care or anxiety. She was deeply, mystifyingly strange. It was kind of interesting – like you'd look at a freak show, half not believing, half marvelling at the contortions it took it be different.

He was a partner in crime to someone he would never know. Even if he stayed a year in this peculiar place, he'd never comprehend her. She was more than curious; she seemed to be dead inside. Not a flicker of reaction when they set the fire to Maitland's studio. Only once had he seen tears, when she talked about her brother, and in the long hours of the night he'd understood why that had touched him. Losing a brother you loved. He fought with the feeling that he'd been expertly, subtly conned.

'You must,' she said now, turning back to look at him with her hands on her hips.

'There's no *must* about it,' he told her.

'I can't do it alone.'

'Yes, you can, Alice,' he said. 'I think you could do anything you set your mind to. And I think you're used to it.'

'I'm not the size of him,' she whispered, with a shadow of a pout. 'Look at me.'

'Alice,' he said,' Alice…'

She walked towards him. She had a sort of swing, like a dancer starting a routine. Or a cat waiting to pounce. 'You've lost your nerve.'

He laughed. 'I never had any bloody nerve,' he told her. 'Don't you know that about me? I've fucked up my entire life. I never used to have the nerve to fire a driver who was cheating on the company, I never had the nerve to talk to my daughters. I haven't got nerve, Alice. I'm angry is what I am, and nowhere to put it.'

'You've got Maitland.'

He stood up and turned away, walking to the window that looked out on the knee-high grass and the rusted gate.

'You don't care about Mike,' she said.

God. If there was one thing he wanted to do at that moment, it was run across the room and hit her. He struggled with it, thinking of all the times that Mike had smiled at him while he told him about Liz and the blackness of the moods, the deadness that ate away at him. 'Being angry is the thing that keeps you going,' Mike had warned him. 'You've got to find something else, John, or it'll take you down with it.'

Well, he was down now. He was so far down that he couldn't see any directions. Sometimes it happened when you were walking – no signs, no clues. You had to stop and read the ground. Maybe if it was foggy. Lost and confused like that.

He and Mike had once been on the top of Helvellyn, and he'd walked forward – he was sure it was the way to go – but the fog was thick. You could hear your voice behind you when you spoke. That's why fog disorientates people. You feel there's someone else beside you, or behind you, or ahead of you. Mike had stopped him – caught his arm just in time. He'd been on the edge of the mountain. And when he'd looked down, the fog went swirling away under him.

'It's for Mike that I don't want to do it,' he said, glancing back at her. 'He wouldn't want me to murder anyone. He wouldn't have even wanted me to go into that studio.'

He saw a movement out of the corner of his eye, and turned back to her. Her arms had risen above her head as if she was calling down the gods. Like a prayer. Then she dropped them.

'Listen,' he said. 'We can get through this another way.'

'What other way?'

'We could just forget, Alice.'

Her eyes widened slightly. 'No. Forget Helen? Never!'

'The studio must be bad enough for Maitland.'

'Bad enough?' she echoed. 'Like losing a brother, or a partner? Like losing someone you love?'

He knew he'd never get out of this argument. She'd had too long to think about it. It was holy crusade to her.

'Helen isn't coming back,' he said quietly. 'Neither of them is.'

She was standing stock still. She had that look that he didn't like – that frozen like, like a film that had been paused.

'I just think…' he began.

'You're going to go home,' she said.

'Yes. I'm going to go home.'

'To nothing.'

'There's nothing here either, Alice.'

'Oh yes,' she said. 'There's what we've done.'

'I'm hardly going to tell anyone, am I?'

'But I could tell them about you.'

Three, four, five seconds of utter silence while he wondered if he had heard her right. 'What?'

'How I watched you set fire to the place and I tried to stop you.'

He stopped, letting the blood beat in his head. Counting his breaths.

'And you were the one who wanted to kill him,' she continued.

He dared not move. Not because he was afraid of her.

But because he was afraid of what he might do.

Just a slip of a girl.

She'd said so herself.

'Alice,' he said slowly. 'My brother wouldn't have wanted this. He wouldn't want it.'

She rocked back and forth on her heels. 'Well, Helen would want it. She wouldn't have let ten years go past, either. She'd have done something straightaway. Found out who was responsible. Killed them with her bare hands. I've let her down for too long.'

'Helen doesn't exist anymore, Alice. She probably never existed the way that you saw her. She wasn't everything you hoped, and so you've made her up in your head. Just in your head.' He paused, hoping that it was sinking in. 'Helen never was the Helen you wanted. And now she's dead.'

He expected her to come for him, but she did the exact opposite. She went to the back door, flung it open, and he heard her run down the steps from the verandah, her bare feet thudding on the wood. He went after her. She was standing in the grass at the back of the house, wavering slightly. Swaying, her fists clenched.

'Alice!'

She took off towards the trees, the thick scrubland. He ran down the steps after her. She was quicker on her feet than he was, and thinner; she wriggled through the bushes, the blackberry trailers, the overhanging branches. Following her, he was scratched by the trailers. The branches were willow, flexible, like small whips springing in his face.

'Alice!'

He could see her ahead of him. Now that they were through the trees, the sound of the sea was louder. She had stopped, glanced back at him, and ran on again until she was at the edge of the cliff. Here she paused, but for a second too long. He grabbed her arm, and for a moment he thought that they were both going to fall. The height was dizzying. And he felt a kind of reflex response in him, a longing to fall, a pull of vertigo. He saw himself fall over the edge and down towards the rocks and the water, and just for that moment it was a fantastic relief.

Alice had gone limp in his grasp, and he pulled them both back from the edge. He looked down and saw that her feet were bleeding; it was nothing but ragged chalk here at the edge. He held her in his arms and was surprised at the heavy thudding of her heart. He could feel it through his clothes. She had gone an awful shade of grey.

'She *was* like I saw her,' she whispered. 'She was.'

'Come back to the house.'

But she resisted him. 'Even my mother wasn't as real as Helen, and I killed my mother.'

He was still in the act of trying to turn her back towards the trees when it registered with him what she'd said. 'Alice, your brother killed your mother. Not you.'

'Oh no,' she murmured.

He dropped his hands from her.

'I killed my mother,' she repeated. 'She was lying in bed, and it was a hot afternoon, and she was drunk. And I took her a drink of water – I took a jug, she'd asked for it – she said she had a headache. And downstairs William had a seizure. He had a seizure while I was trying to get the water, and I'd never seen him like that.'

John took a pace backwards.

'It's… it's a condition that gets worse. He'd lost his sentences. The way to make sentences. He just used a few words. He was so big and so heavy and when he saw me turning the tap, he tried to turn it off. He got up and he hit me away from the tap because of the noise of the water. He couldn't stand some sounds, and running water was one of them.' Her gaze drifted away from him and along the coast. 'And he fell down and he began shaking. And I just stepped over him because my mother was shouting for the water and when I got to the room she told me I was a bloody nuisance.' She gave a small, pained smile. 'I think I'd been told that every day of my life, you know?' she said. 'A nuisance or a pest. She was never interested in anything I did.'

Abruptly, she sat down on the ground. 'Have you ever felt like you were the only person alive in the world?'

'No,' he said, astonished at the bizarre change of subject. He looked past her to the house.

'Not in the mountains?'

He'd told her about climbing peaks, with and without Mike. And she was right. Especially in the early hours, at dawn. 'Yes,' he murmured.

'And everything stands still.'

In his mind's eye he saw the light creeping slowly across Striding Edge. Deep shadow. Bright sunlight. 'Yes, it does.'

'And you feel that you're not really there, but you are. You're strung between the seconds.'

All at once, he saw her in the kitchen of that house with her brother on the floor.

'I went upstairs with the water,' she said. 'And when I got near the bed, my mother knocked the jug out of my hands and it went flying. It went all over the bed. She shut up then, because it was cold, and because it went all over her too, and in that few seconds I saw – you know, in that silent spot – I saw how nice it would be when she stopped shouting, and I picked up the pillow, and I put it over her face.'

The feeling that John had got when they had both been near the edge just moments before came swarming back over him like an all-consuming wave.

'Your brother didn't kill your mother,' he said.

'No.'

'But you told everyone that he did.'

'He was put in a secure hospital,' she said. 'It was for the best.'

'And that's where he died.'

'Oh yes,' she said off-handedly. 'He hanged himself in there.' She glanced up at him, and away. 'Because I told him that he murdered her.'

John could hardly get his breath.

'Because otherwise,' she said, 'he might have remembered that it was me.'

*

John stepped back.

He thought that perhaps he swayed slightly, just like Alice did if she was questioned. He looked up and saw the vast expanse behind them both – the Channel far below, millpond calm, icy blue. And in the other direction was the house, the decaying roof showing beyond the scrub of trees. His car was parked in the lane beyond.

Alice Hauser stood between him and his car, smiling slightly.

'You were going to do exactly the same thing,' he said slowly. 'You were going to kill Maitland and blame it on me.'

And then he knew. He knew that he'd never stand on top of a mountain anymore. He would never go home.

He put out his hands and fastened them around her neck.

She fought like a bloody demon, kicking his legs until he fell to his knees. Scratching his face, his hands. Then quite abruptly she went completely limp and he loosened his grip, only for her to open her eyes suddenly and begin writhing and kicking and hitting him with clenched fists until his ears rang and blood ran into his eyes and he shook his head. Like a dog shaking off water. No no no no. Liz's face flashed in front of him and he started shouting. No no no no. Alice Hauser's eyes widened and he waited. She stopped moving and he waited. She slumped to one side and he fell over with her until they were both lying sideways on the ground and he could feel the stones digging into him, and he waited.

At last, he took his hands away and let her go.

He stood up, and looked down at her.

'Mr Lord,' someone said.

He straightened, thinking he had imagined the voice. And then he recognised it. Turning, he saw Thomas Maitland halfway through the scrub, trying to prise blackberry trailers from his arm, half frozen in that attitude, but with his gaze flickering between him and Alice Hauser at his feet.

'Don't come any further,' he heard himself say.

Maitland didn't take any notice. He emerged from the low line of trees and stood three feet from him, frowning.

'Her brother,' he said.

'Yes, I know,' Maitland answered.

'You *don't* know,' he told him.

He could see what was coming. Maitland would start talking to him in that low voice that he used, and what was he after all, what business did he have? An ex-cop, nobody anymore. And yet here he was walking towards him like he had all the answers. Suddenly it was blazingly clear, the only person who could have killed Helen was him – Alice hadn't done it – Alice had just been lied to – crazy in the head, sick at heart. He recognised that, to be sick down to the last atom, so sick and so dark there was no way out at all – and he knew that, despite all of that, Alice Hauser couldn't have murdered Helen because Helen was her lifeline, the only real thing that she had ever had.

Maitland was holding out his hand. 'Come back to the house,' he was saying. 'We'll sort it all out.'

John began laughing. He knew what it meant. Maitland would sort *him* out. Like he'd done with Helen. But John Lord wouldn't give him that chance.

Maitland was only a foot from him, smiling, when he watched his own hand come up swiftly and connect with Maitland's head, striking with the stone that he had been holding since he had stood up from Alice.

Maitland went straight down.

He landed on his side and rolled on to his back and was still.

Dead still.

If only…

If only he hadn't gone to Maitland's studio, and seen his house. His expensive idyllic-looking house. If only Mike hadn't been travelling that day. If only he hadn't wanted to be buried out by the sea away from everything they had shared together.

If only he'd got a grip of what was happening, years ago, when the first black-grey blanket came down around him and choked the air out of him. He heard Liz now, asking him why he was always angry. And he didn't know why but he knew that he was. He knew that feeling. Furious boiling greedy anger, never satisfied, never done with. But now looking at Alice and Maitland, for the first time in his life he didn't feel angry at all.

He felt wiped clean and empty.

And so tired.

He turned his back on them and the trees and the house and he walked to the edge of the cliff until his heels were on the edge and he looked at the sea. It was so still out there. No wind came barrelling up from the shoreline below, not a breath of air.

He was where Alice had described, between one place and another and yet nowhere at all.

He stepped forward.

31

THE THINGS THAT PEOPLE DO for love.

That's what Christine was thinking as she walked down the hospital corridor. Sun streamed through the corridor windows. She was early, but it had been hard to keep away.

She walked with her hands in her pockets, head down, determined that no one was going to stop her seeing Thomas. They hadn't even thought to tell her until 12 hours after he'd been attacked, and she was furious about it.

It had been almost 9 o'clock at night when Ellis had knocked on her door. Seeing him there, her heart had started beating heavily in her chest.

'Is it Thomas?' she asked. She hadn't seen him all day.

'Yes, it is.'

She'd died a thousand deaths between that door and the chair in her kitchen, until Ellis told her the story.

'And it was all about this missing woman ten years ago?' she'd asked.

'Well, it seems so, yes.'

'She thought that Thomas had killed her partner?'

'Perhaps,' Ellis said.

'What was Thomas doing there?'

'He shouldn't have been.'

'And the man... Is he all right?'

Ellis had shaken his head.

On the way here this morning, she'd been trying to fit all the pieces of the puzzle together. Why had Thomas been trying to find Alice Hauser? What was he going to say to her when he found her? What was he going to do? It was all so confusing, but she was certain of one thing. She'd made a decision. When Thomas came home, she would look after him. She would make sure that he was safe.

She remembered a friend saying that to her one summer – *the things that people do for love* – when they had heard that someone's son had run away with a married woman, someone that they knew to be a bad sort through and through. The foolishness of other people.

All her life, it had been like another world to her – the place where people fought over others and had wickedness in their hearts. That had never been her way. She had been happy in herself and had never had a boyfriend for more than a few months, and time had passed, years of being alone, and it had somehow become her life. All that she'd hoped for as a girl – husband, children – hadn't materialised. It was no use crying over it. It was just the way it had happened. She was 'funny old Christine' now. She'd heard one of the kids say that when she used to volunteer at the school, helping the baby ones with reading. She was just that woman living in the cottage at the corner of the road, never having much to do with anyone, getting along in her own quiet, disorganised way.

Even when Thomas and Fran had moved in, that didn't change.

Not for a long time anyway.

After Thomas had retired, Thomas had helped her around the house every so often. Odd jobs. Helped her once when her car wouldn't start. And when the snow came he would always help her to clear and salt the drive.

It had been an awful time after Fran died. Christine had seen such a change come over Thomas, as if the blood had drained out of him. He had begun to stoop, carrying himself around as if he were dragging a sack of stones and would gladly put it down. That was when the balance changed; she started helping him, looking after him, even feeding him when it looked as if he hadn't eaten. And even though they still lived apart, they were almost like a married couple, knowing each other's ways and times and habits.

Of course, she realised that Thomas never thought of her as anything but old Christine – much too old for him, of course, but then how could you help your feelings? To him, she was just Christine who lived in the next house along the drive, even when they drank together after supper and he would tell her about cases that he'd known in the police force. That was what was so unusual about him. Not revealing the case of Helen McAllister until recently. She'd felt a sort of tremor inside when he'd admitted that he had had an affair. It wasn't the Thomas that she thought she'd known, but it had explained Fran's expressions sometimes, looking aside at her husband as if weighing him up, considering him.

The very first thing that Christine had done every day for years now was to leave her bedroom and go to the landing window, the one where she could see the corner of Thomas's house. This April, she had watched him tying up the roses on the gable end wall; and she had watched him whenever he went out, and she had counted the hours until he came back home again. Every hour, every day, in all seasons.

She'd tried to show him, of course, but he had never understood.

*

When she reached the ward, and was shown the door of the side ward where he was, she hesitated before she pushed open the door.

She hadn't been able to sleep for thinking of it.

For the last few days, from the top window of her house she had seen Thomas starting to dig over the patch of grass at the bottom of his garden, the one near the footbridge. She had watched how diligently he had dug over the soil, how carefully, how slowly. It had almost been as if he were looking for something.

However, by the time that she had got up and dressed and got behind the wheel of her car and was driving to the hospital, she had almost forgotten the thought. Almost… but not quite.

It remained in the corner of her mind as a faint echo.

The things that people did for love.

ABOUT THE AUTHOR

Photo credit © Kate McGregor

Under the names Elizabeth McGregor and Elizabeth Cooke, E.M. Scott has been writing for thirty years and has some 15 novels and one non-fiction work to her name, as well as over a hundred published short stories. Although having worked in various genres, crime is her first love. She lives in Dorset.